Natural TEMPTATION

Other Books by Anna Durand

Natural Obsession (Au Naturel Nights, Book One)
Natural Deception (Au Naturel Nights, Book Two)
Natural Passion (Au Naturel Trilogy, Book One)
Natural Impulse (Au Naturel Trilogy, Book Two)
Natural Satisfaction (Au Naturel Trilogy, Book Three)
The Dixon Brothers Trilogy (Hot Brits, Books 1-3)
One Hot Escape (Hot Brits, Book Four)
One Hot Rumor (Hot Brits, Book Five)
One Hot Christmas (Hot Brits, Book Six)
One Hot Scandal (Hot Brits, Book Seven)
One Hot Deal (Hot Brits, Book Eight)
One Hot Favor (Hot Brits, Book Nine)
One Hot Bash (Hot Brits, Book Ten)
One Hot Moment (Hot Brits, Book Eleven)
One Hot Chase (Hot Brits, Book Twelve)
Lachlan in a Kilt (The Ballachulish Trilogy, Book One)
Aidan in a Kilt (The Ballachulish Trilogy, Book Two)
Rory in a Kilt (The Ballachulish Trilogy, Book Three)
The American Wives Club (A Hot Brits/Hot Scots/Au Naturel Crossover Book)
Brit vs. Scot (A Hot Brits/Hot Scots/Au Naturel Crossover Book)
The MacTaggart Brothers Trilogy (Hot Scots, Books 1-3)
Gift-Wrapped in a Kilt (Hot Scots, Book Four)
Notorious in a Kilt (Hot Scots, Book Five)
Insatiable in a Kilt (Hot Scots, Book Six)
Lethal in a Kilt (Hot Scots, Book Seven)
Irresistible in a Kilt (Hot Scots, Book Eight)
Devastating in a Kilt (Hot Scots, Book Nine)
Spellbound in a Kilt (Hot Scots, Book Ten)
Relentless in a Kilt (Hot Scots, Book Eleven)
Incendiary in a Kilt (Hot Scots, Book Twelve)
Wild in a Kilt (Hot Scots, Book Thirteen)
Unstoppable in a Kilt (Hot Scots, Book Fourteen)
Valentine in a Kilt (Hot Scots, Book Fifteen)
Electrifying in a Kilt (Hot Scots, Book Sixteen)
The Outlands Shifter (The Devil's Outlands, Book 1)
The Outlands Demon (The Devil's Outlands, Book 2)
The Complete Echo Power Trilogy
The Psychic Crossroads Series Collection (Books 1-3)
The Janusite Trilogy (Undercover Elementals, Books 1-3)
Obsidian Hunger (Undercover Elementals, Book Four)
Unbidden Hunger (Undercover Elementals, Book Five)
The Thirteenth Fae (Undercover Elementals, Book Six)
Cyneric (Undercover Elementals, Book Seven)
The Immortal Falls (Undercover Elementals, Book Eight)

Natural TEMPTATION

Au Naturel Nights, Book Three

ANNA DURAND

JACOBSVILLE BOOKS · CHESTERHILL, OHIO

ISBN: 978-1-958144-58-9 (paperback)
ISBN: 978-1-958144-59-6 (ebook)
ISBN: 978-1-958144-60-2 (retail audiobook)
ISBN: 978-1-958144-61-9 (library audiobook)

Manufactured in the United States.

Jacobsville Books
www.JacobsvilleBooks.com

Publisher's Cataloging-in-Publication Data
provided by Five Rainbows Cataloging Services

Names: Durand, Anna, author.
Title: Natural temptation / Anna Durand.
Description: Chesterhill, OH : Jacobsville Books, 2025. | Series: Au naturel nights, bk. 3.
Identifiers: ISBN 978-1-958144-58-9 (paperback) | ISBN 978-1-958144-59-6 (ebook) | ISBN 978-1-958144-60-2 (retail audiobook) | ISBN 978-1-58144-61-9 (library audiobook)
Subjects: LCSH: Man-woman relationships--Fiction. | Vacations--Fiction. | Middle-aged persons--Fiction. | May-December romances--Fiction. | Romance fiction. | BISAC: FICTION / Romance / Contemporary. | FICTION / Romance / Later in Life. | GSAFD: Love stories.
Classification: LCC PS3604.U724 N39 2025 (print) | LCC PS3604.U724 (ebook) | DDC 813/.6--dc23.

<h1 style="text-align:center;font-style:italic">Prologue</h1>

Ryan

The sun gradually sinks toward the horizon, casting a fiery glow on the sky and painting it in shades of blood red with smears of purple, like big bruises on the sunset. I curl my toes deeper into the sand, feeling the tiny grains move beneath my feet. My shoulders are relaxed, my jaw too. The breathtaking scenery of Heirani Motu surrounds me, and the weight I'd felt bearing down on me a few days ago has crumbled away. Still, I can't help wondering if I'll be able to handle swimming in a sea of naked strangers.

Am I ready for this? For a new job in a strange new place? Tomorrow, I'll start my first full week on the island, and my first full day as interim general manager. But this island is nothing like the resort I'd worked at before. This is a nudist resort, after all. The clothes-free kind.

But if I wake up in a cold sweat in the middle of the night...I'll handle it. My best friend taught me how to get through the bad times.

My mind races through an endless list of preparations. Have I double-checked the welcome baskets? Are the trail maps updated? God, I hope the staff remembered to stock extra sunscreen. Then a seabird's cry pierces the air as my thoughts spiral back to the impending arrival of a new crop of guests—my first since I touched down on the island. Can I handle so many new people? All at once? I have no choice. They are my responsibility, and I never let my crew down.

A memory unfolds in my mind as I remember the last time I managed a guest influx this large. It was at a different kind of resort, in a different life. The complaints, the accidents, the sheer unpredictability of human beings, had nearly driven me crazy. Yet now, with so much more at stake, I feel relaxed instead of anxious. Maybe it's the scent of the ocean and rustling of the palm trees that's keeping me centered.

But what if someone gets hurt on the nature trails? Or bitten by shark? Sure, that's likely to happen. I shake my head at myself. "Get it together, Kimble. You've done this before.' "

Yeah, those other instances were at a regular resort where everyone kept their clothes, or at least their swimsuits, on at all times. But I can handle it, for sure. Even as I tell myself the words, I know it's a lie. The pressure to maintain Au Naturel's sterling reputation feels heavier than ever. One misstep, one unhappy guest, and it could all come crashing down.

Don't be an idiot. The whole chain of resorts won't explode just because I flub something.

I turn away from the fading light, my steps purposeful as I head back toward the resort. My mind cranks into high gear as I plot checklists and contingency plans. I need to review the staff schedules one more time, ensure the kitchens are fully stocked, double-check that all the equipment for tomorrow's activities is in perfect working order.

As I walk, I catch my reflection in a nearby window. For a moment, I barely recognize the man staring back at me—all soft smiles and casual certainty, as if I know exactly what I'm doing. *What bullshit.* I force a smile, practicing the pleasant, welcoming expression I'll need to wear tomorrow and every day after.

"Welcome to Au Naturel Naturist Resort South Seas," I say to my reflection, my voice carefully modulated to project confidence and ease. "The one place where you can truly be yourself."

The irony of those words isn't lost on me. How long has it been since I've allowed myself that luxury? I shake off the thought, squaring my shoulders. There's work to be done, and I won't let my personal hang-ups interfere with the guests' experience. They came here seeking freedom, relaxation, maybe even a bit of romance.

It's my job to ensure they find it—even if I can't seem to find any of that for myself.

Suddenly, the breeze wafts a familiar odor toward me. It smells like blood, mixed with the salty sea air. My heart rate spikes as I scan the beach, searching for the source. Could someone be hurt? My mind races through worst-case scenarios—a guest injured on the rocks, a shark attack, or worse. But it's only a mirage, of course. Yet I'm transported back to another night that I've tried to forget, another place, another lifetime on a different continent.

Then it's over as quickly as the memory had begun.

I blink rapidly, my heart racing. The phantom pain in my chest feels all too real, and I can almost taste the coppery tang of blood on my lips. I shake my head in an attempt to clear the memory, muttering to myself. "Not now, Kimble. Focus on this moment, this time."

The rhythmic crash of waves pulls me back to the present. I turn toward the shoreline, watching as the moonlight glimmering on the water surges and recedes in an endless tango. It's mesmerizing, peaceful. I let out a long breath, trying to match the steadiness of the waves with the ocean's rhythm. My heart rate slows, and the memories gradually drift away from me.

"Amazing, isn't it?" I say aloud as I gaze at the ocean, though there's no one else to hear me. "Paradise on earth."

Here I am, surrounded by breathtaking beauty, and all I can think about is spreadsheets and guest complaints. The duality of it all—the serenity of Heirani Motu versus the chaos in my head—it's almost laughable. I close my eyes, letting the sound of the waves wash over me once again. For just a moment, I allow myself to be present, to feel the sand beneath my feet and the caress of the breeze on my skin.

I open my eyes to watch the last sliver of sun disappear beneath the horizon. The colors turn from pink to purple and finally to darkness. My life has been filled with too much darkness, but I've worked hard to live in the light. Can I ever truly do that? Some scars remain embedded in my psyche forever.

With one last look at the darkening sky, I turn back toward the resort. There's still work to be done, even after sunset, and I won't let the ghosts of my past interfere with the promise of tomorrow.

The shrill ring of my phone cuts through the air like a seagull's cry, yanking me back to reality. I fish it out of my pocket, cursing softly when I see the name on the screen: James Bythesea. I take a deep breath, schooling my voice into a mask of calm professionalism.

"James," I answer, my voice steady despite the sudden uptick in my heart rate. "What can I do for you, boss?"

"How is your first week going, Ryan?" James's crisp British accent crackles through the line. "I trust I'm not interrupting anything important?"

A wry smile tugs at my lips. "Not at all. Just finishing up some last-minute preparations for tomorrow's new arrivals."

"Ah, excellent. That's precisely why I'm calling." There's a pause, and I can almost picture James straightening his crisp white dress shirt, even over the phone. "How are we looking for the upcoming season?"

I start walking back toward the resort, sand shifting beneath my feet until I step onto the manicured trail. "We're on track, boss. Bookings are up fifteen percent from last year, and early feedback on our newest adventure options has been positive."

"That's...good." But there's hesitation in his voice that makes my shoulders tense up. "However, I can't help but feel we could be doing better. Eve and Val are expecting significant growth this quarter."

I hold back a sigh. Of course they're expecting growth. Eve and Val Silva, the owners of the Au Naturel chain of resorts, are great people. But they're also dead serious about business. "I understand, James. We've implemented several new strategies to enhance guest experience and boost word-of-mouth marketing. I'm confident we'll see results."

"I certainly hope so, Ryan. The Au Naturel brand is known for excellence, and we can't afford to let standards slip. Not even on a remote island paradise."

His words sting more than they should. I've poured my heart and soul into this resort, using it as a lifeline to pull myself out of the darkness that threatened to consume me after...No, I won't think about that. I know James, as well as Eve and Val, don't think of their resorts as just another line item on a spreadsheet. It's their calling.

"Don't worry, boss," I say, infusing my voice with a confidence I don't entirely feel, "I assure you every guest who sets foot on Heirani Motu will experience nothing short of perfection. You have my word."

"See that they do, Ryan. The future of the resort depends on it." With that ominous parting shot, James ends the call.

I lower the phone, staring at the dark screen. The weight of expectation settles over me like a heavy cloak, and for a moment, I allow myself to feel the full force of it. Then, with a deep breath,

I straighten my shoulders and continue my walk back to the office. Every day is another chance to prove myself. And I won't let anyone down—not James, not the guests, and most importantly, not myself.

As I exhale slowly, I allow the frustration to sift away with every breath. Stabbing a hand through my hair, I mutter to myself once again. "Get it together, Kimble. James won't fire you."

I really need to stop talking to myself out loud.

With a final glance at the darkening horizon, I turn and start the trek back to my office. My feet sink into the cooling sand with every deliberate step, mirroring the weight I feel settling in my chest. The conversation with James replays in my mind, his words a constant reminder of the pressure I'm under.

As I reach the path leading away from the beach, I quicken my pace. My movements are purposeful, every stride reflecting the discipline I've honed over years of managing crises—both personal and professional. The lush foliage whispers around me, but I barely notice its beauty, my mind already racing through tomorrow's to-do list.

"Welcome speech, staff briefing, final room checks," I recite under my breath, organizing my thoughts as I navigate the familiar trail.

The resort's main building comes into view, its warm lights a beacon in the moonlit night. I pause for a moment, taking in the sight of the star-studded sky and the island that has become my home for the past few weeks. This is more than just a job. It's my redemption, my chance to prove that I can still make something meaningful, even after everything that's happened.

I square my shoulders before stepping inside the lobby. The cool air-conditioning hits me as I enter, a stark contrast to the balmy evening outside. I nod at the night staff, who offer cheerful greetings as I urge myself to respond in kind.

On the way back to my office, I can't help wondering what challenges tomorrow's guests will bring. But I push the thought aside. After all, I've faced worse things—much worse. And this time, I'm determined to make this island my new home, permanently.

Once inside my office, I sink into my chair with a sigh. The computer screen flickers to life, its glow casting shadows across my desk. I pull up tomorrow's guest list, each name a potential landmine in the delicate balance of running Au Naturel. I scroll through the document, uncertain of why I'm bothering to do that. The task relaxes me, and that's all that matters.

My gaze dances over the names and any special requests they might have asked for. The Johnsons wanted extra towels. Mr. Patel requested a vegan menu. The Coopers are celebrating twenty years of marriage, so they requested the anniversary package.

I pause, my finger hovering over the trackpad, and try to memorize the first names of all the new guests. That's no easy task. But my previous career taught me to notice everything. Before I know it, I've cataloged all the first names.

With a satisfied sigh, I lean back and clasp my hands behind my head.

I close the guest list and pull out a fresh sheet of paper, clicking my pen over and over. Time to craft the perfect welcome speech. My fingers tap a staccato rhythm on the keyboard as I begin to write.

"Welcome to Au Naturel Naturist Resort South Seas," I say, testing the words. "Where paradise meets...No, too cliché." I cross it out, frowning. The speech needs to be warm, inviting, professional. Just like me, huh? A wry smile tugs at my lips. If only everyone knew how much effort goes into maintaining this facade.

I try again. "Welcome to Au Naturel Naturist Resort South Seas. We're delighted to have you join us on Heirani Motu, where..."

The words flow easier now, my pen racing across the page. I describe the island's lush beauty, the crystal-clear waters, the hidden waterfalls waiting to be discovered. Every sentence is carefully constructed, designed to paint a picture of serenity, sensuality, and adventure. The interim general manager won't be getting any of that.

While I work, I feel the tension in my shoulders begin to ease. This is what I'm good at—setting the stage for others to find their bliss even if I can't seem to find my own, creating an experience they'll remember long after they go home.

I pause, tapping the pen on my chin until inspiration strikes again.

"Remember," I say softly, practicing the words, "at Au Naturel, we celebrate the beauty of the human form in all its diversity. Here, you're free to be your authentic self."

The irony of those words isn't lost on me. I glance up, catching sight of my reflection on the polished desktop. The fading light casts shadows across my face, emphasizing the lines of worry etched around my eyes. I twist my lips into a frown as I mutter, "Authentic self, my ass. When's the last time you let anyone see that, hey, Kimble?"

The reflection offers no answer, just a weary look that speaks volumes. I see the weight of expectations in the set of my shoulders, the guard I've built in the tightness around my mouth.

This is who you are now. The capable resort manager. The professional.

But even as I speak the words, a part of me rebels. Is this really all I am? A collection of polite phrases and efficient gestures, hiding behind a mask of competence? I spin my chair around, unwilling to look at my own reflection anymore, unable to face the questions in my own eyes. The speech lies finished on the desk, a testament to the persona I've crafted. It's good. It's exactly what the guests need to hear.

So why does it feel like I'm lying?

I take another deep breath, squaring my shoulders. The dimly lit office feels like a cocoon, shielding me from the world outside. But I can't hide here forever.

Shake off the memories, Kimble. Look to the future.

My perusal of the guest list proved there will be loads of hot women on the island for the next two weeks. Why I thought about that I can't explain. It's not like I can have a fling with a sexy guest. Can't even remember the last time I had sex.

And you won't be having any on this island either, Kimble. Keep it professional, remember?

I step out the door, leaving the sanctuary of my office behind. Tomorrow will bring its own challenges, but I'll face them the way I always do—one carefully measured step at a time. The door clicks shut behind me, and I head for my private bungalow. Just another night in paradise, with the weight of the world on my shoulders and a heart I don't dare to unchain.

Chapter One

Meredith

As the wheels of the small jet touch down on the grass landing strip, my heart leaps into my throat. This is it. I'm really doing this. Whenever I've dreamed about taking a vacation, I would imagine Cozumel or Italy or maybe even Amsterdam—but never an adults-only nudist resort on a private island in the South Pacific. Yet here I am at the Au Naturel Naturist Resort South Seas. And I'm about to strip naked in front of a bunch of strangers. Fortunately, I have my three best friends with me to take the plunge together.

As I descend the steps of the jet, with our pilot's chivalrous assistance, I give him a smile. "Thank you, Rene. I love your Australian accent. And I can tell you're a gentleman with a naughty streak, just the kind of man I like."

He winks and chuckles. "Don't tempt me, love."

As my shoes touch down on the grass, I know for sure that I'm finally here on the magical island of Heirani Motu. The vibrant colors and luscious aromas of the island drench my senses like warm honey. Lush green palms sway gently in the breeze, framing a sky so blue it almost hurts to look at it. The air is thick with the scent of tropical flowers and salty sea spray.

Mm, this is heaven.

"Welcome to paradise, ladies and gents!" Rene calls out with a grin. "Watch out for the mosquitos, they're as big as Godzilla!"

His corny joke breaks the tension, and I can't help but laugh along with the other guests.

Then a handsome young man approaches us, clipboard in hand. He's clearly an employee of the resort. "I'm Emilio, your assistant manager. If you'll follow me, I'll escort you lot to the resort and get you checked in at the front desk."

Emilio has a smooth New Zealand accent and a cheerful attitude.

As we make our way up the winding trail, my three best friends crowd around me, buzzing with excitement.

"Can you believe we're actually here?" Lila gushes, her green eyes wide as she takes in our surroundings. "It's like stepping into a dream."

"A very naked dream," Maya quips with a wink. "Hope you all remembered to pack your birthday suits."

Zara smirks, linking her arm around mine. "Oh, this is going to be such an adventure. I can feel it in my bones."

I grin. "Well, ladies, are you ready to unleash your wild sides?"

Lila shakes her head. "Honey, my wild side's been caged up for so long that it's gone feral. Watch out, island men!"

As we emerge from the wooded path and onto a sprawling patio overlooking the sea in the distance, my breath catches. The view is spectacular, but that's not what draws my eye. Standing near the edge is quite possibly the most gorgeous man I've ever seen. Tall and lean, with tousled blond hair and piercing hazel eyes. He exudes an aura of quiet authority that makes my pulse quicken.

"Who's the stud?" I murmur to Zara.

She follows my gaze and smirks. "That, my dear, is Ryan Kimble. In the brochure, it said he's the interim general manager and a former Navy SEAL. Didn't you read your welcome packet? If you had, you'd know who he is. Ryan is filling in while the regular general manager and his wife are away."

My gaze remains glued to Ryan as he moves to address the group. The way he carries himself, shoulders back and spine straight, exudes confidence and control. And wow, is that sexy.

"Welcome everyone," he begins, his voice as deep and smooth as aged whiskey. "I'm Ryan Kimble, and on behalf of the entire staff, I'd like to say how happy we are to have you here at Au Naturel Naturist Resort South Seas."

As he continues speaking, my mind wanders to decidedly less wholesome places. I wonder what that tanned skin would feel like under my fingertips. How those strong arms might feel wrapped around me. And oh yes, how his cock might feel inside me.

"Earth to Meredith," Maya whispers, elbowing me gently. "You're drooling."

I blink rapidly, realizing I've completely zoned out. And I whisper too. "Sorry. Just...taking in the scenery."

Zara snickers. "Oh, we noticed. Planning your island fling already?"

"Maybe. A girl can dream, right?"

But honestly, I doubt a hunk like Ryan would want to have a fling with a post-menopausal woman. Must be some fit and sexy older men around here too. Well, there's always Rene, I guess. But I just can't picture myself getting it on with him.

As we await the welcome speech, my thoughts drift back to the brochure. It had promised "two weeks of sun, sand, and freedom that will provide the no-holds-barred experience of a lifetime." My inhibitions are already starting to slip away just thinking about that, replaced by a giddy sense of possibility.

Watch out, Heirani Motu. Meredith Hayes is ready to play.

I can't help but marvel at the resort's design. The open-air architecture seamlessly blends with the lush surroundings, almost as if the buildings grew organically from the island itself.

"Can you believe this place?" I whisper to Lila, gesturing at the vibrant greenery and colorful flowers surrounding us. "It's like we've stepped into paradise."

Lila grins, her eyes sparkling with mischief. "Oh, honey, paradise is just the beginning. Wait until you see what else this island has to offer."

I had thoroughly researched the resort beforehand, poring over the website for weeks to make sure this was the perfect playground for me and my friends. "Did you know there are dolphins that swim along the shore? And strange flying foxes that come out at night? They're officially called monkey-faced bats, but 'flying foxes' has a better ring."

"Ooh, wildlife," Maya chimes in. "As long as they don't interrupt my tanning time, I'm cool with that. Not sure about monkey-faced bats, though. Sounds creepy."

"Speaking of animal life," Zara whispers, nodding toward a group of muscular twenty-somethings, "I spy a few specimens I wouldn't mind studying up close."

I roll my eyes but can't help laughing. "Focus, ladies. This is only day one, so there's no rush."

"Sure, yeah," Lila teases with a knowing roll of her eyes. "So, the 'wildlife.' Is that what we're calling it now?"

As we go on bantering, I only half listen to my friends. In a matter of minutes, I'll be baring it all in front of complete strangers. My heart races with a mix of exhilaration and nerves like nothing I've experienced before. But this isn't fear. It's freedom.

"You okay, Mer?" Zara asks, noticing my sudden quiet.

I take a deep breath. "Yeah, just...processing. This is really happening, isn't it?"

"Second thoughts?" Maya inquires gently.

I shake my head. "No, not at all. After losing Brian, I never thought I'd do something this...daring."

Lila squeezes my hand. "Be proud of yourself, honey. Brian wore you down and ignored you, treating you like a roommate instead of a wife. Now, it's time to take charge of your life and embrace new experiences."

"Thanks," I whisper, blinking back unexpected tears. Then I straighten my shoulders, pushing the bittersweet memories aside. "All right, enough of that. We came here to have fun, right?"

Zara smacks my arm. "That's the spirit. Now, about those young studs over there..."

I laugh, grateful for the distraction. "Down, girl. Let's at least get through the introductions before you start planning your conquests."

As my friends continue their playful debate over which guests look the most "delicious," I find my gaze drawn back to Ryan. There's something about him, an air of quiet intensity that's utterly magnetic. I shake my head, reminding myself that I'm here to relax and have fun, not get tangled up in complicated emotions. Still, as the resort staff begins to gather for introductions, I can't quite shake the feeling that this vacation might hold more surprises than I bargained for.

I pull the welcome packet out of my purse, flipping through the glossy pages absently. The promise of a wild adventure has me tapping my toes in anticipation.

"Ladies, it's showtime," Zara whispers, nudging me forward.

We join the crowd, moving even closer to the temporary dais where Ryan stands. I catch snippets of conversation—hushed giggles, speculative murmurs about what awaits us. My own curiosity bubbles up, threatening to overflow.

Then Ryan steps onto the platform, and the world narrows down to only him. He spreads his arms wide, and I swear the air crackles with electricity. Apparently, tropical islands melt my brain.

"Welcome to Au Naturel Naturist Resort South Seas," Ryan begins, his voice rich and warm. "We're thrilled to have you as our guests for the next two weeks, on this privately owned island that offers the ultimate in discretion and luxury."

I lean in more, hanging on every word like a nerdy schoolgirl with a crush on the football star. There's something about the way he speaks, confident yet approachable, that draws me in.

"I'm Ryan Kimble, interim general manager. But you can call me Ryan," he continues, gesturing to the staff behind him. "And these amazing people are my partners in bringing you the best vacation experience of your lives."

My gaze flicks to Zara, finding an echo of my own excitement in her eyes. We exchange a silent nod, a promise of what's to come.

Ryan's lips pucker briefly, the expression almost imperceptible. "Please don't hesitate to ask any of us whatever questions might come to mind. Your welcome packets include a list of our rules. Please abide by them."

A hand shoots up from the crowd, and a man's voice calls out, "Rules? I thought this was supposed to be a naughty place!"

I stifle a laugh, curious to see how Ryan will handle this.

He doesn't miss a beat, a hint of amusement in his tone. "Don't worry. We have only a few restrictions. It's all common-sense stuff and common decency. But you'll find a plethora of opportunities to explore the sensual side of life while you're here on the island of Heirani Motu."

As Ryan continues, I find myself wondering just what those "opportunities" might entail. And whether I'll have the courage to seize them. Telling myself I'm on board for a naughty holiday isn't the same as actually doing it.

Buck up, woman. This is your time to escape from life back home. Seize it.

I lean in, hanging on Ryan's every word as he delves deeper into the resort's philosophy. His voice, rich and confident, sends a warm shiver down my spine.

He sweeps his hazel eyes over the crowd. "Remember, this is an adults-only, clothes-free naturist resort. The few exceptions to that rule are outlined in your packets." Ryan gestures to the far side of the patio. "In consideration of our clothes-free mandate, we provide a few amenities other tourist destinations don't offer. The terracotta bowls located throughout the resort offer free access to sunscreen, insect repellent, and condom packets."

Wait. Condoms? Big bowls of them? Yeah, he just said that. Sure, I'm itching for some hot romance, but I hadn't expected terracotta bowls full of rubbers. Guess I don't need to worry about the box of condoms I bought back in the airport gift shop. When in Rome, dive into the debauchery. Don't think that's quite how the saying goes.

But Ryan is still talking, and I find myself mesmerized all over again.

"And also," Ryan explains, "we remind you that our in-house pharmacy can provide whatever medication refills you might need. We also have a medical doctor and a nurse on staff."

As he speaks, my attention drifts. I begin to consider my options for a vacation fling and sneak a few glances at some of the younger male guests. To my surprise, more than a few are eyeing me appreciatively. Maybe being fiftyish isn't such a drawback after all. I wonder if Ryan is younger than I am.

I take a deep breath, inhaling the sweet scent that seems to permeate the island. And I whisper to myself, "You've got this, Mer. Time to live a little for once in your life."

As Ryan's speech winds down, a surge of determination washes over me. This is it. My chance to rediscover myself, to embrace life with everything I've got. I square my shoulders, a silent vow forming in my mind: *No more holding back. No more what-ifs.*

"And now," Ryan announces, "off with your clothes!"

There's a moment of hesitation, then a flurry of movement. Shirts fly, pants drop, and suddenly the patio is awash in a sea of bare skin. I take a deep breath and peel off my sundress, tossing it aside. And just like that, I'm naked. In public. The tropical breeze caresses my skin, and I can't help but smile. It feels...liberating. Exhilarating, even.

"Well, would you look at that," Lila giggles beside me. "Mer has the girls out and proud!"

I laugh, giving a little shimmy. "Might as well put them to good use. Think they'll help me snag that cabana boy?"

"Honey," Zara chimes in, "with those puppies, you could snag the whole kennel if you wanted."

We dissolve into laughter, the sound mingling with the excited chatter around us. I catch Maya eyeing a group of young men nearby, her cheeks dappled with pink.

"Earth to Maya," I tease. "Did you see something you like?"

She grins, a mischievous glint in her eye. "Just thinking about the, um, *scenery.*"

"Speaking of scenery," Lila interjects, "we'd better stock up on lube. Otherwise, we'll be suffering from what I like to call the Sahara Desert Effect. We are mature women, after all."

I snort, shaking my head. "Always the practical one, aren't you?"

As we banter, I can't help but marvel at how natural this feels. Here we are, naked as the day we were born, cracking jokes like it's any other girls' trip. But it's not, is it? This is the start of something new, something life changing. I glance around, taking in the diverse array of bodies on display. Young, old, fit, curvy—everyone seems so comfortable in their own skin. It's infectious, really. I stand a little straighter, feeling a newfound confidence course through me.

"Ladies," I announce, "I think this is going to be one hell of a vacation."

Chapter Two

Ryan

I stand on the patio dais, alone yet surrounded by people, taking a deep breath as I watch the new arrivals strip down. Their whoops and laughter echo across the patio, a cacophony of uninhibited joy. My jaw clenches. *Stay professional, Kimble. You've faced tougher challenges.* But have I? Even my SEAL training didn't prepare me for managing a nudist resort. I can almost hear Tucker's gravelly voice and his laughter when I informed him of my new job. He thought it was funny, but he wasn't being a douche. He's genuinely happy for me.

Tuck knows about my...issues. And he helped me figure out how to cope.

A peal of feminine laughter draws my attention. A lithe brunette tosses her sundress aside, stretching languorously while she tips her head back and grins. My gaze snaps back to the resort entrance. *Focus on the job, not the guests.* I smooth my crisp white uniform, the starched collar a stark contrast to the carefree atmosphere. My fingers brush the name tag—"Ryan Kimble, Interim General Manager." The cool metal grounds me just enough to keep me from acting like a human statue.

You've got this, Kimble. Second chances don't come easy, so fight for it, man.

As I turn away, a flash of caramel-brown hair catches my eye, and I get a glimpse of amber eyes. What is that woman's name? I'd been watching her out of the corner of my eye during my entire welcome speech. Though she's now facing away, I'd recognize that luscious hair and those transfixing eyes anywhere. My heart thuds traitorously, and my cock jerks too. My own body is trying to encourage me to break my rules for this job. No romance. No sex either.

My phone chirps, mercifully distracting me. It's Tucker: *How's paradise treating you? Still got your clothes on?*

I chuckle despite myself. Leave it to Tucker to cut through the tension. I type back: *All good here. Professionalism is my middle name.*

His reply is almost instantaneous: *Bullshit. It's Theodore and we both know it. Proud of you, man. You've come a long way, and you've got this.*

Suddenly, I'm standing up straighter and lifting my chin. Maybe I do have this, just like I told myself a moment ago. Maybe Heirani Motu is exactly where I need to be. I type: *Thanks, Tuck, no need to worry about me.*

He sends me a thumbs-up emoji, then signs off. I square my shoulders and stride toward my office. Time to get to work.

I pivot smoothly, as the first guests enter the lobby, my practiced smile sliding into place. I extend my hand to a sun-bronzed couple. "Welcome to Heirani Motu. I'm Ryan, your interim general manager. How may I assist you today?"

The woman beams, her enthusiasm infectious. "Oh, this place is just gorgeous! We're looking for some information on activities."

I nod, gesturing toward a nearby rack. "Of course. You'll find our full range of pamphlets right over there. Emilio, our assistant manager, can help you. We also have two activity coordinators who can provide more details."

Emilio appears at my side as if he'd been hiding behind me, though I doubt that. His curly hair is hair tousled by the island breeze, and he grins at the couple. "Did someone say activities? I've got you covered, mates."

"Ooh, what a lovely accent," the woman says. "Is that Australian?"

"New Zealand. I'm a proud Kiwi."

While Emilio leads the couple away, I catch Marley's eye across the lobby. She gives me a subtle thumbs-up, mouthing '"you're doing great!" I manage a small smile in return, grateful for her support.

A booming voice cuts through the chatter. "My god, would you look at this view?"

I turn to find a barrel-chested man with a salt-and-pepper beard, his eyes wide with wonder as he gazes out the floor-to-ceiling windows at the entrance to the lobby.

"It's certainly breathtaking, sir," I agree, stepping closer. "Hei-rani Motu is home to some of the most diverse wildlife in the South Pacific. Our nature trails offer—"

"Nature trails?" He claps a hand on my shoulder. "Tell me more, son. Can't wait to explore this wicked paradise."

I slip into my well-rehearsed spiel, grateful for the distraction. "We have several guided hikes that showcase our local flora and fauna. The waterfall trail is particularly popular, featuring a rope bridge and a natural swimming hole. For the more adventurous, we offer zip-lining tours through the canopy."

His eyes light up. "Zip-lining? Now that's what I'm talking about!"

I find myself warming up to the topic too, though I doubt I'll have time for recreation of any sort. "We also offer day trips to the nearby Fiji Islands, and even shopping excursions to New Zealand for those looking to mix a bit of urban exploration with their tropical getaway. You have to wear clothes off the island, of course."

As if he wouldn't have figured that out on his own. *Duh, Kimble.*

While I speak, I can't help but marvel at how easily the words flow now. A few weeks ago, I was floundering, unsure if I could handle this role. Now, it almost feels...natural.

Almost.

Because even as I maintain my professional demeanor, a part of me remains hyper-aware of every bare shoulder, every flash of skin in my peripheral vision. This job is unlike anything I've ever done before, and the constant balancing act is...challenging, to say the least. But I'm determined to make it work. For my career, for my future, and maybe, just maybe, for a chance at finding a real home here at a nudist resort. Normal life hadn't turned out so well for me. Might as well try something vastly different.

My mind drifts back to earlier, when the guests first began to disrobe. I'd steeled myself for this moment, but nothing could have prepared me for the sight of the most beautiful woman I've ever seen. She smiles at me as if she knows me, her smile radiant, the caramel-brown waves of her hair catching the sunlight as she sheds her dress. I force my gaze upward, meeting her amber eyes. They're sparkling with mischief, and I swear she just winked at me.

"Keep it together, Kimble," I mutter under my breath, gripping my clipboard tighter. The familiar weight grounds me, a shield against the sudden rush of heat coursing through my body. I scan the crowd, focusing on faces, not bodies. *Remember, professionalism first,* I remind myself. But it's a losing battle. My eyes keep drifting back to that gorgeous woman—her confident stance, her easy smile. Even the wrinkles around her eyes are enchanting.

"All right, everyone," I call out, my voice remarkably calm. "If you'll gather round, we'll get started with our welcome orientation."

After a brief pause to make sure everyone is listening, I step onto the temporary dais with my clipboard in hand. The wood creaks beneath my feet, but I doubt it will collapse. But yeah, I suffered a brief moment of concern about that. My voice sounds authoritative as I speak, and I suddenly realize that's not an act. "Welcome to Heirani Motu. We're thrilled to have you here at Au Naturel Naturist Resort South Seas. Before we dive in, I'd like to emphasize our core values: respect and consent."

A murmur of approval ripples through the crowd. I continue, outlining our amenities and activities, careful to keep my gaze at the eye level of every guest. But whenever my focus passes over a certain guest, my heart rate spikes. No woman has ever affected me this way before.

"While this is a clothes-free resort," I explain, "we recommend wearing sandals or sneakers outdoors, and you may want to place a napkin or handkerchief under your bottom when you sit down. That includes the dining hall especially."

The guests haven't made any lewd jokes. What a relief.

I glance at my clipboard briefly, then face the crowd again. "Remember, photography is strictly prohibited without explicit consent from all parties involved. Please place a red sticker over your phone's camera when you aren't photographing. If your phone has multiple cameras, slap those dots on all of them."

As I speak, I can't help but admire the guests' confidence. Their unabashed attitudes, their comfort in their own skin...it's admirable. And it's a stark contrast to my own rigid posture in my resort uniform. *I could never go naked in public,* I think, even as a small part of me wonders what it might feel like to be so free.

A voice pipes up from the crowd, breaking through my reverie. "Hey, does this mean we can finally tell people we're going to a nude beach without lying just so we'll seem totally based?"

The quip catches me off guard, and a ripple of laughter spreads through the group. I feel the corners of my mouth tug upward, my stoic facade cracking just a bit. It's been a while since I've allowed myself a genuine smile. The young man who spoke is still grinning.

A slight chuckle tumbles from my lips. "Well, I suppose that's one perk of our clothes-free policy."

More chuckles follow, and for a moment, I'm transported back to family gatherings, to easier times filled with warmth and laughter. But the memory twists, turning bittersweet as I find my thoughts reeling backward in time to a far less pleasurable moment.

I clear my throat, pushing the darkness aside. "Now, let's talk about our nature trails. We have several routes of varying difficulty..."

As I continue the orientation, my eyes scan the diverse group before me. It includes a kaleidoscope of body types, ages, and backgrounds—all united in their embrace of a unique experience. It's oddly beautiful, this celebration of the human form in all its variations.

"Our main waterfall trail is a particular favorite," I point out, my voice rock steady. "It offers breathtaking views and a chance to connect with the island's natural beauty."

I catch a glimpse of that woman again, her eyes sparkling and her lips curled up at the corners. For a moment, I allow myself to wonder what it would be like to hike that trail with her, to share in the wonder of Heirani Motu's hidden treasures and share an erotic moment with her beneath a shimmering waterfall. Her water-slicked body would shimmer, as droplets dapple her skin.

But then shame washes over me, hot and familiar. I'm not the man I once was—trusting, open. Tragedy left its mark, deeper than any physical scar.

"Remember," I add, pushing the memories aside, "safety is our top priority. Always stay on marked paths and respect wildlife habitats."

As I wrap up the orientation, I realize something has shifted. The anxiety has faded away. Here, surrounded by people embracing new sides of themselves without shame, the idea of holding onto that fear seems...trivial. So, I step down from the dais, my clipboard no longer a shield but simply a tool.

"Any questions?" I ask, surprised to find I'm genuinely curious about what these people might want to know.

While I mingle with the guests, their enthusiasm begins to infect me too. I can't help but feel a spark of pride for Heirani Motu, this slice of paradise I've been entrusted to manage.

"Where's the best spot for stargazing?" a silver-haired woman asks.

"The secluded cove on the north side of the island," I reply, gesturing toward the lush tree line. "It's a bit of a hike, but the view is unparalleled. You'll feel like you can touch the Milky Way."

I find myself relaxing into the role, answering questions about hidden waterfalls and the best times for wildlife spotting. It's almost...fun. The thought of James and Holly's suggestion about a long-term future with Au Naturel flits through my mind. Maybe this is more than just a temporary escape.

A tap on my shoulder pulls me back to the present. I'm in the lobby now, the orientation simply a vivid memory.

"Ryan?" It's Marley, her freckled face wrinkled with a mix of apology and urgency. "Sorry to interrupt, but I've got a question about today's schedule."

I turn to face her, pushing thoughts of the past aside. "No problem, Marley. What's on your mind?"

She explains a conflict between two activities, her hands gesturing animatedly. I listen, considering the options.

"Let's move the nature walk to three pm," I decide. "That'll give the zip-lining group time to finish and join in if they want. Good catch, Marley."

Her face lights up. "Thanks, boss. You're doing such a great job with all of this, Ryan. Seriously, the resort's never run smoother."

Her praise makes me want to clear my throat and avoid her gaze, though I tamp down that instinct. "I appreciate that. But it's a team effort. Your attention to detail makes my job a lot easier."

She beams, and I'm reminded of how often I've commended her during staff meetings. It's not just empty praise. Her work ethic is impressive. I've only known Marley for two weeks, yet she's already become a trusted ally. While she heads off to adjust the schedule, I allow myself a small moment of satisfaction. Maybe I'm not just running from my past here. Maybe I'm building something new.

I slip away from the lobby, seeking a rare moment of solitude. The worn path through the woods leads me to a small clearing, a hidden oasis with two chaises. I stretch out on one, and the woven material softly creaks beneath my weight. While the chirping of tropical birds and the distant rush of breakers on the shore fill my ears, I perform one final self-appointed task.

"Breathe," I mutter to myself, closing my eyes. But I can't shake the image of that beautiful woman's radiant, unguarded smile. It stirs something in me I thought was long dead.

I jerk upright on my chaise. "No, you moron, you are not going there."

Not today, at least. Maybe once I've settled in a bit more...

But no, I shouldn't go there at all.

With more effort than the task normally requires, I force my mind to show me the day's events, cataloging challenges and successes in a personal inventory of my day so far. The orientation went smoothly, despite my, ah, distractions. I make a mental note to commend Emilio on his quick thinking with a lost luggage situation and Marley's good work too. Rene Walker made the guests feel at home the second they stepped off the Cessna jet.

This job, it's...good. I'm good at it. Damn good, actually. Hell, I rock my job.

A realization hits me. I've been so focused on maintaining distance that I haven't made sure my staff receives the praise and time off they need. We all need moments like this, I decide, and already I'm planning how to encourage little breaks now and then. Might even do a staff retreat of some sort.

But not today.

The peace of the clearing has done its work. I stand, stretching my whole body, and groan deeply as I make my way toward the beach, approaching the water's edge. Waves crash rhythmically, the vast expanse of blue stretching to the horizon. I tip my head back, eyes closed, letting the sound wash over me.

"Yeah, you *can* do this," I whisper. "One day at a time."

With a deep breath, I open my eyes. The calm of the ocean has settled something within me, but I know the underlying turmoil remains. There's still so much unresolved, so much pain I've buried.

I turn, striding back toward the main building with renewed purpose. My office beckons, offering a sanctuary of spreadsheets and schedules. *Keep your distance*, I remind myself firmly as that mystery woman's beautiful eyes flash through my mind unbidden. *Focus on the job. Nothing else matters.* But I have to know her name or else I'll go mad. A tiny indiscretion won't hurt anything. So, I sort through the passport photos for each guest. And there she is—Meredith Hayes, age fifty-two. Is she married? I didn't see any wedding ring.

Even as I settle in behind my desk, a treacherous part of me whispers that maybe, just maybe, something else does matter after all.

Chapter Three

Meredith

As I gaze past the patio, a gentle breeze brushes against my skin, bringing with it the soothing scents of afternoon in the tropics. My throat suddenly feels parched, and my mouth waters at the thought of a cool, fruity cocktail. I half expect to see staff members bustling about with trays of drinks. And I can almost taste the sweetness and tanginess on my tongue. The sound of clinking glasses and soft chatter fills the air, accompanied by the occasional burst of laughter. I can also hear the distant sound of waves crashing against the shore.

"Should we head to the lobby for our welcome cocktails?" I ask Zara.

Her light laughter almost seems to tinkle like wind chimes. "Oh, Mer, didn't you read the welcome packet? The drinks are on the auxiliary patio."

"Right, of course." I hesitate, feeling a bit sheepish. Guess I should've read the welcome packet more thoroughly. "Lead the way, oh wise one. I wonder how many tiny umbrellas had to die for our drinking pleasure."

"Probably an entire rainforest's worth," Maya giggles like a schoolgirl, not like the mature college behavioral counselor she is. Her blue eyes are sparkling in the sunshine as she points toward a sexy man with a buff bod and salt-and-pepper hair. "Mm, can I get one of those to go?"

I roll my eyes at her. "This isn't a buffet, Maya."

"Not yet. But who knows..."

This is what happens when four widows who met at a group counseling session decide to relieve our dwindling sorrow with a crazy vacation. And that's how I met Maya, Lila, and Zara—because we lost our husbands. The vacation idea had been two-and-a-half years in the making. Once we resolved to put the past behind us, this trip was inevitable. Hence, our wild holiday on the other side of the world.

As we saunter toward the larger patio, I shake my head, wondering if I could have a little something steamy with the interim general manager. I know his name, but I wonder if he knows mine. Ryan had been glancing at me often during his welcome speech this afternoon. That suggests he is interested.

But I don't see him now.

We reach the bar where a colorful array of tropical concoctions is spread out before us. I grab a vibrant blue drink, complete with pineapple wedge and, yes, a tiny umbrella. Then I notice Maya has just reached for a second cocktail.

"Careful there, Ms. Kozlow," I admonish. "Any more of those and you'll be pink from head to toe."

"Oh, hush," Maya retorts, but her cheeks are already flushed. "I'm just embracing the island spirit."

As we sip our drinks, my gaze wanders to the snakelike pool below. Guests splash and laugh, their bodies glistening in the sunshine. I watch a group of twenty-somethings engaged in a heated game of volleyball, their movements fluid, their laughter carefree. They all look so...comfortable, so at ease with their nudity and with this whole experience.

Zara gives me a knowing wink and a smile. I take a deep breath, feeling the warm island air fill my lungs, and release it gradually.

You're ready for this, Mer, I remind myself. *Ready for all of it.*

I raise my glass. "To new adventures."

My friends echo the sentiment, our glasses clinking as we imagine the promise of memories to come. Yeah, I might be going a tad overboard with the purple prose. Hey, I never said I was a writer. I'm a bank teller, for pity's sake.

"Ladies, shall we check out our accommodations?" I suggest, draining the last sip of my drink.

My friends nod their agreement.

The sweet, tropical flavor of my cocktail lingers on my tongue as I lead the way into the main resort building. The cool air offers a surprising respite from the balmy atmosphere outside. As we follow the corridors, our bare feet pad softly on the carpeted floors. I guess they don't want anyone to slip on polished wood, so they went for soft carpeting instead.

Maya and Lila dash ahead, clearly too excited to do anything but grin and laugh. I feel exhilarated too, minus the giggles.

Lila raises her key card and grins. "Room 304."

She fumbles with her key card, and the door swings open to reveal a spacious suite bathed in natural light.

"Oh. My. God." Maya's jaw drops as she takes in the panoramic view from the open patio. "Mer, you have to see this!"

I step out onto the balcony, drinking in the breathtaking vista. The sinuous pools wind their way through lush gardens, beyond which the mountains rise majestically, their peaks kissing the azure sky. The ocean glimmers in the distance, a ribbon of turquoise on the horizon.

"Not too shabby," I concur, but my casual tone can't mask my awe.

We spend the next hour exploring each of their suites, oohing and aahing over the luxurious amenities. As I flop onto Zara's king-size bed, a twinge of disappointment hits me, and I sigh.

"I can't believe I'm all the way across the resort from you guys."

But Zara pats my shoulder. "Look on the bright side, honey. You'll have all the privacy you need for any...late-night visitors."

I pretend to be horrified and overdo it a touch. "Please. I'm here to relax, not..."

"Not what?" Lila waggles her eyebrows. "Have mind-blowing, earth-shattering, tropical-island sex?"

The four of us dissolve into uproarious laughter. When we flop backward onto the bed in unison, we laugh even more. Once we catch our breath again, we discuss ordering room service for the four of us, but I make my excuses and leave my friends behind. They don't mind. And I need a bit of alone time after that long plane ride in premium economy class. We pooled our resources to pony up for the extra fees that granted us a teeny bit more comfort. It was still a far cry from first class.

After walking out of Zara's amazing suite, I set off toward my bungalow. It lies in a more secluded area. I had reserved the bungalow only because the resort was almost booked up when we made our reservations. I would've preferred to stay closer to my friends. But as I exit the main building, I lift my chin and feel a bounce in my step that I hadn't noticed before.

Is this freedom I'm feeling? Yes, it is.

The path to my bungalow is a feast for the senses. Vibrant hibiscus and fragrant frangipani line the walkway, their petals dancing in the gentle breeze. The air is thick with the heady scent of ylang-ylang, its sweet perfume mingling with the salty tang of the sea. I pause to admire a towering breadfruit tree, its large, glossy leaves creating dappled shadows on the ground. Nearby, a cluster of bird of paradise flowers reveal their vibrant orange and blue petals reminiscent of exotic tropical birds ready to take flight.

A melodious trill catches my attention, and I pause, watching a brightly colored bird flit from branch to branch. I swear its song is beckoning me, as if it's crooning, "You belong here, Meredith."

Jeez, I really have gone sappy. So what? I'll embrace the schmaltz.

As I approach my bungalow, my heart quickens with anticipation, though I can't quite explain why. A woven basket sits by the door, overflowing with local fruits and treats. The attached card tells me the basket includes feijoa, guava, and several other exotic fruits I've never heard of before.

I lift the woven lid, inhaling deeply as a burst of sweet, tropical scents wafts up to greet me. The feijoas are oval-shaped and green, their skin slightly bumpy under my curious fingers. I've never tasted one before, but the card promises a flavor somewhere between strawberry and pineapple. Next, the guavas beckon with their yellow-green hue and intoxicating aroma. I can't resist picking one up, marveling at how its soft fuzz tickles my palm. The basket seems like a cornucopia of surprises. There's a spiky red fruit that must be rambutan, according to the card, its wild exterior hiding the translucent flesh within.

My hand hovers over the doorknob, and I take a deep breath. "Well, Mer, here goes nothing. Let's hope my bungalow is as amazing as the suites my friends have."

I twist the knob and step inside, my jaw falling open in awe. The bungalow is indeed a paradise within paradise. Two words whisper out of me: "Holy shit."

Sunlight streams through floor-to-ceiling windows, illuminating a spacious living area that flows seamlessly into an open-air deck. The décor is a perfect blend of tropical luxury and intimate comfort—all natural materials and sensual curves.

I run my fingers along the silky-smooth surface of a driftwood coffee table. "This is...absolutely incredible."

My gaze is drawn to the hallway where I can just glimpse a sliver of the large bedstead. I race down the hall and spread my arms wide, smiling as I throw my head back. The bed is draped in gauzy white curtains that billow gently in the ocean breeze. It's an invitation to indulgence if I've ever seen one. I swear I can already feel the fabric brushing against my skin even from across the room.

"Well, hello there, you sexy thing," I purr as I leap onto the bed, giving the mattress a playful pat. "I have a feeling we're going to become very good friends."

I continue my exploration, each discovery more wonderful than the last. The bathroom is a work of art with a freestanding tub big enough for two people—or more, my mind helpfully supplies. The gorgeous tub takes center stage, while an outdoor shower promises the exhilarating feel of warm water and tropical air on bare skin.

While I picture the possibilities, a tiny shiver of anticipation races down my spine. "Babe, you've outdone yourself this time. A nudist resort? My girlfriends would never have thought of that on their own."

Stepping onto the deck, I'm greeted by a private infinity pool that seems to melt into the ocean beyond. The view is breathtaking—endless shades of blue stretching to the horizon. I close my eyes, letting the warm sun caress my skin. For the first time in years, I feel truly alive, every nerve ending tingling with possibility.

"Look out, Heirani Motu," I declare to the sea and sky. "Meredith Hayes is ready for adventure."

As if in response, a gentle breeze wraps around me like a lover's embrace, carrying the intoxicating scent of tropical flowers. Laughter spills out of me, light and carefree. I've never felt this free, not in my entire life. Years of sadness hadn't left much time for frivolity.

My mind drifts to Ryan, his easy confidence and that devastating smile. Then I recall his welcome speech and the other guests gathered on the patio, who ranged from young to old, all of them beautifully uninhibited.

"Two weeks," I muse, trailing my fingers along the railing. "Two weeks to be whoever I want to be, to do whatever—and whoever—I want."

With a contented sigh, I turn back to the bungalow. It's time to unpack and maybe take a dip in that inviting pool. But as I cross the threshold, I can't shake the feeling that I'm stepping into more than just a room. I'm stepping into a whole new chapter of my life. And I can't wait to see how the story unfolds.

As I wander back into the living room, my mind still reels from the luxurious nature of my surroundings. The large flat-screen TV catches my eye, and for a moment, I'm tempted to sink into the plush sofa to lose myself in a bit of mindless entertainment. But as I reach for the remote, a pang of guilt stops me.

"What are you doing, woman?" I chide myself. "You're on a tropical island paradise, and you're about to watch TV? Come on."

I toss the remote aside and walk to the window, gazing out at the lush landscape. The distant roar of a waterfall reaches my ears, and suddenly, I remember the rope bridge I'd read about in the resort's brochure.

"Now that's more like it," I grin, grabbing my phone, my sun hat, and a bottle of water. I had already smeared sunscreen over myself earlier.

As I amble out of my bungalow, the temperate air wafts around me once again. The path to the waterfall trail is clearly marked, winding through a verdant jungle that teems with life. Exotic birds call to each other in the canopy above, their melodies a siren song drawing me deeper into the heart of the island. As the trail gradually steepens, I feel a slight burn in my thighs. It's been too long since I've challenged my body like this. As I round a bend, the rushing of water grows louder until, suddenly, there it is—a breathtaking cascade tumbling over moss-covered rocks.

"Wow," I breathe, drinking in the sight.

The rope bridge stretches across the gorge, swaying gently in the breeze, suspended high above the deep gorge. Its wooden slats are only slightly weathered despite frequent use. The ropes that hold it together show no fraying and seem strong enough to bear the weight of a single person at a time or even couples or small groups too. The bridge seems to dance between the lush green trees and the sparkling waters below in a gentle, lulling rhythm.

I take a deep breath, steeling myself for the crossing. The first step onto the bridge sends a jolt of excitement through me as it sways beneath my feet. I grip the ropes tightly as I make my way across, one step at a time, until I've found my footing. At the half-way point, I pause to take in the view. The waterfall roars below, mist rising in ethereal swirls.

Once I'm safely across the bridge, I throw my arms up and whoop. I've conquered my first challenge of the trip. Energized, I opt to explore further down the trail. The path narrows, winding deeper into the jungle. Vibrant flowers peek out from the undergrowth, their heady scent intoxicating. Lost in the beauty around me, I barely notice as the well-worn trail gives way to a less traveled path. The canopy grows denser, filtering the sunlight into dappled patterns on the forest floor. The air grows thick with humidity, and I can feel beads of sweat forming on my skin.

As I push through a particularly dense patch of foliage, I suddenly emerge into a small clearing. My breath catches in my throat at the sight before me. A hidden waterfall, smaller than the main one but no less beautiful, cascades down a rocky cliff face into a crystal-clear pool below. The sunlight sparkles on the water like diamonds.

"Oh my," I whisper, in awe of the secluded paradise I've discovered.

Without a second thought, I fling my sun hat away. The heat and humidity have left me feeling sticky and uncomfortable, but the cool, inviting water calls to me like a siren's song. I wade into the pool, sighing with pleasure as the refreshing water envelops my body. I dip my head back, letting my hair fan out around me. For a moment, I float here, weightless and free.

Then I hear a rustling in the underbrush ahead of me. My heart leaps into my throat as I freeze, wondering what creature I might encounter. But instead of some exotic animal, a familiar figure emerges from behind a large fern.

"Ryan?" I gasp, surprised to see the resort manager out here on the trails.

He looks equally startled to see me, his eyes widening as they take in my nude form. I feel warmth in my cheeks, abruptly aware of my nakedness in a way I hadn't been back at the resort.

"Meredith?" he queries, his voice a bit husky. "I didn't expect to run into anyone out here."

Ryan's crisp, white resort uniform stands out against the lush greens of the surrounding jungle. The fabric is neatly pressed, just as it had been during his welcome speech, and it accentuates his muscular frame. The faint scent of laundry detergent clings to his uniform, while my skin smells of sunscreen and sweat.

His gaze flickers over me, and I feel a rush of heat that has nothing to do with the tropical climate.

"I, um, I was just exploring," I stammer, suddenly feeling tongue-tied. "I didn't realize I'd wandered so far off the main trail. Hang on, how did you know my name? I don't recall introducing myself."

He scratches the back of his neck, wincing guiltily. "Well, I, sort of...looked at everyone's passport photos until I found yours."

Ryan stalked me? Oddly, that fact turns me on. "I'm not upset, sweetie. Actually, it's rather flattering."

He takes a step closer, managing to peek at me sideways. "This is a beautiful spot, isn't it? Not many guests find their way here."

"I probably should have brought a map. Good thing you stumbled onto me, or who knows how long I would've been lost in the woods." His rapt focus on my face makes me shiver faintly, and I'm acutely aware of the water lapping at my skin. "It's like a little slice of paradise, don't you think?"

He smiles, and I feel my heart skip a beat. "That it is. Though I have to say, the view just got even more spectacular."

I blush at his words as if I'm a virgin, which I haven't been since prom night many years ago. Part of me wants to sink deeper into the water, to hide from Ryan's gaze. But another part, a bolder part I'm just discovering, wants to stand up and let him look his fill.

As I settle for treading water, keeping my shoulders above the surface, I try for a casual tone. "I didn't realize the staff got to enjoy the island too."

Ryan chuckles, the rich sound sending a tingle of arousal down my spine. His eyes never leave mine as he speaks. "We're encouraged to explore during our off hours, so I decided to go for a walk on my lunch break. Even a few minutes of time off helps us better assist all our guests. It was James and Holly's idea—they're my bosses. Though I have to admit, this is a first for me."

"What, stumbling onto a naked guest in a hidden pool?" I tease, surprising myself with my boldness.

His grin widens. "Something like that."

We stare at each other for a long moment, the air between us charged with unspoken tension. I can feel my heart pounding, and not just from the exertion of my hike. Ryan takes another step closer, his feet at the water's edge now. I can see the muscles in his arms flexing as he grips the strap of his backpack tighter.

"I—I should probably head back," I tell him, though I make no move to climb out of the pool. "My friends will be wondering where I've disappeared to."

Ryan nods and sighs, a flicker of disappointment crossing his face before his professional mask slips back into place. "I understand. Please let me walk you back to the main building."

And he does exactly that. He escorts me. No copping a feel. He doesn't even glance at my boobs. Ah, well, there's always tomorrow.

Chapter Four

Ryan

Did Meredith notice when my gaze flicked down to her tits? I got the impression she was admiring the scenery and didn't pay any attention to me. Not that I care. But damn, a man only has so much willpower, and Meredith is a beautiful, sensual woman. The fact that I caught her swimming in the waterfall pool with no clothes on doesn't help.

Of course she was naked, you moron. It's a nudist resort.

As I lead Meredith back to the main resort building, she insists on chatting like any normal person would. I do my best, but my attraction to this woman is hard to resist. When she tells a joke, I smile and manage a slight chuckle. She is one of the nicest people I've ever met, but that only makes it harder for me to stay professional around her.

"So, Ryan," Meredith says, her voice as silky as warm honey, "you never did tell me how you ended up working at a nudist resort. Seems like an...interesting career choice."

I clear my throat, trying not to let my eyes wander to her tits again. "It's a long story."

She bumps her shoulder into mine in a playful gesture. "I've got time. And I literally can't leave the island unless Rene flies me to Fiji."

I sigh, knowing I shouldn't encourage this conversation but unable to resist. "Let's just say I needed a change. A big one."

"Okay. I can relate to that. It's why I'm here, actually."

As we walk, her arm brushes against mine, sending electricity through my body. I clench my jaw, reminding myself of the rules I'd written for myself which are somewhat stricter than the guidelines for my staff members. But with every step, every smile she throws my way, I feel my resolve weakening. I shouldn't even be entertaining the idea, but something about Meredith draws me in.

I know the dangers of letting my guard down, of allowing even a small crack in the wall I've built around myself. Yet, the more time I spend with this woman, the more I find myself wanting to know her—beyond the polite small talk and surface-level pleasantries.

Her laughter is infectious, her enthusiasm for life palpable. How can one person be so endlessly cheerful? It's a stark contrast to my own subdued nature, and maybe that's part of the allure. She represents everything I've shut out: spontaneity, joy, the pursuit of real happiness. Why do I crave her attention like this? It's been years since I've felt this kind of pull toward someone, and it's as disturbing as it is exhilarating.

"What kind of change are you looking for?" I find myself asking.

She tilts her head, considering her answer. "I'm not entirely sure. Freedom, maybe. A chance to rediscover myself, for sure." Her amber eyes meet mine. "What about you? Did you find what you were looking for here?"

I hesitate, torn between maintaining professional distance and opening up. But I give in and answer her question—sort of. "I found...peace. And a fresh start."

Meredith's smile softens. "That sounds nice."

We've reached the main building, but neither of us moves to go inside. The balmy evening air wraps around us like a cocoon, filled with the chirping of night insects and the distant crash of waves.

Meredith lowers her voice to barely above a whisper. "Ryan, I realize you're trying to keep things professional. I know it's ridiculous, considering that we just met earlier today, but I can't help feeling like there's...well, something between us. "

I swallow hard, my heart suddenly pounding. "Meredith, I—"

"You don't have to say anything," she interrupts gently. "I just wanted you to know that if you'd ever like to talk or anything else, I'm here."

The invitation in her words is clear, and it takes every ounce of willpower I possess not to pull her into my arms right then and there. Instead, I take a deep breath, forcing myself to re-member I'm the general manager. I need to stick to the rules and my duties.

"I appreciate that, Meredith. But as a staff member, I can't—"

"Of course, I understand." A flicker of disappointment flashes on her face before she masks it with a smile. "I didn't mean to make you uncomfortable. Let's just pretend I didn't say anything, okay?"

I nod, relief and regret warring inside me. "That's probably for the best."

We stand here for a moment, gazing at each other, and I wonder if she feels the same tension as I do. The hot kind. I should walk away, end this conversation before it goes any fur-ther. But my feet seem to be rooted to this exact spot, and my eyes are locked on Meredith's. Then she takes a step closer, near enough that I can smell the faint scent of coconut sunscreen on her skin.

"You know, Ryan, sometimes the best things in life happen when we let go of the rules a little."

My throat tightens, and it feels like invisible hands are squeez-ing my throat. "Meredith..."

She reaches out, her fingertips barely brushing my arm. "I should find my friends. We all promised to have lunch together in the dining hall."

The touch of her fingers on my arm sends a jolt through me, and I have to fight the urge to pull her into my arms and kiss her. Instead, I take a step back, putting some much-needed distance between us.

I clear my throat, my voice now sounding strained even to my own ears. "The dining hall, right. It's, uh, just through those doors and to the left. But I'd be happy to escort you."

Meredith's hand falls back to her side, but her eyes never leave mine. "You're so sweet, Ryan, but I can manage on my own. Thank you for the directions and—the company."

I paste on a polite smile, not trusting myself to speak. As she turns to go, I can't help but admire the way her hips gently sway and the graceful curve of her back. Just before she reaches the swinging doors, she glances over her shoulder, catching me staring.

"See you around, Mr. Interim General Manager," she says, with a knowing smile that makes my dick twitch.

I watch her disappear into the building. My chest feels like a lead weight has landed on it.

Dammit. This is exactly what I was trying to avoid. I run a hand through my hair, frustrated with myself for letting things get this far. I should have shut it down immediately, maintained a professional distance. But something about Meredith makes it impossible to keep my walls up. Though I shouldn't do it, I can't stop myself from striding into the dining hall to grab a table in the far corner, partially hidden by a potted plant. From here, I can see Meredith and her friends, but they can't easily spot me. I tell myself I'm just doing my job, keeping an eye on the guests, but deep down I know that's bullshit. I'm here because I can't stay away from her.

Strictly so I won't look like a stalker, I amble over to the buffet and grab some food and a glass of Noni juice. It has antioxidants or something. Then I settle into my secluded corner, the plate before me offering up a colorful array of island delicacies. The *lomi lomi* salmon looks amazing—cubes of cured salmon nestled among diced tomatoes and onions, the vibrant reds and pinks a feast for the eyes as much as the palate. I take a forkful, savoring the delicate balance of salt and citrus that dances on my tongue.

And still, I keep glancing sideways at Meredith.

Next, I try a thick slice of pineapple coconut bread, its golden-brown color enticing me. The sweetness of the pineapple melds perfectly with the rich coconut, and I find myself tearing off chunks with my fingers, propriety be damned.

My continuing struggle to avoid looking at Meredith has given me a crick in my neck, but I still can't stop watching her. She's laughing with her friends now, her head thrown back, exposing the graceful curve of her throat. I force myself to rip my gaze away, instead focusing on the plate in front of me.

But it's no use. My focus is drawn back to her like a magnet—the industrial-strength kind. She's gesturing animatedly now, telling some story that has her friends in stitches. I find myself wishing I could hear what she's saying and be a part of that easy camaraderie.

Suddenly, Meredith's eyes flick in my direction.

I duck my head, pretending to be fascinated by my food, but I can feel the weight of her focus on me.

Meredith slides her chair closer to Lila while laughing at something Maya says. Even from this distance, the joy she exudes from every pore is infectious. I find myself smiling despite my best efforts to maintain a neutral expression.

Since I've finished my main course, I decide to amble over to the buffet again and snag more grub. If Meredith sticks around for much longer, I'll gain ten pounds before I walk out of the dining hall. But the moment I settle in at my table again, I realize there's another problem.

Meredith and her friends have moved two tables closer to me, apparently because the table had become wobbly. Now that the ladies are only a few yards away, the acoustics in this section seem to amplify every word the women speak. So, I bow my head and focus on my eating, as if that will help.

"Fancy meeting you here."

That voice startles me. I raise my head to see Zara standing by my table, a knowing smirk on her face.

"I'm just having lunch," I tell her stiffly.

Zara raises an eyebrow. "Uh-huh. And the fact that you have a perfect view of a certain someone has nothing to do with it?"

My face grows warm because I've been caught red-handed like a kid with a cookie jar. I'd bumped into Zara earlier, before I found Meredith swimming alone at the hidden pool in the woods. Do older women gossip? While I ponder that notion, I mutter and stab at my salad with more force than is necessary. "I don't know what you're talking about."

Zara laughs heartily enough that everyone must hear her. "Oh, sweetie, you're not fooling anyone—least of all me." She slants toward me, her voice now a conspiratorial whisper. "You know, Meredith's been talking about you. A lot."

My head snaps up involuntarily. "She has?"

"Mm-hm." Zara is clearly enjoying herself. "She wanted to know all about the handsome, brooding general manager who rescued her from certain death at the waterfall."

Zara is teasing me, I know. Certain death? That ridiculous. Besides, this conversation is beginning to sound like high school all over again. I'm forty-two years old, for Pete's sake, not sixteen.

I grunt noncommittally, trying to appear unaffected by what Zara said. But inside, my heart is racing. Meredith's been asking about me?

As Zara continues to prattle on, I try to tune her out, but her statement about Meredith keeps whirling through my mind. I shouldn't care what a guest thinks of me, no matter how sexy she is. I shouldn't want to know more about her either. But I do.

"Look," I say, cutting Zara off mid-sentence, "I appreciate the, ah, information. But there's nothing going on between Meredith and me. There can't be. It's against resort policy."

That's not technically true. But I'll keep that information to myself.

Zara rolls her eyes dramatically. "Oh please. Rules are made to be broken, sweetie. Especially when there's chemistry like what you two have."

I open my mouth to protest, but Zara holds up a hand to stop me. "Save it, handsome. I've seen the way you look at her. And trust me, she looks at you the same way when you're not watching."

Finally, Zara saunters away. I try to focus on my food, but my eyes keep drifting to Meredith. As if she can sense my gaze, she glances up just in time to catch me staring. A slow smile spreads across her face, and she wiggles her fingers at me in a sort of wave. I quickly look down at my plate, my heart pounding. This is ridiculous. I'm acting like a lovesick teenager, not a professional resort manager. I need to get a grip. But as I force myself to eat, I can't help but overhear snippets of conversation from Meredith's table.

Maya's voice carries over to me. "So, Mer, what's the deal with you and the hot staff guy? Ryan, right?"

I nearly choke on my salad.

"Oh, there's no deal," Meredith replies, but I swear I can hear the smile in her voice. "He's just...nice."

"Nice?" Lila scoffs. "Honey, that man is a living, breathing Greek god. And the way he looks at you? Definitely more than just 'nice.'"

"Lila's right," Maya chimes in. "That man's icy exterior melts like a glacier on the sun when you're around."

I shift uncomfortably in my seat, torn between wanting to hear more and knowing I should leave. This is inappropriate on so many levels. But I've never thought of myself as icy, and that's rather disturbing to hear. Professional, yes. But I'm no iceberg.

"Okay, fine," Meredith admits with a sigh. "He's...intriguing. And yes, incredibly attractive. But he's made it clear nothing can happen between us. Resort policy forbids it, I guess."

"Since when has that ever stopped true love?" Zara chimes in, having rejoined her friends. "Rules are made to be broken, sweetie."

I can practically hear Meredith rolling her eyes. "It's not love, Zara. I barely know him. This conversation is embarrassingly juvenile."

"But you want to know him better," Maya suggests slyly. "Come on, you can at least admit it to us. We're your best friends."

There's a pause, and I find myself holding my breath, waiting for Meredith's response.

"Maybe I do want that," she finally admits, her tone softer than usual. "But it doesn't matter. He's not interested."

I grip my fork tightly, fighting the urge to stand up and tell her how wrong she is. Instead, I force myself to stay seated, my food forgotten as I strain to hear more.

Lila clucks her tongue. "Oh, honey, if you think that man isn't interested, you're blind. The sexual tension between you two is thick enough to cut with a knife—one of those high-carbon steel blades."

I nearly choke on my drink at Lila's words. The conversation at Meredith's table has taken a turn I wasn't prepared for. Part of me knows I should leave, that eavesdropping like this is wrong. But a stronger part keeps me rooted to my seat.

"It isn't like that," Meredith protests, but even from here I can hear the uncertainty in her voice.

Zara huffs. "Oh please. I just talked to him, and let me tell you, that man is one step away from spontaneous combustion every time he looks at you."

Is it really that obvious? Shit, I need to work on my poker face.

"Zara!" Meredith hisses. "Keep your voice down. He might hear you."

"Good," Maya declares. "Maybe then he'll finally make a move."

Meredith growls at her friends. "He can't do that. I'm sure he has to abide by some kind of fraternization policy—with guests and employees. I respect that, even if it's...disappointing."

I shift uncomfortably in my seat even as a surge of longing at Meredith's words hits me in the chest. She's disappointed that we can't be together? It doesn't matter how either of us feels, though. But does the resort have that kind of policy? I never bothered to check because I never imagined I'd lust for a guest.

Lila huffs. "Well, if you ask me, sometimes rules need to be bent a little. Especially when there's clearly something special brewing."

"That's right," Maya agrees. "Life's too short to let bureaucracy get in the way of potential happiness."

Fortunately, the four ladies have finished their meal, and they stand up, heading toward the dining hall entrance. I watch as Meredith and her friends amble out of the dining hall, their laughter fading as they disappear through the doors. The remainder of my food sits untouched in front of me, my appetite gone. I can't stop replaying their conversation in my head, especially Meredith's words.

She's disappointed. And she wants to know me better.

I shake my head, trying to clear it. This is exactly why fraternization policies exist—to prevent this kind of distraction, this emotional entanglement. But knowing that Meredith feels the same way I do only makes it harder to resist the temptation.

With a heavier sigh, I stand up and bus my tray. As I'm heading out of the dining hall, I catch a glimpse of Meredith through the window. She's standing by the pool, her hair catching the sunlight as she throws her head back in laughter at something Zara said.

Time to re-read the fraternization policy.

Chapter Five

Meredith

The sun-warmed grass tickles my feet as I step onto the lawn, and a hint excitement zings through me. I can't help but grin as I take in the sight of my friends, all of us as bare as the day we were born, gathered for what promises to be the most unusual game I've ever played. Miniten is a lot like tennis, I've been told, but on a smaller court. It's also only for naturists, also known as nudists.

"Ladies, welcome to miniten!" Marley's cheerful voice rings out as she approaches, fully clothed and holding what look like over-sized oven mitts—except they're made of wood. "This is the sport of champions...Well, nude champions, at least."

I snicker, nudging Zara. "Champions of what, exactly? Best tan lines?"

Zara rolls her eyes, but I can see the smile tugging at her lips. "Speak for yourself, Mer. Some of us are working on our all-over glow."

Marley hands out the strange box-shaped contraptions—thugs, she calls them—and I slip mine over my hand, flexing my fingers experimentally as I curl them around the bar that will help me hit the tennis ball. It feels oddly empowering, like I'm about to engage in some quirky, nudist version of a gladiatorial sport.

"All right, people," Marley continues, demonstrating with her own thug. "The rules are simple. Use this to hit the tennis ball. No rackets, just good old-fashioned hand-eye coordination and a dash of naturist pride."

While Marley explains the finer points of the game, I scan the resort grounds, moving only my eyes, a part of me hoping to catch a glimpse of Ryan's muscular form somewhere in the crowd. But he's nowhere to be seen, and I push down a twinge of disappointment. *Focus, Meredith. You're here to play a ridiculous game and have fun with your friends, not moon over the first attractive man you've met in years.*

The match begins, and soon the air is filled with laughter, shouts of triumph, and the occasional yelp as the ball finds its mark on bare skin. I throw myself into the game with gusto, relishing the feel of the warm breeze on my body and the camaraderie of my friends. Lila and I take on Maya and Zara, whupping them handily before we invite a couple of guys to try their hands.

Hours later, pleasantly exhausted and sun-kissed, we make our way to the resort's spa. As I sink into the warm, fragrant waters of the hot tub, Zara nudges me with her elbow. There's a mischievous glint in her eyes.

"So, Mer, I noticed you checking out the scenery earlier. Looking for something in particular? Or someone in particular?"

I feel a blush creep up my cheeks, grateful it can be blamed on the heat of the water. "Zip it, lady, I'm trying to relax."

"Oh, come on," Lila chimes in. "We've all seen the way you look at Ryan. Why not invite him to join you in the pool behind your bungalow?"

I splash water in their direction, laughing despite myself. "You two are impossible. Can't a girl appreciate the view without being interrogated?"

As we dry off and dress, my friends start chattering about heading to the game room to mingle. But the thought of more socializing suddenly feels overwhelming. I guess miniten wore me out.

"You guys go ahead," I suggest, waving them off. "I think I'll head back to my bungalow and order in."

Alone in my room, I peruse the room service menu, my gaze lingering on dishes described as "sensual" and "indulgent." Without quite knowing why, I find myself ordering a spread that sounds more like foreplay than dinner. The menu is filled with mouth-watering images of delicately plated dishes, each one adorned with vibrant colors and drizzled with exotic sauces that make my stomach growl.

A gentle knock at the door signals the arrival of my decadent spread. I swing it open to find a smiling attendant wheeling in a cart laden with covered dishes. The aromas wafting from beneath the silver domes are intoxicating, a blend of exotic spices and subtle floral notes that make my mouth water. I thank the attendant, a sweet young man who grins at the size of my...tip. Once he's gone, I eagerly lift the first dome. A plate of oysters nestles in a bed of crushed ice, their shells glistening like polished onyx. Beside them, a small dish of mignonette sauce shimmers, the red wine vinegar dotted with finely minced shallots. I lift one to my lips, savoring the briny taste and slippery texture as it slides down my throat. The mignonette adds a tangy kick that makes my taste buds sing.

I move on to the next dish, a vibrant salad of mixed greens topped with juicy pomegranate seeds and crumbled goat cheese. The dressing is light and citrusy, perfectly complementing the sweet-tart burst of the pomegranate. But as I uncover the main course—a perfectly seared piece of mahi-mahi atop a bed of coconut rice—I can't help but imagine sharing this meal with someone special. Someone with sandy blonde hair and hazel eyes that seem to look right through me in the sexiest way.

Stop it, woman. You can find another man, one who will embrace the hedonist in you.

I've just about convinced myself of that when a knock comes at the door. I ease it open, unsure of who might be visiting me now. I hadn't ordered any more food.

Standing before me, looking equally surprised, is Ryan.

His eyes widen as he notices my state of undress—as if he hasn't seen my nakedness before. "I...uh, room service?"

I blink, suddenly very aware of my bare breasts and the slickness between my thighs. "Ryan? What are you doing here?"

He clears his throat, desperately trying to maintain eye contact. "Marley needed the night off, so I'm covering some deliveries. I didn't realize...I mean, I should have checked the room number."

As he stands there, awkwardly balancing the tray of food, I can't help but notice the way his muscles flex under his shirt. A thrill runs through me, and I find myself wondering if this unexpected turn of events might lead to something more exciting than a solitary dinner.

As I smile at him, I experience a mixture of nervousness and excitement fluttering in my belly. "Well, since you're here...I may have ordered way too much food. Would you like to join me?"

Ryan hesitates, his hazel eyes darting between me and the tray. "I'm not sure if that's appropriate, Meredith. I'm technically still on duty."

"This late in the evening? Oh, come on," I tease, leaning against the doorframe. "I'll even put on a robe if it makes you more comfortable. Unless...you'd prefer I didn't?"

A hint of a smile tugs at the corner of his mouth. "You're making it very difficult for me to refuse."

I step back, gesturing for him to enter. "That's the idea."

While Ryan sets the tray down on the nightstand, I can feel the tension between us crackling like electricity. I hate to shatter the mood, but I have to remind him. "Don't you need to deliver that food to its rightful owner?

"Oh, yeah. Right." He blushes again and clears his throat, raising one finger. "Gimme a sec."

He races out of the room, only to return one minute and thirty-five seconds later, flushed and breathless. Yeah, I counted the seconds. Then he slams the door shut. "Delivery...done."

I move closer to him. "Thank goodness. Are we going to share all these delicious treats you brought me tonight?"

Ryan roams his gaze over me, his professional demeanor visibly slipping while his voice grows deeper and rougher. "Why don't we find out together?"

Suddenly, I can't catch my breath. Is this really happening?

He reaches for a strawberry, dipping it in chocolate sauce. Then he lifts it to my lips. "Open up."

I part my lips, letting him feed me the fruit. The chocolaty flavor hits me first, followed by the strawberry sweetness that explodes on my tongue in a rush of sensual flavors, and the juices dribble down my chin. "Your turn, honey."

With every morsel, this dance becomes more daring, more sensual, intensifying my desire more every minute. My nipples harden into tight pearls that ache for his touch. Just the scent of him, all woodsy spice and sweaty male, turns me on even more. Normally, I don't get wet without lube. But I have a feeling Ryan will do much better than that.

His drops to a husky tone that makes my knees weak. "You know, there are more interesting ways we could enjoy this meal."

"Like what?"

He picks up a small bowl of honey. "How about we get a little...messy."

I can't believe this is happening, can't believe all-business Ryan is suggesting something so deliciously naughty. But I'm not about to let this opportunity slip away. "Oh, sweetie, I thought you'd never ask."

While Ryan drizzles warm honey over my collarbone, I shiver with delight. His eyes have darkened with desire, and his expression is rife with erotic determination. He leans in, his tongue following that sweet trail, and I can't help but moan.

"God, Meredith," he growls, his breath hot against my skin.

I shiver again and moan as Ryan curls his tongue inside my navel to lap up even more of the honey. His touch is both tender and electrifying.

"Oh, Ryan." I arch into him, my fingers tangling in his hair while he nips at my neck. "I want to taste you too."

Then he pulls back, smirking in the sexiest way. "Be my guest."

He sweeps me up in his arms, carrying me into the bedroom where he deposits me on the plush mattress. The gauze curtains flutter faintly. Then he scurries away, only to drag the room service cart into the bedroom too. He strips his clothes off swiftly.

Damn, that man has an incredible body.

Emboldened by his striptease, I tell him, "Lie down, please. On your back."

He obeys immediately. Wow, no man has ever done that before—not without complaining.

The dim lighting casts a soft glow on our naked bodies as I reach for the maple syrup, my hand trembling slightly with anticipation. As I drizzle the thick liquid over his skin, it pools into a sticky mess on his chest. The sight alone is almost too much to bear, and I can't help but let out a low moan of hunger. I'm struck by how beautiful he is—all lean muscle and sheer determination. I lean in, savoring the sweetness on my tongue and the salt of his skin. I love that we're tasting each other this way, taking turns, reveling in the intimacy.

Ryan follows my every move with hooded eyes, his breaths coming in short gasps as I lean forward to trail my tongue along his collarbone. The taste of syrup mixed with sweat makes my core clench with the need to take him inside me. I can feel myself getting wetter by the second, aching for him to fill me completely.

With a growl, he grabs me by the hair and tugs me closer, crushing his mouth to mine in a bruising kiss that leaves me breathless. His mouth tastes like sin itself—heady and intoxicating—and it makes me crave his cock even more. Our tongues dance while I trace lazy circles around his nipples with my fingertips, feeling them harden beneath my touch. His body responds to every caress, every languid lick of my tongue.

Ryan's breathing grows ragged while I work my way down his body. When I reach his dick, it's already hard and straining. I pause to look up at him through my lashes.

"You don't have to—" he starts, but I silence him with a wicked smile.

"Oh, I want to," I purr, before taking him into my mouth.

The sound Ryan makes—half groan, half growl—sends a thrill through me.

Slowly but surely, I make my way down his chest, leaving a trail of syrup-covered kisses in my wake. I pause at his abs, reveling in their definition and tracing every ridge with my index finger before gliding it down lower still. As I tease him mercilessly, swirling my finger around the base of his cock before finally taking him into my mouth, I experience a sense of erotic power like nothing I've felt before.

My late husband never would've let me do this to him.

Now I lose myself in the taste of Ryan, the feel of him, the sounds he's making. I can feel him throbbing against my tongue as I work him slowly at first, then faster and harder until he's panting from the need to come. His hands roam over my back and ass possessively, caressing every curve before finally settling between my thighs where I'm so wet for him that my cream drizzles down my inner thighs.

As he approaches climax, every muscle in his body freezes. He lies there immobilized by the need to let go, unable to speak or breathe. I tighten my lips around his throbbing length, flicking my tongue teasingly at the sensitive underside. His muscles tense as I apply just the right amount of pressure, my hand moving in rhythm with my mouth. The veins on his shaft pulse against my tongue and my cheeks hollow out, creating a delicious suction that pushes him over the edge.

When he comes, he explodes into my mouth, and his back arches upward. I devour every last drop of his hot release, the flavor of him as intoxicating as any drug. I swallow eagerly, savoring the taste and feel of him inside my mouth, relishing in the power I hold over him in this moment. The feeling of power that rushes through me makes me feel desired in a way I haven't experienced in years.

Ryan's body trembles with aftershocks while I slowly pull my mouth away from his dick, licking my lips and smiling up at him. The heat between them us has become a palpable energy even as we both bask in the afterglow his pleasure. Can't believe how much I loved doing that for him.

After a moment, Ryan pulls me up and onto his lap for a deep, passionate kiss. Our tongues tangle, our need for each other too ravenous to deny. Then he murmurs against my lips, "Your turn, Meredith."

I bite my lip, anticipating what he might do to me, certain it will be incredible. Ryan's hands roam my body, leaving trails of invisible fire in their wake. His lips brush against my ear as he whispers, "Lie back for me, beautiful."

That simple command does me in. I comply immediately, sinking into the plush pillows.

His gaze roams over me hungrily as he reaches for the bowl of melted chocolate. "Now, let's see how sweet you really are."

The warm, silky chocolate drips onto my skin, pooling in the hollow of my throat before trickling down between my breasts. I gasp at the sensation, arching my back as Ryan's tongue follows the decadent trail. He takes his time, savoring every inch of me as if I'm the most exquisite dessert he's ever tasted.

His mouth closes around my nipple, and he sucks gently while his fingers trace lazy circles on my inner thigh. The delicate sensation drives me crazy. I can barely catch my breath, it feels so good. I moan, tangling my fingers in his hair and tugging him closer. The contrast between the cool air and his hot mouth pushes me to arch upward into his touch. The roughness of his palms turns me on even more.

"Ryan," I gasp as he moves lower, his tongue dipping into my navel. "Please..."

"What are you begging for, Meredith? Tell me, and I'll give it to you." He smirks again. "Maybe."

I catch my bottom lip between my teeth, suddenly shy despite our intimate position. But the hunger in his gaze emboldens me. "I want your mouth on me. Everywhere."

A slow, salacious grin spreads across his face. "Your wish is my command."

Ryan spreads my thighs gently, his breath hot against my most sensitive area. I hold my breath, unable to move even one millimeter. His every move kindles a white-hot fire inside me. When his tongue finally wraps around my clit, I cry out and clench the sheets while my neck arches. Ryan groans against my flesh, the vibrations sending shockwaves of pleasure through my entire body. He licks and suckles with exquisite precision, alternating between long, languid strokes and quick flicks that have me writhing beneath him. His strong hands grip my thighs, holding them open as he devours me.

"Oh god, Ryan," I moan, grinding my mound against his face. "Don't stop, don't stop."

He redoubles his efforts, thrusting two fingers inside me as he focuses on my clit. The dual sensation is overwhelming, and I can feel myself hurtling toward the edge. He pulls my nub into his mouth, raking his tongue over it again and again. My legs thrash while the pressure builds, my hips buck, and I fist my hands in the pillow. I'm gasping for breath, crying out, desperate for a climax.

Just when I think I can't take anymore, Ryan curls his fingers, hitting that perfect spot inside me. My whole body goes rigid, and blinding waves of pleasure crash over me again and again. I cry out Ryan's name, my body arching off the bed one last time as I ride the crest of my orgasm. He doesn't let up, his tongue and fingers working in perfect harmony to prolong my ecstasy until my entire body goes limp and I'm oversensitive from everything he did to me.

When I finally come down from my high, Ryan crawls up my body, dropping soft kisses along the way. He claims my mouth in a deep, hungry kiss that leaves me deliciously languid and satiated. I can taste myself on his tongue, and that sends a fresh wave of desire rippling through me. Moonlight streams through the windows as I watch Ryan pull on his clothes without leaving the bed. His lean muscles flex in the silvery glow. My body still tingles from our earlier intimacy, but I'm not ready for this night to end.

"That was..." I fan myself with one hand, struggling to find the words to describe what we just did.

Ryan chuckles and pats my hip. "I believe the word you were looking for is 'mind-blowing.' "

"Mm, definitely. But I think I need another taste to be sure, though."

He glances at the clock on the nightstand, then slides off the bed. "Sorry, I need to go. Wouldn't appropriate for me to spend the night."

"Appropriate?" I almost screeched that word. Can anyone blame me? I've been dismissed. "You can't run out on me now."

He leans over to kiss my forehead. "Good night, Meredith."

Oh, like hell he's getting away with that. I reach out to him and whisper, "Stay. Please spend the night with me."

Ryan pauses, his hand on the doorknob. I swear I can see the conflict in his eyes, desire warring with something else—responsibility? Fear? But I can't imagine what he might be afraid of—certainly not me.

"Meredith," he whispers, his voice husky. "Please don't make this any harder than it already is. Getting fired on my first real day as general manager would...suck."

I sit up, letting the sheet fall away. "Who cares? We're at a nudist resort, for heaven's sake. Anything goes here, right?"

He wipes a hand over his mouth. "I just...I need to keep some boundaries. For now."

Despite my disappointment, I paste a tight smile on my face. "I understand."

Ryan crosses the room in two quick strides, cupping my face in his hands. His kiss is gentle, almost reverent, and makes my heart pound.

"Goodnight, Meredith," he murmurs against my lips before slipping out the door.

I flop back onto the bed with a frustrated groan and mutter to the empty room, "Damn that man and his self-control."

As I drift off to sleep, I make a silent vow. I'm going to show Ryan exactly what he's missing out on. And I have a feeling he won't be able to resist for long.

Chapter Six

Ryan

An array of tiki torches flickers all along the beach, casting dancing shadows across the sand. I catch Meredith's eye from across the party, and my heart skips a beat. She's radiant in the warm glow, her golden-brown hair gleaming with streaks of firelight. I can't resist picturing my fingers knotted in those locks as I tug her head backward while I fuck her up against a palm tree. But I can't do that. I won't do it. Not in public. At forty-three, I'm hardly a kid, but next to her timeless beauty at fifty-two, I feel like a fumbling teenager. What if she just sees me as her hot island fling—a "boy toy" to play with and discard?

She doesn't seem like that type. But then, I barely know her—except in the biblical sense.

Meredith saunters over to me, those hips undulating in a hypnotic rhythm, and gives me a playful wink. "Quite the shindig, isn't it? Though I must admit, the view just got a whole lot better."

I fight back a grin. "It's...lively."

Her laughter, sensual and inviting, makes my dick twitch. "Oh, come on, you can do better than 'lively,' Ryan. Where's that clever wit you showed me last night?" Her amber eyes dance with mischief like they had last night. "Speaking of which, where were you hiding all morning? I was up at the crack of dawn, ready to continue our...'negotiations.' "

I clear my throat a little too loudly, disconcerted by the memory of our intensely erotic encounter. God, I want nothing more than to whisk her away right now and pick up where we left off. But I shouldn't. I can't. I won't.

So instead, I stammer like a frigging moron. "I, uh, had some work to catch up on."

Meredith arches an eyebrow. "All work and no play makes Ryan an uptight boy." Her fingers graze my arm, leaving tingles in their wake. "Perhaps we should remedy that..."

I swallow hard, trying my damnedest to remain composed. "Meredith, I really shouldn't—"

As the music swells, her fingers twine with mine. "Dance with me, sweetie."

Her sultry breaths tickle my ear. Without waiting for a response, she tugs me gently away from the crowd, and I let her lead the way. The farther we go from the beach party, leaving the flickering torches behind, the drier my mouth becomes. The raucous laughter and chatter fade away, replaced by the soft lapping of waves against the shore. Moonlight bathes the deserted stretch of beach in an ethereal glow, transforming Meredith's hair into a shimmering halo.

"It's magical out here," I murmur, drinking in the serenity. But even as I speak the words, my body grows tense.

"Oh, no, *you* are magical, Ryan. Last night, you made me come so hard I swear I saw stars."

I have no idea how to respond to that statement, so I don't even try. We walk in companionable silence, our bare feet sinking into cool sand. With every step, our shoulders brush and her presence alone relaxes me. Yet I'm hyper-aware of her proximity, the gentle sway of her hips, the intoxicating scent of coconut and something uniquely Meredith.

"So, Ryan Kimble, tell me something I don't know about you."

I hesitate, caught off guard by her directness. "I, uh...I make a mean pineapple upside-down cake?"

Meredith's laughter echoes off the trees. "Somehow I doubt that's the most interesting thing about you."

Our fingers are still entwined, and I give her hand a gentle squeeze. "Maybe not. But I'd rather hear about you. What brought you to Heirani Motu?"

She pauses, her head down, and rubs her arms as if she's cold. But I doubt that's the case. We are on a tropical island, after all—not in the arctic circle. The moonlight catches the amber flecks in her eyes, making them shimmer faintly. I also notice, however, that she's begun to sniffle. It only lasts a moment, then she straightens and clears her throat. No trace of anxiety or sadness remains. Her lips curve into a soft, inviting smile. She doesn't speak, but her gaze holds mine. Her body language is open, one hip cocked slightly as she leans toward me, closing the already small distance between us.

God, she's beautiful. And vibrant. And everything I shouldn't want. My eyes flick toward the ocean and its vast expanse that mirrors my tumultuous thoughts and mood. I take a small step back.

"We should probably head back," I say, the statement sounding hollow even to my own ears.

Meredith's brows furrow. "Are you okay, Ryan? You seem...tense."

I run a hand through my hair, a nervous habit I can't seem to shake. "It's just, you know, work responsibilities and all that."

But even as I speak those words, I can feel my resolve wavering. The moonlight, the gentle crash of waves, the intoxicating presence of Meredith—it's all conspiring against my better judgment. I find myself torn between duty and desire, professionalism and the raw need to connect.

Meredith takes a step closer, her voice dropping to a whisper. "Ryan, I need to tell you something." She hesitates briefly, then seems to make a decision. "I've never felt this...alive before. This connection between us, it's more than physical. It's like you see the real me, and I see you."

My pulse accelerates. Her words echo my own unspoken thoughts, and I feel as if my carefully constructed walls have begun to crumble. How she does this to me, I can't explain.

"I realize we barely know each other," she continues, her fingers brushing my arm. "But I'm willing to take a risk here. Are you?"

Without meaning to do it, I stretch my hand out to cup her cheek. Her skin is warm and impossibly soft under my palm. I have to remind myself that she's not some naive girl. Meredith Hayes is a mature woman who knows what she wants.

I trace my thumb along her jawline, and I'm acutely aware of every point where our bodies connect. "I want to take the risk. God, I want to. But there's so much you don't know about me, about my past."

She leans into my touch, her gaze locked on mine. "Then tell me. I'm here, Ryan. I'm listening."

As I close my eyes, I'm torn between the intoxicating pull of her presence and the weight of my responsibilities, my guilt. When I open them again, I see nothing but acceptance in her gaze, and for a moment, I let myself hope for a miracle. Then I lean in, drawn by an irresistible force—Meredith. The moment our lips meet, the kiss becomes charged with passion, hunger, and a hurricane of emotions that sweeps away all my carefully constructed defenses. Her lips are soft yet insistent, tasting of salt and tropical fruit. I pull her closer as she threads her fingers through my hair. Our need for each other erupts into a desperate, tongue-tangling, groping exploration of each other's mouths and bodies.

The sounds of the beach party fade away, replaced by the thundering of my heartbeat and the soft sighs escaping Meredith's lips. Time seems to slow, stretching this moment into eternity. It's just us, two souls connecting under a vast canopy of stars, with the gentle lapping of waves as our soundtrack.

When we finally peel our mouths apart, breathless and gasping, reality comes crashing back. My mind races, panic rising like bile in my throat. What am I doing? I'm the general manager, for pity's sake. I have a job to do, responsibilities that can't be ignored.

"I...I shouldn't have done that," I stammer, stumbling backward. "Meredith, I'm sorry. This isn't...I can't..."

The confusion in her eyes makes me hate myself for putting that look on her face. But how can I explain? How do I tell her about the guilt that haunts me, the vows I've made to never let myself be vulnerable again?

"Ryan, it's okay," she tells me, reaching for me. "We're both adults here. We can figure this out."

I shake my head, my thoughts a jumbled mess. "No, you don't understand. My job, my past...there are things you don't know about me. Things that make this impossible." I veer away from her, my feet already shuffling back toward the flickering lights of the party. "I have to go. I'm sorry, Meredith. I just...can't."

"Ryan, wait!" Meredith calls out, her voice a mix of confusion and anguish. I feel her hand brush against my arm, but I jerk away from the touch, unable to face her. The warmth of her touch lingers, a stark contrast to the cold dread settling in my stomach.

The heaviness of my footfalls makes me sink into the sand with every step. But I can't stop running, not even when the earth shifts under my feet, and I almost fall down. As I put more distance between us, every step feels like some kind of betrayal. The sounds of the beach party grow louder as I approach, but they're muffled by the roaring of my own pulse in my ears.

"Ryan!" Meredith calls again, her voice tinged with desperation. "Please, don't run away from this!"

Her words hit me like a physical blow, but I can't bring myself to turn around. If I look at her now, see the hurt and confusion on her face, I know I'll crumble. And I can't afford to fall apart, not here, not now.

I reach the edge of the party where the flickering tiki torches cast long, dark shadows across the sand. A few curious glances are thrown my way as I hurry past, but I ignore them.

Once I've slammed the door of my bungalow behind me, I sag against it, my eyes closed.

No matter what I might feel for Meredith, I can't drag her into my world.

After a restless night's sleep filled with visions of Meredith writhing, moaning, and coming apart for me, I know I need to do something or I'll go crazy. She is the most incredible woman I've ever met. And she loves to get naughty, that much I learned from our encounter in her bungalow. That gives me an idea. Fortunately, the resort shop offers plenty of options for adults who enjoy a little kink—or maybe more than a little.

Still, I don't feel like outing myself as a potential sex fiend, so I wait until after the shop closes. Then I use my master key to get back inside and grab what I need. I left a note for Mariel explaining that I'd paid for an item, though I fibbed about why I bought it. For a friend, I told her. Yeah, she'll believe that.

What did I buy? A vibrating sex toy that comes with a remote control so I can make Meredith come whenever I feel like it—in her bungalow, in the woods, on the beach, or...in public.

Fuck, I'm getting hard just thinking about that.

I sneak back to my bungalow, heart racing as I clutch the discreet black bag. What am I doing? This is insane. I'm the general manager. I should be focusing on work, not plotting ways to secretly pleasure a guest. But I can't get Meredith out of my head. The way she looked at me on the beach, vulnerable yet determined. The taste of her lips, the softness of her skin. God, I want her so badly it physically hurts.

Pulling out the toy, I slide my hand up and down its length, getting aroused simply by feeling its sleek and curved shape. And by thoughts of what I could do to Meredith with this device. The remote feels heavy in my palm. Images flood my mind—Meredith writhing in ecstasy as I control her pleasure from across the room. Her trying to maintain composure during dinner as waves of sensation wash over her.

My cock strains against my pants. This is wrong. So wrong. But I can't bring myself to put the toy and remote back in the bag. *Shit.* What am I thinking? I can't do this. It's completely unethical. I'm letting my desires cloud my judgment.

I sink onto the edge of my bed, head in my hands. God, I'm a mess. One kiss from Meredith and I'm ready to throw away everything I've worked for. My professional integrity, my vows to never let anyone get close again. All of it, crumbling because of one amazing woman. But it's more than simple physical attraction. There's something about Meredith that calls to me on a deeper level. Her warmth, her wisdom, the way she seems to see right through my carefully constructed walls. And the pleasure she gave me last night...it was more than hot sex.

And that terrifies me.

I leap off the bed and begin pacing the length of my bedroom. The toy sits on my nightstand, a tempting reminder of my momentary lapse in judgment. I can't use it. I won't. But I also can't bring myself to return it.

With a frustrated groan, I grab my running shoes. I need to clear my head, to put some distance between my dangerous thoughts and the woman who inspires them. The pre-dawn air is cool against my skin as I set off down the beach, my feet pounding out a steady rhythm in the sand. I run until my lungs burn and my legs ache, pushing myself to the limits of exhaustion. But even physical exertion can't drive Meredith from my mind. Her throaty laughter echoes in my ears, and the ghost of her touch traces over my skin.

As the sun begins to peek over the horizon, painting the sky in vibrant hues, I slow to a stop. I'm far from the resort now, alone on a secluded stretch of beach. The waves lap gently at the shore, a soothing counterpoint to my ragged breathing. I bend over, hands on my knees, as I try to catch my breath and calm my carnal fantasies.

What am I going to do about Meredith? I can't avoid her forever, not on an island this small. And if I'm being honest with myself, I don't want to hide from her. Despite my best efforts to maintain professional distance, she's gotten under my skin in a way no one has in years.

I straighten, thrusting a hand through my sweat-dampened hair. The logical part of my brain knows I should put a stop to this, draw a firm line and stick to it. But my heart...it wants to take that risk Meredith spoke of last night. As I start the long trek back to the resort, I try to sort through the jumble of emotions swirling inside me. *Good luck with that, pal.*

The sun climbs higher in the sky as I make my way along the shoreline. My muscles ache from the punishing run, but it's nothing compared to the ache in my chest. Images of Meredith flash through my mind—her radiant smile, the warmth in her amber eyes, the softness of her lips against mine. God, that kiss. It was like being struck by lightning, every nerve ending in my body coming alive at once.

I pause to catch my breath, staring out at the endless expanse of turquoise water. The ocean has always had a calming effect on me, but today it only serves as a reminder of my inner turmoil. The vastness of it all makes me feel small and insignificant in comparison.

As I near the resort, I spot a familiar figure walking along the beach. I freeze, my gaze locked on the figure moving toward me. I recognize Meredith's graceful gait. She hasn't seen me yet, her gaze fixed on the horizon as she meanders along the water's edge. For a moment, I consider ducking behind some nearby rocks to avoid an encounter. But something stops me. Maybe it's the way the morning light catches her hair, turning the golden-brown strands into spun gold. Or maybe it's the memory of her words from last night, her willingness to take a risk on whatever this is between us. For reasons I can't explain, I find myself calling out to her before I can stop myself.

"Meredith!"

She whirls around at the sound of my voice, her eyes widening in surprise. For a moment, we just stare at each other across the sand, letting the crash of waves fill the silence between us. I close the distance, unsure of what I'm going to say but knowing I need to say something.

Her face lights up. "Ryan? I didn't expect to see you out here."

"Couldn't sleep," I admit, running a hand through my damp hair. "Needed to clear my head."

Meredith searches my face. "About last night..."

"I'm sorry," we blurt out simultaneously. And we smile at the same time too.

"You go first," she offers.

Her beautiful body and that smoky laugh make the decision for me. "How wicked would you like to be, Meredith?"

She edges closer. "What did you have in mind?"

I must be smirking like the devil himself. "Ever hear of remote-controlled sex toys?"

Meredith's grin broadens. "That sounds deliciously wicked."

"Tomorrow, I'm leading a sightseeing trip to Fiji." I pull her closer. "Come with me. You'll need to wear clothes, which means I can slip the device inside you. Then you'll be at my mercy, coming whenever I allow it."

Will I survive doing that to her? It'll be worth a heart attack. I've never been this horny before, and I know one thing for certain.

I will need to fuck her afterward and fuck her hard.

<h1 style="text-align:center">Chapter Seven</h1>

Meredith

Palm fronds whisper above me, thanks to a sultry breeze, as I make my way toward the open-air café. My mind has become a whirlwind of conflicting emotions lately, but I know one thing for certain. I can't wait for Ryan to slide that toy inside me. But he won't do that until tomorrow. *Damn.* The gentle island breeze caresses my skin, but I barely notice, too consumed by thoughts of Ryan's intense gaze, the way his strong hands felt on my body, and the frustrating coldness that followed our first sexual encounter.

But he's not playing it cool anymore. He wants to control my pleasure from afar. That's as hot as hot can get.

I pause to appreciate the breathtaking view of Heirani Motu's lush landscape. The vibrant greens of the rainforest blend seamlessly with the golden sands and crystal-clear waters, a paradise that usually soothes my soul. Today, though, it only serves as a backdrop to my internal struggle.

Maybe that's the appeal, I admit to myself, a wry smile tugging at my lips. *The chase, the mystery...God, Meredith, when did you become such a cliché?*

Since the day I met Ryan Kimble, that's when.

As I approach the café, my eyes are drawn to a familiar figure seated at one of the tables. Lila, my free-spirited best friend, is hunched over a sketchpad, her curly auburn hair forming a fiery halo around her face. Her hand moves across the paper with practiced grace, capturing the essence of the island's beauty. A smile tugs at my lips at the sight of her. Lila's presence is always a balm to my restless spirit, her artistic soul a perfect complement to my more practical nature. That's why Lila and I became friends. She was the first person I met at our group therapy sessions.

As if sensing my approach, she raises her head, her face lighting up with a radiant smile. "Meredith! I was just thinking about you. Come, sit with me and tell me everything."

I laugh, shaking my head as I slide into the chair across from her. "Everything? That's a tall order, my friend. I'm not sure I even understand everything myself."

Lila sets her sketchpad aside, leaning forward with an eager gleam in her eye. "Oh, now you have to spill. I know that look, Mer. Something's happened, hasn't it?"

"Maybe." I bite my lip, torn between the urge to confide in one of my best friends and the desire to keep my encounter with Ryan a titillating secret. So I hedge, unable to prevent a secretive smile from tugging at my lips. "Let's just say Heirani Motu is living up to its reputation as a place of new beginnings where anything goes."

"Ooh, mysterious," Lila teases, rubbing her hands together. "Come on, give me something to work with here. I'm an artist, Mer. I need details to paint the full picture."

I lean back in my chair, letting out a deep sigh. "It's... complicated. There's this man, and the connection between us is electric. But he's like a riddle wrapped in an enigma, hot one minute and cold the next. I can't figure him out, and it's driving me crazy."

"Ah, the dance of attraction. It's like a masterpiece in progress, isn't it? Bold strokes of passion, subtle shades of intrigue...Tell me, does this mystery man make your heart race?"

I close my eyes briefly, remembering the intensity of Ryan's gaze and the way he turns me on so easily. "Does my heart race? Absolutely. Like a hummingbird on caffeine."

Lila reaches out to squeeze my hand. "Then maybe the mystery is part of the masterpiece. Embrace it, honey. Let the colors blend and see what beautiful creation emerges."

I open my eyes, meeting Lila's gaze. "When did you get so wise, oh great artist?"

She laughs, the sound as melodious as the island's songbirds. "I've always been wise, my dear. You've just been too busy chasing your own tail to notice."

As we share a moment of laughter, I feel some of the tension rush out of my body. The mystery of Ryan still lingers, but with Lila's encouragement, I find myself more excited than anxious about what lies ahead. Whatever this island has in store for me, I'm ready to embrace it with open arms.

But I still want to know more about Ryan Kimble.

I lean in closer, my voice dropping to a conspiratorial whisper. "Okay, so here's the thing. Last night was...incredible. Like fireworks-exploding, earth-moving incredible."

Unconsciously, I trace patterns on the table's weathered surface, mirroring the electric sensations still lingering on my skin from the other night. I can't help imagining Ryan's fingers moving over my body instead of the table, arousing me more with every leisurely swipe. I want to touch myself, under the table, and relieve this delicious ache. But instead, I clench my fingers on my thighs.

"It was that good, huh?" Lila's emerald eyes widen, a mischievous grin spreading across her face. "Come on, spill the beans, Mer. I demand all the juicy details. Well, maybe not *all* of them, but you know what I mean."

I laugh. "It involved some playfully naughty things, moonlight, and the kind of kiss that makes you forget your own name. That's all I can tell you."

"Meredith Hayes, you minx!" Lila exclaims, her sketchbook momentarily forgotten. "I knew this island would work its magic on you."

"It was magical last night and this morning." My smile falters a touch. "But he still won't tell me anything about himself."

"Have you confessed all your secrets and old wounds to him?"

I wince and scratch my cheek. "Not exactly."

"And that's Meredith for 'hell no.' Right?" Her tone remains casual, but that's just what Lila is like. Even an asteroid hurtling toward Earth couldn't faze her. "Men can be more complex than a coral reef ecosystem sometimes. Did you try talking to him about it?"

I bow my head and moan pitifully. "I wanted to, but he seemed so closed off when I tried to talk about his past. It seems like he's built more than a wall around himself. He's erected an entire castle, and I'm not sure how to scale those ramparts. God, I'm sick of metaphors."

As I speak, I can't help but wonder if Ryan's behavior is a defense mechanism or if I completely misread our connection. The memory of his touch, so tender and passionate last night, seems at odds with his absolute refusal to talk about his past this morning. It's a riddle I'm determined to solve, even as part of me wonders if I'm setting myself up for heartbreak.

Lila leans toward me, her expression gentle yet with a touch of mischief. "Oh, my dear Meredith, don't you see? Life's greatest adventures often begin with a dash of mystery." She gestures expansively at the lush island around us. "This paradise isn't just about shedding clothes. It's about peeling away our inhibitions, our fears, all the things that hold us back."

I can't help but smile at her. "You always know just what to say, don't you?"

"It's a gift," she winks. "But seriously, embrace this feeling. The thrill, the uncertainty, it's all part of the journey. Your heart knows what it wants, even if your head's a bit confused right now."

Her words resonate with truth, stirring something deep inside me. I take a deep breath, inhaling the sweet scent of plumeria carried on the breeze. It reminds me of Ryan for some strange reason. "You're right. I can't let fear hold me back. Not here, not now. If there's one place in the world where I can be myself, completely and without shame, it's here on Heirani Motu."

"That's my girl," Lila beams. "Now, go hunt down your hot young mystery man and unravel that enigma."

I turn to leave, but Lila's voice stops me.

"Remember, confession is a two-way street, Mer. You need to share your past with Ryan too."

"Thanks, Lila. I'll do that."

But will Ryan reciprocate? I'm praying he will.

With newfound determination, I bid Lila farewell and make my way to Ryan's office. My heart races as I approach the door, and I feel a bit nauseous from sheer anxiety. So, I take a moment to calm myself with slow, deep breaths. Then I knock on the door.

"Come in," Ryan calls out.

I shut the door after me and lean back against it. "Hello there, handsome."

Ryan's hunched over his desk, surrounded by a sea of papers. His brow crinkles as he concentrates on whatever, but I notice a slight tension in his shoulders that wasn't there yesterday.

I clear my throat deliberately. "Busy day?"

His head pops up, and freezes. For a split second, I see a flash of something in those hazel eyes—desire? regret?—before his professional mask slips back into place. "Meredith. Yeah, just, uh, catching up on some work."

I step closer, my voice gentle. "Wow, that's quite the workload. Anything I can help with?"

Ryan shifts uncomfortably, his eyes darting between me and the papers. "I appreciate the offer, but I've got it under control."

I bite the inside of my lip while I search for a way to breach his defenses. "You know, all work and no play...well, it doesn't suit this place, does it?"

A ghost of a smile tugs at his lips before he catches himself. "Someone has to keep things running smoothly."

I lean against his desk, and my proximity clearly affects him. "True. But I think there might be something else on your mind. Or maybe...someone?"

"Meredith, I have a job to do."

"But you take breaks, I know that. You found me at the hidden waterfall because you wanted some relaxation." I reach out, my fingers lightly brushing his arm. "It's okay, Ryan. Whatever's going on in that head of yours, you can talk to me. Last night was...special. At least, it was for me. And I'm looking forward to the Fiji outing."

The tension in the room is palpable. While I watch Ryan wrestle with his emotions, or maybe it's his demons, I can see the internal struggle playing out on his face. His hazel eyes darken with desire, but there's a flicker of hesitation, of something deeper holding him back.

His voice has become rough and strained. "Last night was...incredible. I shouldn't want to do it again, but I've been fantasizing about fucking you all day long." He snatches up a sheet of paper, waving it around. "This is what I'm supposed to be focused on, but all I can think about is you. God, I can smell how turned on you are."

The heat in his words triggers a slickness deep inside my body that spreads into my folds. But he won't distract me that easily. "We could have some fun right here, right now—or anywhere you want to take me. But only if you share a few pieces of yourself with me first. Or would you rather I go first?"

He runs a hand through his tousled sandy hair, a gesture I'm quickly coming to recognize as a sign of his inner turmoil. But it isn't pain holding him back. It's sheer lust. When he pulls me onto his lap, straddling his thighs, I need to bite my lip to stave off the orgasm I can already feel rising within me. I've grown so slick that my cream is rubbing off on his pants. I gasp as Ryan's strong hands grip my hips, pulling me firmly against him. His dick has begun to stiffen, and I can't resist rubbing my cleft against his khakis as if I were riding his cock instead of his pants. His eyes, dark with desire, lock onto mine.

"Christ, Meredith," he growls, "I need to feel you wrapped around me, but...not here." He grasps my ass firmly with both hands, rocking my hips into him and making me gasp. "Come to Fiji with me and the tourists. Like I told you, I have...plans for you that require us both to be clothed. At least while we're in Fiji. I can hold out that long, can you?"

His actions betray his words as his fingers dig into my flesh, holding me in place. I can feel his rod pressing against my cleft, and I roll my hips experimentally, eliciting a groan from deep in his chest.

"If you can wait, I can too." I whisper, trailing my fingers along his jawline. "We're both adults. We both want this. Whatever you've got planned, I'm game."

Ryan nostrils flare like a bull's, his grip on me tightening almost painfully. "You have no idea what you're agreeing to."

I lean in close, my lips brushing his ear as I whisper, "Then show me."

"Last chance to back out," Ryan warns.

Instead of answering, I crush my mouth to his in a searing kiss. Any remaining hesitation melts away as he responds with equal fervor, pressing me against the door. His hands roam my body, hungry for any contact, though I desperately need to feel his skin on mine. I gasp as Ryan's lips trail down my neck, his faint stubble grazing my sensitive skin. I tangle my fingers in his hair, pulling him closer. The heat between us is intoxicating, driving all thoughts from my mind except the desperate need for more.

"Ryan," I breathe, arching against him. "Please..."

He groans, pressing his forehead to mine. "Meredith, we can't. Not here."

The longing in his voice matches the ache in my core. I roll my hips against him, relishing his sharp intake of breath.

"Why not here?" I challenge, nipping at his earlobe. "No one will know."

Ryan's hands tighten on my thighs. For a moment, I think he'll give in to the passion simmering between us. Then he sets me down carefully, putting space between our bodies. "I have plans for you, and nothing will get in the way of what I want—you, at my mercy, begging me to make you come."

Holy shit, that sounds amazing. And I don't even know what his mysterious plans for me are. Don't give a damn. Ryan wants to play, and I won't do anything to shake his naughty mood.

Ryan swings the door open and lays a hand on my back to give me a gentle shove out of the room. I'm about to complain, but then he pecks a kiss on my forehead.

"See you later, Meredith," he virtually purrs while smirking. "You'll have the rest of today and all of tonight to wonder about what I'll do to you tomorrow. You will not touch yourself in any erotic way, but feel free to fantasize. Tonight, in my bedroom, I'll be stroking myself to a hard, hot climax while thinking of you."

And with that, he shuts the door.

I stand here, stunned, my body still thrumming with unfulfilled desire. The door clicks shut behind me, leaving me alone in the hallway, my mind reeling from Ryan's words and actions.

"Oh, you insufferable tease," I mutter under my breath, pressing my thighs together in a futile attempt to ease the ache between them. The memory of his touch, his scent, the heat of his body against mine—it's all seared into my senses, leaving me dizzy.

I take a shaky breath, trying to compose myself. As I knife a hand through my tousled hair, I can't help but replay Ryan's parting words in my mind. The image of him stroking himself, thinking of me, sends a fresh wave of heat coursing through my body.

"No touching, huh?" I lean against the wall, trying to steady my racing heart. Ryan's command echoes in my mind, both thrilling and frustrating me. "No touching? Easy for him to say."

I push off the wall and start walking, not entirely sure where I'm headed. My body feels like a live wire, every nerve ending hyper-aware and longing for Ryan's touch. The gentle island breeze caresses my skin, and I shiver, imagining it's his fingers trailing along my arms. As I wander the resort grounds, I find myself drawn to the beach. The sound of waves lapping at the shore calls to me, promising if not relief, at least a distraction. I kick off my sandals and let my toes sink into the warm, wet sand, relishing the sensation. The sun is beginning to dip toward the horizon. I take a deep breath, inhaling the salty air and trying to calm my racing thoughts. I find a secluded spot near some rocks and sit down, wrapping my arms around my knees. The gentle rhythm of the waves helps to soothe my frayed nerves but does little to quell the desire still simmering within me.

"Get it together, woman," I mutter to myself, resting my chin on my knees. "It's just one night. You can handle this."

But as the sky darkens and the first stars begin to twinkle overhead, I find my thoughts wandering back to Ryan. What is he doing right now? Is he still working, or is he thinking about me too? The image of him in his bedroom, stroking himself while fantasizing about me, explodes in my mind unbidden. I groan softly, burying my face in my hands.

"Oh god, this is torture," I half whine to the night air.

The breeze carries the scent of jasmine, mingling with the freshness of the ocean. I lean back on my elbows, tilting my face up to the star-studded sky. The vastness above me is a stark contrast to the intimate, heated moments I shared with Ryan. I breathe deeply, letting the sound of the waves wash over me.

But instead of calming me, every rhythmic crash of water on sand seems to echo the pulsing need in my core. I can almost feel Ryan's hands on me, his lips trailing fire across my skin. My breath catches as I remember the intensity in his eyes, the raw desire barely contained beneath his professional facade. I shift restlessly on the sand.

"Damn you, Ryan. How am I supposed to make it through the night like this?"

Only then do I realize a salient fact. Ryan got me hot and bothered as a devious means of making me forget that I wanted to have a serious conversation with him.

That sneaky rascal.

Chapter Eight

Ryan

I slip into the massage workshop, trying to blend in with the walls. My interest in the workshop isn't just about gathering data and crunching numbers to find out how successful this event will be, though, not anymore. I need to understand what makes this place tick, what draws people here. But as I wander into the room, the scent of lavender and sandalwood washes over me. I guess that's common with an activity like this. I scan the room to get a read on the participants. The scents I detected a moment ago must have been massage oil. I can't deny it's, ah, kind of nice.

I give the room one more quick scan before I take up my position in the corner. The guests in attendance nod and smile as they amble past me. I offer similar greetings.

But then *she* walks in. Meredith. The most beautiful, sensual woman I've ever known. She glides into the room with effortless grace, her loose waves of caramel brown hair catching the sunlight that streams through the windows. Meredith's eyes widen briefly as she swivels her head to scan the space, and a soft smile curls her lips.

The lighting casts a warm glow on her skin, and I imagine running my fingers along—

No, you moron, focus. This is work, not playtime.

As Meredith settles onto a massage table, she chats with Zara, her partner for this session. With enormous effort, I manage to look away, reminding myself why I'm here. This is information gathering for the resort, and I need to remain laser focused on that task. Massage workshops could be a lucrative option moving forward.

But while Maya, the workshop leader, begins her instructions, my gaze keeps drifting back to Meredith. The way she closes her eyes and breathes deeply, clearly embracing the experience. The gentle curve of her neck as she tilts her head. The laugh that escapes her lips at something Maya says. It's hard to focus on anything but Meredith when she's right here, clearly enjoying herself. I want to usher her out of the room so I can kiss her senseless, but I hold back. Professional distance and all that crap.

I'm so damn sick of being professional. That's why I've orchestrated that naughty surprise for Meredith tomorrow.

The quiet chatter of the other guests fades from my awareness. Why? Because Meredith just smiled and gave Maya the thumbs-up sign. The gesture wasn't even aimed at me, yet it makes me feel...aroused.

"Now remember," Maya reminds us. "Today is about discovery—of yourselves, of others, of the incredible potential within your own bodies. Ryan, thank you for making this workshop possible. I never imagined I'd have this chance."

"No problem. Mind if I sit in on the session? With my clothes on, that is."

"Sure thing, hon." She winks. "And if you get the hankering for it, go ahead and strip."

A nervous laugh splutters out of me. "Uh, thanks. But I'm still on the clock."

While Maya begins the workshop, I find myself thinking back on how far I've come. I had made sure James and Holly were fine with my plans for guest-led events, and they agreed it was a great idea. The resort is all about empowerment, about shedding inhibitions along with clothing. But this island has also empowered me in ways I couldn't have predicted.

Meredith has been a big part of my transformation. But I still need to tell her about my past, no matter how much I'd rather not do that. It's time for me to man up.

In the background of my thoughts, I hear Maya's voice. "We'll be exploring different massage techniques, but more importantly, we'll be exploring boundaries, communication, and trust."

Her words inspire me to come back to the present. I notice a flicker of uncertainty cross Maya's face, but she pushes through it, her confidence growing with every moment. That's the magic of this place. It brings out the best in people, helps them find strength they didn't know they had and limits they didn't know they could shatter.

Meredith raises her hand. "So, are we massaging each other? I mean, do we each get a partner?"

"Yes, you will—but only if you're comfortable with that."

I cross my arms, tipping my head to the side, curious about Maya's response. Part of me hopes Meredith will choose to let someone else massage her, while another part wants to shield her from prying eyes. Including my own, if I'm being honest.

Maya spreads her arms. "Remember, this is about your journey, at your pace. Now, let's begin."

While Meredith settles into the massage routine, I find myself wondering what it would be like to serve as her partner for this workshop, to feel her skin under my hands, to rub her clit...*Dammit*. I need to get out of here before I do something stupid. Like volunteering to be her guinea pig. As I slip out, I catch Meredith's eye. She smiles, and for a moment, I forget how to breathe.

This is going to be a long day.

I slip into the far corner of the room, leaning back against the wall with my ankles crossed. It's a comfortable pose, one that lets me observe without drawing attention. Maya speaks in a soothing yet confident as guides the group. I'm proud of how she's grown into her role so quickly.

"Ryan!" Lila's voice cuts through my thoughts. She grins and winks. "Why don't you hop up on the table? I'll give you a deep tissue massage."

I shake my head. "Thanks, but I'll pass. I'm just here to observe. And I'm on duty, anyway."

My gaze flicks to Meredith, and I can't help hoping she'll offer to rub me down instead. God, what I wouldn't give to feel her hands on me again like she'd done the other night when we pleasured each other in her bungalow. But that's exactly why I can't let it happen. If she touches me, even innocently, I'll be harder than the coral reefs that surround our little island paradise.

"Don't be shy, Ryan," Lila teases. "You're so tense. Let me work out those knots."

I wave her off, grateful for the loose-fitting shirt that hides my body's reaction to the very thought of Meredith's touch. "Really, I'm good. You guys carry on."

My gaze is drawn back to Meredith like a magnet. She's listening intently to Maya's instructions, nodding along with every new lesson. A stray lock of hair falls across her face, and I have to physically restrain myself from rushing over there to brush it back.

Shit, what is wrong with me? I'm acting like a horny teenage virgin. Time to get out of here before I drag Meredith down to the floor and do something that will surely get me fired.

"I should get back to work," I mutter, more to myself than anyone else. "Enjoy the workshop, everyone."

As I escape out the door, I catch one last glimpse of Meredith. She looks up, our eyes meeting for a brief, electric moment. The gentle strains of a ukulele float through the air thanks to the band I'd hired. They sound great. Despite my feet trying to lead me away from the massage workshop, I can't help but peek back into the workshop room. Meredith's eyes are closed, her face the picture of serenity.

Maya's soothing voice guides the group. "Breathe deeply, letting the tension melt away with every exhalation. In, out. In, out."

I watch, mesmerized, as Meredith's chest rises and falls in a steady rhythm. God, she's beautiful. The urge to join her, to feel her hands on me, is almost overwhelming.

"Get it together, dumbass," I grumble to myself, ordering my feet to move. "Back to work. You know, the thing you get paid to do."

I shuffle back to my office and wind up knee-deep in invoices once again. When there's a knock at the door, I leap out of my chair. Anything to escape the drudge work. I call out, grateful for the distraction. "Come on in."

A couple shuffles in, their skin an angry shade of lobster red. *Ouch.* I guess these two didn't read the welcome packet closely enough.

"Mr. Kimble," the woman begins, "we fell asleep on the beach and—"

"Say no more," I interrupt, already reaching for the aloe vera gel I keep stocked for just such occasions. "Let's get you taken care of."

As I'm explaining the best practices for applying aloe to soothe and cool their scorched shoulders, my walkie-talkie crackles to life.

"Ryan, we've got a situation at bungalow twelve," Emilio informs me. "It's a guest with a rather, um...delicate issue. Could you help out, mate?"

I sigh inwardly. No rest for the jerk who keeps fantasizing about a guest. I've just finished up with the sunburned couple, anyway. "Be there pronto, Emilio."

As it turns out, bungalow twelve houses a burly man with an angry-looking rash in places I'd rather not think about. Emilio is blushing and squinting at the same time, like he can't quite convince himself to look at the poor guy.

"It's not contagious," he assures me, scratching furiously. "But damn, is it uncomfortable."

"No problem. I've got just the thing," I tell him, thankful for my extensive first-aid training. As I'm handing him a tube of anti-itch cream, my walkie-talkie crackles again.

"Ryan, the miniten net's down," Marley reports. "A gust of wind snatched it away. We're all tied up with other guests at the moment."

"I'll handle it," I reply, already heading for the door. So much for a quiet afternoon of paperwork.

As I'm jogging toward the miniten court, a flash of brown hair catches my eye. Meredith. She's walking down the main trail toward the beach, a towel slung over her shoulder. Before I can stop myself, I'm veering off course, following her at a discreet distance. The rational part of my brain screams that this is a bad idea, but I can't seem to help myself.

"What are you doing, dumbass?" I mutter under my breath. "You're supposed to be fixing the net, not stalking guests."

But even as I chastise myself, I can't tear my gaze away from Meredith's retreating figure. The sway of her hips, the bounce of her hair, it's like catnip to me. I'm so caught up in spying on her that I nearly trip over a root. *Smooth, Kimble. Real smooth.* Shaking my head, I force myself to turn back toward the miniten court.

Work first, fantasies later.

But even as I set about fixing the net, my thoughts keep drifting back to Meredith, wondering what she's doing on the beach, imagining her stretched out on the sand...This woman is going to be the death of me, I swear. The moment I finish my task, I realize it's time for my mid-afternoon break. That gives me a perfect excuse to hunt for a certain guest.

I find her on the beach. She won't see me. I'm hiding behind a tree.

Meredith dips her toes into the lapping waves, laughing softly as she makes curling shapes in the sand. Her laughter carries on the breeze.

"Oh!" she exclaims, jumping back as a larger wave splashes her legs.

I grin at her surprise. It's been so long since I've felt this...alive. This drawn to someone.

Then I swerve my gaze toward the ocean, catching something in my peripheral vision. I immediately recognize the telltale signs of one of our famous island rainstorms. It isn't here yet, but it will arrive at any moment.

I jog over to where she's still playing in the waves and call out, "Meredith! Time to go!"

She whirls around, her face alight with joy—at seeing me? Not sure. Just as the rain abruptly pours down, her mouth stretches into a wide grin. "Ryan! Isn't this amazing?"

I'm about to respond when a crack of thunder splits the air. Without thinking, I rush forward, sweeping Meredith into my arms, carrying her up the trail toward a large palm tree. "We need to get to shelter. But don't worry, frequent rainstorms are common on South Pacific islands."

"My hero," she teases, her breath warm against my neck.

The palm tree's broad leaves provide a makeshift shelter from the rain. Leaves drip with crystal droplets that catch the sunlight. Meredith's hair is slicked back in a manner that makes her look even more beautiful. The sound of rain mingles with the crashing of waves. Her flushed cheeks and parted lips feel like an invitation to ravish her mouth. As our eyes lock, our lips meet too, and suddenly, we're kissing like the world might end at any second. The wind howls around us, and the rain pelts our bodies, but we're lost in the chaos of our need for each other. It's all-consuming, intense, a wild frenzy of passion born from the tempestuous atmosphere surrounding us.

"I've wanted to do that for days," Meredith whispers when we finally stop kissing, both gasping for breath.

"Me too," I admit. "But we shouldn't go any further, not yet, not until we've—"

Had a serious talk about our pasts. That's what I meant to tell her.

But she silences me with another kiss, and I lose myself in the moment, the rain, and Meredith. But sooner than I'd like, I need to get back to work. The rain has ended, anyway. I need to get back to work, anyway. That means the serious talk I wanted to have with her will have to wait.

I don't see her again until evening.

The veranda thrums with excitement as guests gather for the dance competition Marley and Emilio had suggested. Colorful lanterns hang above our heads and sway in the evening breeze, casting an orange and pink glow over the makeshift dance floor. I adjust my collar, feeling both out of place and fascinated by what's to come. Dancing? Not my thing.

Meredith sidles up to me, her eyes alight with humor. "Come on, Ryan. Show us your moves."

I shake my head, smirking. "Can't. I'm judging tonight."

"Sounds like an excuse to me," she teases, and she sidles even closer. "Afraid you can't keep up?"

I swallow hard, assailed by mental images of holding her close while our bodies writhe in sync with the music. Damn, I want to do that. But I'm on still on the clock, and screwing Meredith on the dance floor wouldn't make a good impression on my staff or the guests.

"Rules are rules," I tell her, hoping my voice doesn't betray the lust coursing through my body.

As the music starts, I take my seat at the judges' table, grateful for the barrier between myself and the only woman who has ever me turned into a lust-drunk moron. Meredith joins her friends, throwing a playful wink my way before twirling onto the dance floor.

I try to focus on the other couples, but my eyes keep drifting back to her. The way she moves, uninhibited and joyful, mesmerizes me. I shift uncomfortably, glad for the tablecloth that hides my stiffening dick. After what feels like an eternity of torture, I finally announce the winners have been chosen, including two runners-up. All three winners receive gift cards.

"And now, the moment you've all been waiting for," I declare, lifting a ridiculous, cheesy trophy carved into a coconut shape. "The first place winner is...Barb Larson! Come get your trophy!"

Everyone grins and chuckles as I hand over the silly trophy. Barb, a grandmother of five, hoists her trophy and grins. "The coconut is mine, people!"

Meredith catches my eye, her smile softening into something more intimate. Now that my duties for the evening are over, I wend my way through the crowd to find Meredith. Hand in hand, make our way down the main path. Outside her bungalow, we halt and face each other.

She presses her body to mine. "Stay with me tonight?"

I cluck my tongue. "Sorry, I can't. It would ruin tomorrow's surprise."

"You're such a tease," she whispers, then pulls me in for a deep kiss.

Back in my own bed, I toss and turn, my mind racing with possibilities. The toy I bought sits on my nightstand, and just looking at it gets me aroused. All I can do is close my eyes, take my stiffy in my hand, and beat off until I'm too tired to think about Meredith. But I keep picturing her expression and her reactions, the way she'll squirm and gasp while I'm remotely detonating her. Sleep finally claims me, but all my dreams involve Meredith, the toy, and the erotic torment I have planned for us both.

When I leave my bungalow in the morning, I wonder if what I did last night will show on my face. But no one gives me horrified looks.

And now, I'm standing on the patio delivering another speech.

"Listen up, everyone," I call out, clapping my hands to get their attention. "Remember, we're heading over to Fiji today. That means clothes on at all times."

I catch Meredith's eye and fight to suppress a grin. She's wearing a flowing dress that barely reaches her knees makes her look both elegant and irresistible.

"Rene's got the jet prepped and waiting on the grass strip," I continue. "Head on down, and we'll be taking off shortly."

As the guests wander out to the jet, I gently touch Meredith's elbow and murmur, "Can I have a word?"

"Of course."

I lead her away from the group. Once we're hidden from view by the foliage, I turn to face her. "I've got a surprise for you."

My voice comes out gruff. That's what happens when I spend hours jerking off to thoughts of her. I think I shouted at one point too.

Meredith's eyebrows lift. "Oh? I do love a surprise—from you. What have you dreamed up for me, sweetie?"

Instead of answering, I reach into my pocket and pull out the slender, curved toy. Her eyes widen as I back her up to a tree and lift the hem of her dress. She's already growing slick, that much I can feel even through her panties.

"Ryan," she gasps. "What are you—"

I silence her with a quick, ravenous kiss, then gently slide the toy inside her panties. Thank goodness she wore underwear. The toy nestles between her labia perfectly and covers her clit too. I can't stifle my groan at the thought of what's to come and what I'll do to her today. The mere thought of switching the vibrator on when she least expects it makes me breathe harder.

"There." I smooth her dress back down. "Now, whenever I want, I can do this."

I pull out my phone and tap the screen.

Meredith's eyes flare wide for about two seconds. Then she catches her bottom lip between her teeth, releasing it little by little while her tits heave. "I'm at your mercy, hm?"

I can already smell her cream, and it takes every ounce of my self-control not to take her right here, right now. "Consider this payback for all the times you teased me mercilessly with that body. By the time we return to the island, you'll be begging me to let you come."

Meredith's tits bounce with every labored breath she takes. Her cheeks are flushed too. They've turned the same shade of dusky rose as her nipples.

"You're evil," she declares, but there's a wicked gleam in her eye that tells me she's loving every second of this.

I clasp her hand. "Come on. We don't want to keep Rene waiting."

As we walk toward the airstrip, I can't help but think that this day trip to Fiji is going to be the longest—and most exhilarating—flight of my life. I guide Meredith toward the jet, her hand warm in mine and the faint scent of her cream teasing my senses. The other guests are already boarding, their excited chatter blending into the background. All I can hear, see, or think about is *her*. When Meredith's steps falter slightly as we approach the steps, I know the toy is working its magic.

And I haven't even turned it on yet.

"You okay there?" I ask with false innocence, unable to keep the smirk off my face.

She shoots me a look that's equal parts lust and exasperation. "You're enjoying this way too much."

"Guilty as charged."

Meredith and I are the last passengers to step onto the jet. I can't help but marvel at her composure under the circumstances. I know she must be experiencing intense, arousing sensations inside her body. Yet even while she greets our fellow travelers, she remains cordial, and apparently, relaxed.

"Beautiful day for flying, isn't it?" Meredith suggests to Zara, her voice only slightly breathier than usual.

I watch her interact with her friends, feeling a surge of admiration. This woman, who only took up nudism a few days ago, is now embracing adventure in ways I never imagined. Her courage, her willingness to push boundaries, those traits are among the many things about her that impress me. Once we settle into our seats, a realization hits me. Meredith's transformation isn't just physical. It's ignited something in me too. I've spent so long playing it safe, hiding behind rules and professionalism. But now...

I slant toward her, my lips brushing her ear. "You're incredible, do you know that?"

She turns toward me, her brows lifting. "What brought that on?"

"Just...you. Everything about you." I take a deep breath, steeling myself. "I think it's time I started facing my own fears too."

Meredith wraps her hands around mine. "Together?"

I feel as if a weight has lifted off my shoulders. "Yeah, together."

While the jet's engines roar to life, I make a silent vow. No more hiding. No more letting fear hold me back. Meredith has shown me that life's too short for that bullshit.

And as we take off, soaring over the pale blue expanse of the South Pacific, I can't help but feel we're flying toward something far greater than just a day trip to Fiji.

Chapter Nine

Meredith

I wriggle in my seat, hyper-aware of the small silicone device nestled between my thighs. My pulse races. Just knowing Ryan could set it vibrating at any moment gives me a thrill so intense that I might orgasm at any moment. But Ryan is in control of my pleasure, and I think he's going to draw it out all day long.

What have I gotten myself into?

Ryan is chatting with a gray-haired couple in the back row. He doesn't even glance at me. When the jet hits a pocket of turbulence, I grip the armrests hard enough that I might split the leather with my nails. The toy remains cupped intimately against me, like a lover's palm. A shiver rushes through me that has nothing to do with the plane's movement.

"You okay, Mer?" Maya asks, plopping down beside me. "You look a little flushed."

I smile tightly. "Just excited for the trip."

"Me too," Lila chimes in, taking the seat on my other side. "I can't wait to see Fiji—all of it."

As my friends chatter about our upcoming adventures in Fiji, I try to focus on their words instead of the tantalizing pressure between my legs. But it's no use. My body has become so sensitized that I can barely stand it. My nipples have become tight beads that must be visible beneath my thin dress. No one seems to notice, though.

Ryan walks past me as casual as you please, without even glancing my way.

I sneak a peek at him as he nears the front of the plane and turns sideways to speak to a pair of guests. His expression remains pleasant as he chats with the younger couple, who I've heard are newlyweds. But I swear I see a hint of a smirk playing at Ryan's lips as he throws me a sidelong glance. I suspect he relishes tormenting me this way.

Of course he does, the sexy bastard.

Zara waves a hand in front of my face. "Earth to Meredith. Where'd you go just now?"

I blink several times as I realize I had completely zoned out. "Oh, sorry. Just daydreaming about those beautiful beaches we'll see."

"Uh-huh," Maya agrees with a knowing grin. "I bet you were thinking about our hot tour guide. What was his name again? Rufus?"

"Ha-ha. As if you don't know his name." I peer into her eyes as if I'm deeply concerned. "Did you hit your head coming onto the jet? Maybe you've got an aneurysm, and that's why you can't remember names. Our tour guide is Ryan."

Lila leans over to peer down the aisle. "Look at that fine ass. I don't blame you for wanting to jump his bones, Mer."

"Stop talking about Ryan's ass. Please."

Zara wags her eyebrows. "We can still enjoy the view."

She said that just as Ryan strode past us. Whether he heard it, I don't know for sure. But he seems...quite pleased with himself.

"Oh, you've got it bad, Mer, don't you?" Maya suggests. "I've never seen you so antsy. Must be jonesing for—"

"Shush," I hiss.

My friends all smirk at me.

I roll my eyes, but inwardly, I'm panicking. Are we that obvious? Am I that obvious? What if someone figures out what's really going on? Another wave of turbulence hits and I bite back a gasp as the toy shifts a teeny bit. Ryan still hasn't turned it on, but just knowing it's there, waiting, has me balanced on a razor's edge.

But god, I love the sweet torture he's giving me.

I did come to Heirani Motu for adventure, didn't I? Well, this definitely qualifies. As anxiety and excitement war within me, I can't help but wonder what other surprises Ryan might have in store for me.

The cabin door swings open and Rene swaggers out, his gray hair tousled and his blue eyes twinkling with scampish humor. "G'day, folks! Just thought I'd pop out and let you know the good news. We don't need a pilot anymore!"

A ripple of nervous laughter spreads through the cabin.

Rene grins, clearly enjoying himself. "Yep, our good mate AI is taking care of everything. I'm thinking of catching some shut-eye or maybe skydiving. Anyone care to join me?"

Despite my predicament, I find myself grinning and laughing. There's something infectious about Rene's carefree attitude.

"All right, all right, I'm only pulling your leg," Rene chuckles. "We're on autopilot at the moment, smooth sailing ahead. Now, who's ready for a proper Fiji welcome?"

As Rene launches into a colorful description of Fiji's attractions, I wriggle in my seat, acutely aware of the toy nestled between my thighs. Every tiny movement sends a jolt through me, and I'm torn between wanting to squirm and staying perfectly still.

Rene disappears into the cockpit, shutting the door behind him.

A moment later, his voice crackles over the intercom. "Ladies and gents, if you look out your windows, you'll see a pod of humpback whales frolicking in the waves. Quite a sight, eh? I'll descend to a lower altitude so you can get the best view."

My friends practically leap over me in their excitement, pressing their faces against the glass. Lila breathes, "Oh my god, Mer, you have to see this."

I hesitate, not trusting myself to move. "I'm good here, thanks."

No, my voice didn't sound oddly strained. Nope, not at all.

Liar.

That's when I feel his presence. Ryan leans in close, his breath warm against my ear and his voice low and teasing. "Having trouble, Meredith? I could always help you up if you'd like a better view."

Through gritted teeth, I whisper, "You're making this very difficult for me, you know."

He smiles with a wicked glint in his hazel eyes. "That's rather the point, isn't it?" Then, in a louder voice, he declares, "Come on, I know a spot where we can get an even better view of the whales."

Before I can protest, he's gently pulling me to my feet. I follow him to the back of the jet on shaky legs because the toy just shifted again. We settle into two empty seats, far from prying eyes. As I gaze out at the majestic whales breaching the waves, I can't help but wonder if I'm in over my head. But with Ryan's calming presence beside me and the thrill of the unknown buzzing through my veins, I realize I don't really give a damn. This is exactly the kind of adventure I came here for.

I still have my face plastered to the window as the whales recede from view. Once our whale-watching experience is over, Ryan excuses himself and heads back to the cockpit.

"Duty calls," he tells me with a wink and a sparkle in his eyes.

I watch him go, admiring the confident set of his shoulders and tightness of his tush.

No sooner has he disappeared than I feel a sudden, delicious vibration between my thighs. My breath catches, and I grip the armrests of my seat.

"You okay, Mer?" Lila asks, leaning toward me. "You look sort of, um, flushed."

I fake a smile, desperately trying to keep my voice even. "I'm fine. Just...excited about the sight-seeing tour."

The vibrations intensify, and I bite my lip to keep from gasping. That devious man is playing with the remote and having a ball torturing me. My cheeks burn, but I can't deny I love every minute of it. Can't wait to find out what he'll do next.

"Are you sure you're okay?" Zara presses, her brows furrowed. "You're squirming like you've got fire ants in your panties."

I laugh, but voice comes out a bit too high-pitched. "Just restless, I guess. Long flight and all that."

"Long flight? It's only an hour from Heirani Motu to Fiji."

"Well, it, uh, feels longer. And I'm fine, I swear."

Zara shakes her head but then turns her attention to Lila and Maya. As my friends chatter around me, oblivious to my predicament, I'm caught between embarrassment and arousal. But secretly, wickedly, I hope Ryan doesn't stop.

While the jet begins its descent, Rene's voice crackles over the intercom. "Ladies and gents, we're approaching the Suva airport. Hope you're ready for some fun in the sun!"

As we file out onto the tarmac, Rene gives us all a cheeky grin and an exaggerated wink. "Enjoy yourselves, folks. Fiji's full of...delights."

I catch Ryan's eye as he guides us toward a waiting bus. God, I want to hold his hand, to pull him close and...to make him turn that vibrator on again. But he's all business now, efficiently herding us along. We settle into the bus seats, and just as I think I'm safe, another wave of vibrations hits me. I gasp, drawing concerned looks from my friends.

"Meredith?" Lila asks, touching my arm. "Are you having a hot flash or something?"

I laugh nervously, fanning myself, and lie my ass off. "Must be the tropical heat."

Not sure how I'll survive this intoxicating torture Ryan's putting me through.

The bus lurches forward, and I'm immediately enveloped by the sensory overload of Fiji. I glimpse the endless expanse of turquoise ocean as the salty sea breeze wafts in through the open windows, mingling with the sweet scent of tropical flowers.

"God, it's gorgeous here," I murmur, running my fingers along the smooth velvet of the bus seat.

Lila clutches her hands to her chest, poking her head out the window, and grins. "I can't wait to hit the beach!"

The chatter around me rises and falls like waves, punctuated by bursts of laughter. I close my eyes, letting the sounds of Fiji soothe me. Suddenly, a subtle vibration starts up again, and I'm once again breathless squirming.

"What's up with you today?" Lila asks, concern in her voice. "You're gripping that chair pretty hard, just like on the jet."

I shake my head, feeling my hair brush against my neck. The simple sensation has me biting my lip. "I'm fine, I swear."

As we pull up to the Fiji Museum, I spot Ryan at the front of the group, the picture of professionalism. But I know better now. That man has a naughty streak five miles wide. Inside the museum, I try to focus on the exhibits, but Ryan's teasing hasn't stopped. I'm examining a traditional Fijian war club when he suddenly appears beside me.

"Enjoying the tour?" he asks casually.

I turn to him and feign a scowl. "You're making this tourist excursion very...stimulating."

A ghost of a smile crosses his face. "Good."

Ryan glances around. Then in one swift motion, he pulls me into a hidden alcove. His hand grips my waist possessively, and his lips crash into mine with a wild hunger. I gasp, my lips parting, and he takes advantage of the moment to thrust his tongue into my mouth, tasting me, exploring every millimeter. Ryan Kimble is a consummate kisser. My hands find their way to his shoulders, drawing him closer, our bodies melding together as if we're two puzzle pieces meant to fit together. His other hand roams over my body, squeezing my ass, fingering the hem of my skirt. I can feel his hard length pressing into me, and I instinctively grind against him.

The kiss deepens as we consume each other with ravenous hunger. He nips at my lower lip, eliciting a gasp from me, and I moan deeply, thrusting my hands into his hair, crushing my body to his. He trails his lips down my neck, leaving a trail of wet kisses in his wake. His hand travels up my thigh as he hikes my skirt up inch by inch. I can feel his fingers grazing my panties, searching for a way around them.

I melt into him, all thoughts vanishing from my mind. When we finally break away, I'm breathless.

"Damn," he growls against my neck. "You're so fucking wet for me I can smell it."

"Ryan, I—Please do something before I go insane."

But he's already slipping away, leaving me dazed and wanting more.

And I still have the toy buried between my folds.

Later, at the Suva markets, I try to lose myself in the vibrant chaos. The Handicraft Centre is a riot of color and texture, with intricate weavings and carvings catching my eye at every turn.

"Look at this!" I call to my friends, holding up a beautifully painted tapa cloth.

As we wander through the Flea Market, the aromas of spices and tropical fruits fill the air. I can't resist buying a ripe mango. Its juice dribbles down my chin as I sink my teeth in the tender flesh, and my friends give me quizzical looks.

"Messy, but worth it," I laugh, wiping my mouth and chin.

Our final stop is the Grand Pacific Hotel. As we settle in for coffee, I'm struck by the Old-World elegance of the place. The barista presents me with a work of art—a cappuccino adorned with a delicate fern design.

I inhale the rich aromas. "Now that is a sensory experience."

I take a sip, savoring the creamy texture and bold flavor. Beside me, Lila bites into a flaky pastry.

"Oh my god," she moans. "You have to try this."

I accept a piece and bite into the tender, flaky flesh that melts on my tongue. Its buttery, slightly sweet flavor is divine. For a moment, I forget about Ryan's teasing, lost in this simple pleasure. But as I catch his eye across the room, I know our day of erotic teasing is far from over.

Next, we visit Thurston Botanical Gardens. As we step through the wrought-iron gates, the lush greenery envelops us. Ryan's powerful voice rallies the group to attention. "Feel free to explore at your own pace. We'll meet back here in an hour."

I breathe in the heady scent of orchids and frangipani, which reminds of of Heirani Motu. But the gardens here lack the wildness of that island. As the others disperse, Ryan settles a hand on the small of my back, guiding me down a secluded path.

"God, Meredith, I've been dying to get you alone ever since the museum."

"I've been feeling the same way."

He brushes his thumb over my lips. "You bring out the raunchy side of me, Meredith, and I love it."

We round a corner, and suddenly we're in a hidden alcove, surrounded by vibrant tropical flowers.

Ryan slings his arms around my waist, pulling me flush against him. "You are so beautiful, Mer. But when you come, you're like a firework bursting in the sky."

I barely have time to process his words before his lips claim mine. The kiss begins gradually as a gentle exploration, but it swiftly ignites into a conflagration so hot it could melt granite. My fingers tangle in his sandy hair as his tongue teases mine. A moan spills from my lips.

His answering growl sends a warm shiver up my spine. As our kisses grow even more intense, more passionate by the second, I lose all sense of time and place. There's only Ryan, his strong hands roaming my body, the intoxicating taste of him on my tongue. Just when I think I might combust from the rising tension, Ryan reaches into his pocket. With a wicked smile, he presses a button, and suddenly the vibrator nestled between my thighs comes to life.

Despite the gentleness of the vibrations, I gasp and jerk. My knees nearly buckle at the unexpected sensation. I cling to him, my human anchor. "Ryan, oh god..."

He holds me steady. "Don't go off yet, baby. We're just getting started."

The world slowly comes back into focus as Ryan and I cling to each other. The humid air makes find beads of sweat trickle down my skin. My body trembles with unfulfilled desire while my every nerve sings from the lingering vibrations. I press my face into the crook of his neck, inhaling his scent—a mix of salt, sun, and something uniquely him.

"You okay?" Ryan asks, tracing his fingers on my back in soothing patterns.

I nod, not trusting my voice just yet. My mind races. I struggle to make sense of what's happening between us because this feels like more than just a holiday fling, more than the wild adventure I'd initially wanted. There's an intimacy here that both thrills and terrifies me.

"Ryan, what are we doing?"

"I'm not entirely sure. But I know I don't want to stop."

Neither do I. But before I can respond, we hear voices approaching. Ryan steps back, his professional mask slipping back into place. But his eyes...they tell a different story.

Later, as the group settles in at Eden Bistro & Bar, Ryan appears at my side. The mischievous glint in his eye proves he's not done teasing me yet. "Care for a change of scenery?"

I raise an eyebrow. "What did you have in mind?"

He leads me to a swanky restaurant just down the street. Once we're seated, I can't help but tease him. "Special treatment for the troublemaker, huh?"

Ryan stares down at his men, clearing his throat. "I just...wanted some time alone with you."

"Oh?" I lean forward, enjoying his momentary discomfort. "And why's that?"

He takes a deep breath and finally looks up at me. "Because you're not just someone to fuck and play with, Meredith. You're...becoming important to me."

My heart skips a beat.

"I know it's complicated," he continues. "But I can't deny what I'm feeling."

While I process his words, a realization slams into me. I don't want this to end when my vacation does. The thought of returning to my old life, leaving Ryan and Heirani Motu behind, feels impossibly wrong.

"What if..." I start, surprised by my own boldness. "What if I didn't go home after two weeks? Maybe I'd like to stay after that."

I feel a delicious tingle as Ryan's fingers brush my thigh under the table. He's been teasing me relentlessly with that damn toy all afternoon, and I'm about ready to combust.

"You're killing me, Ryan."

He smirks. "Just wait."

Once we've enjoyed our expensive snacks, which were delish, he leads me back to the tour group.

Rene's booming voice cuts through the chatter. "All right, mates! Who's up for some sightseeing?"

As the group climbs onto the bus, Ryan pulls me aside. "I've got other plans for us. This was just a quick visit to make sure Rene doesn't think we got lost and fell down a mountain."

My pulse quickens. "More surprises? You've been one busy boy, haven't you?"

"Trust me," he urges, leading me away.

We hike through a lush park where the air is heavy with tropical scents that I can't even describe. Ryan's hand in mine feels right, like it belongs there. As for the toy...Yeah, it's still there and still driving me crazy.

"Almost there," he advises, guiding me off the path.

We emerge into a secluded clearing that I can honestly describe as a hidden paradise. A small waterfall tumbles into a crystal-clear pool, surrounded by vibrant flowers.

"Ryan, it's breathtaking."

He tugs me closer, and soon, our lips are fused, our tongues tangling in an erotic dance. Then suddenly, the toy between my thighs springs to life.

I gasp against his mouth. "Oh god..."

"Let go, Meredith," he whispers. "I want to see you come undone this time."

The intensity builds to an almost unbearable peak, every wave of pleasure more powerful than the last. My body arches against Ryan's. My nails dig into his shoulders as I cry out, the sound echoing off the rocks. The most earth-shattering orgasm of my life crashes through me like a tidal wave, leaving me trembling and breathless. My mind goes blissfully blank, every thought and worry drowned out by a sea of ecstasy.

As the aftershocks ripple through me, I collapse into Ryan's arms, utterly spent. My legs are useless, like overcooked noodles, and I'm grateful for his strong, steady hold. He strokes my back tenderly, his touch sending little sparks through my oversensitized flesh. The tranquil sound of the waterfall mingles with our heavy breathing, creating a serene backdrop to our stolen moment.

I close my eyes and let the warm, humid air envelop me. The scent of blooming hibiscus and wet earth fills my lungs, grounding me in the present. Ryan's heartbeat is a soothing rhythm against my cheek, and I feel a deep, unexpected contentment washes over me. This is more than just a physical release. It's a connection, an intimacy that goes beyond the here and now. We remain rooted to this spot for what feels like an eternity, neither of us willing to break the fragile spell. My fingers trace lazy patterns on his back, and I can feel his breaths ruffling my hair. There's a softness to this moment that makes my heart ache in the best possible way.

Slowly, reality begins to seep back in. I lift my head to gaze up at Ryan. He brushes a strand of hair from my face, his touch lingering on my cheek. I wonder if he's feeling the same thing I am—this delicate balance between desire and something deeper.

I nuzzle his cheek. "That was...incredible."

"You're incredible, Meredith. And I'd love to know more about you, all the things you've held back. I'll do the same."

I pull back to look into his eyes. "I want to share everything with you, Ryan. It's time we opened up to each other. But after what you did for me a few minutes ago, I need you inside me, every inch of you. Right now."

"Anything for you, baby."

In response, I crush my lips to his in a searing kiss. He unzips his pants while clutching me to his body, and we don't even stop kissing while he rips my panties to shreds. We're both so desperate to for him to take my body that our brains shut down. We come together in a frenzy of passion, our bodies colliding, our hands groping. Then he shoves his knee between my thighs to spread them and punches into me. I throw my head back and swallow a shout. The fullness of him feels incredible. The world fades away, until nothing exists but Ryan inside me, our bodies moving together in frenetic harmony.

Afterward, we fall into a heap on the grass, tangled in each other's arms, basking in the afterglow. I trace lazy patterns on Ryan's skin, marveling at how right this feels.

Ryan brushes hairs away from my face. "We should probably head back soon."

"I suppose so," I agree, exhaling a long sigh, not wanting this moment to end.

But we behave like adults and straighten our clothes while stealing kisses and touches all the while. As we begin our trek back to the bus, Ryan takes my hand, lacing our fingers. I smile up at him, probably seeming like an infatuated fool.

"This has been the most amazing day, Ryan. Thank you."

He kisses my hand. "It's not over yet. We still have the flight back to Heirani Motu."

"Promise to behave yourself this time?"

"Now where's the fun in that?" He kisses each of my knuckles in turn. "But if you don't want me to use the toy anymore..."

"Oh, I never said that."

We reach the airport shortly, rejoining our group on the tarmac. My friends give me knowing looks, but I can't bring myself to care. As we board the plane, I catch Ryan's eye, and we're both grinning like idiots. I guess we've given up on hiding our feelings for each other.

The toy stays in my purse—at least until we're back at the resort.

Already this vacation has surpassed my wildest dreams, and we're just getting started. I can't wait to see what other adventures await us on Heirani Motu.

<h1 style="text-align:center">Chapter Ten</h1>

Ryan

The jet's engines hum as we climb aboard, our bodies weary but our spirits soaring. Rene and I help all the ladies get up the stairs, and we provide the same courtesy to the men who have arthritis or bad knees. Yes, Au Naturel is a full-service resort.

"Looks like Suva did a number on you lot." Rene grins and winks. "But it's the good kind of exhaustion, eh?"

I settle into my seat, stealing a glance at Meredith from across the aisle. Her cheeks are flushed, and she clutches her oversized purse close. I know what's hidden inside, and the mere thought of it makes my dick begin to rouse. But as we take off, my mind wanders to all the possibilities that little toy represents. I imagine Meredith's soft skin and the hungry noises she makes. But exhaustion falls over me like a lead blanket, and I know we're both too spent for any adventures tonight.

Back at the resort, we part ways with lingering backward gazes.

Meredith blows me a kiss. "Sweet dreams, Ryan."

I watch her retreating figure until she disappears into her bungalow.

Hours later, I leave my bungalow and slip out into the night. Why? Because Meredith texted me: *Come to the beach now—and be naked.* The moon hangs low, casting silver light across the resort grounds as I race toward my destination. When I approach the main trail, I finally ditch my T-shirt and shorts. I move quietly, acutely of every twig and leaf beneath my feet. A secret rendezvous in the dead of night is crazy, but I can't deny I'm itching to find out what Meredith has in mind.

I halt at the trail's end, letting myself catch my breath.

The beach stretches before me, a pale ribbon in the darkness.

And there she is.

Meredith stands at the water's edge, her curvy silhouette etched against the shimmering ocean. My breath catches. She's a vision, wild and free, her hair dancing in the sea breeze.

As I draw closer, I feel my heart beating faster. This feels forbidden, exhilarating. For a moment, I forget about my past, about the weight I carry. Here, now, there's only Meredith and the promise of the night ahead.

"Well, well, look who's right on time," Meredith says. "I was starting to think you might stand me up."

"And miss out on a moonlit rendezvous? Not a chance."

She steps closer, and I drink in the sight of her. The moonlight caresses her curves, casting a silvery glow on her skin. She reaches out to trace a fingertip along my jawline. "You know, Ryan, I'm glad that serious face of yours wasn't permanent. You have a beautiful smile."

I catch her hand in mine, pressing a kiss to her palm. "You brought out my lighter side. I didn't know I could feel this...light. As if a weight has been lifted."

"Well, I intend to bring out a lot more than that tonight."

"In what ways?"

She nods toward a blanket spread out on the sand. "Why don't we get more comfortable and find out?"

As we settle onto the blanket, the rhythmic lapping of waves on the shore provides a sensual soundtrack.

"Close your eyes," she whispers.

I comply, helpless to resist her, and my other senses begin to heighten in the darkness. I feel something soft brush against my wrists—silk, I realize. My breath hitches as Meredith gently binds my hands.

She brushes her fingers over my cheek. "Is this okay?"

"Yeah, it's more than okay." But I'm somewhat surprised by how much I trust her. "I like this. Keep going."

"Glad you said that," she whispers into my year. "Because after what you did to me in Fiji, turnabout is fair play."

I feel Meredith's fingers trail down my chest, caught in a whirlwind of emotions—exhilaration, apprehension, and a deep-seated need I can't quite name. The silk scarf around my wrists is both a tether and a release, challenging everything I thought I knew about myself.

"You're thinking too hard," Meredith tells me. "Let go, Ryan. I've got you."

I swallow hard, fighting against years of carefully constructed walls. "It's not that easy."

She pulls back, and I swear I can feel her gaze on me even with my eyes closed. "Why not, sweetie?"

"I'm...not used to this. Being vulnerable." The single word—vulnerable—seems alien to me.

Meredith cups my cheek with her hand. "Open your eyes, Ryan."

I obey, and the tenderness I see in her gaze nearly undoes me.

"We'll go as slow as you need," she assures me. "But I want you to know something. Your vulnerability? It's beautiful."

Something shifts inside me at her words. I lean into her touch, allowing myself to truly let go for the first time in years. "You're different, Mer."

"Good different?"

"Definitely good. You seem...freer."

"I feel freer," she admits. "Being here, with you, it's awakening things inside me that I didn't even know existed."

"I know exactly what you mean."

While she lays her hands on me in the gentlest way, I'm struck by how attentive Meredith is to my reactions. Every touch, every kiss is carefully calibrated to my responses. She pushes my boundaries with exquisite care, always asking me how I feel, always making sure I'm comfortable. As we lose ourselves in each other under the starlit sky of Heirani Motu, I realize that for the first time in years, I am truly, blissfully alive.

Once it's over, we lie tangled together on the blanket, our breathing slowly returning to normal. The stars twinkle above us, a silent audience to our intimacy. Meredith's head rests on my chest, and I absently run my fingers through her hair.

"That was...life-altering, Mer. I know that sounds dumb, but it's how I feel."

"It was the same for me. What we just did was beautiful."

I tip my head back to take in the full panorama of the night sky, feeling more at peace than I have in a long time. "I never expected this when I came here."

"What do you mean?" Meredith props herself up on one elbow to look at me.

I hesitate, weighing my words carefully. "I came here to escape, to hide from my past. But with you...I find myself wanting to open up, to share things I've kept locked away for so long."

"I'd like that, Ryan. I want to know you—all of you."

As the first light of dawn breaks over the horizon, we reluctantly part ways. I steal one last kiss before slipping back to my bungalow, my heart feeling lighter than it's been in years.

The next day, I'm helping Marley set up for a morning yoga class when I spot Meredith across the lawn. She's chatting with a group of guests, smiling and laughing. Our eyes meet briefly, and my heart suddenly beats faster.

"Are you sleeping standing up, boss?" Emilio's voice breaks through my reverie. "Or are you planning on starting this class sometime soon? Marley's waiting for your thumbs-up."

I clear my throat, tearing my gaze away from Meredith. "Right, sorry. Go ahead, Marley."

She turns toward the guests gathered on the lawn, each standing on a yoga mat. "Let's begin with some deep breathing exercises..."

Throughout the day, Meredith and I dance around each other, stealing glances and "accidental" touches. During lunch, she brushes past my table, her hand ghosting over my shoulder.

"Oops, sorry about that." She winks, but her tone is anything but apologetic.

I struggle to keep my expression neutral. "No problem at all, Ms. Hayes."

Later, in the privacy of my bungalow, I sink onto the bed, my mind a whirlwind of conflicting emotions. As much as I loved last night and our little game this morning, I'm beginning to feel the old anxieties creeping in again.

Because I still haven't told her about my past.

"What are you doing, moron?" I mutter to myself, running a hand through my hair.

I can't deny the pull I feel toward Meredith. It's more than just physical attraction. It's a connection I've never experienced before. She sees past my carefully constructed facade, challenging me to be vulnerable in ways that both terrify and exhilarate me.

But as I gaze out at the stunning Heirani Motu sunset, reality crashes in. This is a vacation fling, nothing more. In a week,

Meredith will leave, and I'll still be here, trapped by my past and my responsibilities.

"You're playing with fire," I warn myself. Yet even as I speak the words, I know I'm already burning.

Chapter Eleven

Meredith

As I dangle my feet in the infinity pool, tiny wavelets lap at my ankles, tickling my skin. The blue of the water seamlessly melds with the ocean horizon. Lila's laughter rings out, drawing my gaze to where she's perched on the pool's edge, her auburn curls catching the light.

"I swear, that zip line was trying to kill me," she jokes. "My stomach dropped faster than my body."

"Baloney," Zara teases, splashing water in Lila's direction. "You were squealing like a toddler the whole time. And half expected you to propose marriage to the tour guide."

"He was pretty cute," I admit. "But Cooper's taken. Or did you not notice the wedding ring on his left hand?"

"What a bummer," Maya declares with no small amount of sarcasm. "This island is like a buffet of hot men. We must sample liberally!"

As my friends dissolve into giggles, I feel a pang of guilt. If only they knew about Ryan and all the naughty things we've done together. Just thinking about our secret encounters gets me wound up. I take a sip of my piña colada, hoping the cool sweetness will calm the butterflies in my stomach.

Zara waves a hand in front of my face. "Wake up, Mer. You zoned out there for a second. Daydreaming about our next adventure?"

"Just enjoying the sunshine, that's all."

Maya sinks back in her deck chair and sighs. "Every morning, I wake up thinking I'm still in my boring apartment back home."

Lila shakes her head. "Get your mind out of the city, girl. We're surrounded by naked gods with equipment that would make any woman blush."

As my friends launch into a debate about which excursion to tackle next, I find my thoughts drifting back to Ryan.

"What do you think, Mer?" Lila asks, pulling me back to the present. "Waterfall hike or snorkeling tomorrow?"

I hesitate, wondering if I can engineer another clandestine meeting with Ryan instead. Guilt gnaws at me just for thinking about that, but the excitement of our stolen moments was intoxicating. "How about we play it by ear? This is a vacation, after all. No need to over-plan."

My friends go back to checking out hot young studs—until I announce that I'm starved. That spurs Maya to suggest we finally try the open-air restaurant.

I take another sip of my drink, the fruity sweetness doing little to quell the bittersweet cocktail of disappointment swirling within me. I haven't seen Ryan yet today. When we settle into our seats at the open-air restaurant, the scent of grilled seafood mingling with the salty air does little to raise my spirits. I miss Ryan. Still, I can't help but smile as I take in the vibrant scene around us—other vacationers chatting animatedly, the rhythmic crash of waves in the distance, and the lush greenery framing our view of the crystal-clear sky.

"I'll have the mahi-mahi with mango salsa," Zara announces, closing her menu with a flourish. "And a piña colada, because why not live a little?"

"Make that two piña coladas," I add, catching the waiter's eye.

As we place our orders, I notice how each of my friends approaches the menu differently. Maya meticulously weighs her options, while Lila confidently chooses without hesitation. It's these little quirks that make our group dynamic so special.

Once the waitress bustles away, Zara leans toward me. "So, Ms. Hayes, what's your secret?"

I nearly choke on my water. "Secret? What do you mean?"

"Oh, come on. You've got this...glow about you. Like you've stumbled onto hidden treasure on this island."

The others lean in, clearly intrigued. I force a laugh, desperately searching for a plausible explanation. "Oh, that? Must be all this sun and relaxation. You know how I burn easily—I'm probably just one shade away from 'cooked lobster.' "

My attempt at humor seems to work. But as I take a long sip of my newly arrived piña colada, I wonder why I need to be secretive at all. Would Ryan care? I should ask him first.

As our laughter subsides, Zara's eyes light up. "Ladies, have you heard about the water volleyball tournament the resort's throwing?"

"Are you serious?" I ask. "Nude water volleyball?"

"Oh absolutely." Zara bobs her head enthusiastically, her curls bouncing. "It's this afternoon. Apparently, they're transforming the curvy pool for the big event, net and all."

"That sounds incredible," Maya agrees. "I've never been very athletic, which you guys know. But I'd love to give volleyball a go."

Zara launches into a detailed description of what she believes water volleyball will be like. But I can't stop picturing Ryan in the nude, spiking the ball and making his balls flap too. But I assume the general manager won't participate in that event. It wouldn't be professional.

Lila snaps her fingers in my face. "What about you, space cadet? Game for a little silly fun before the tournament?"

"Uh, what?" I smile, trying to disguise the face that I have no idea what Lila is talking about. "Oh, I don't know. Whatever you guys want."

Zara shakes her head in mock disappointment. "You weren't listening at all, were you?"

"Sorry, no, I zoned out for a minute."

"No kidding." Zara sighs. "Coconut painting, Mer. Yay or nay?"

"Sure, let's do that." I have no idea what coconut painting is, though it sounds bizarre.

Later that afternoon, I find myself wandering down to a secluded beach I'd seen on the map of the resort. The warm, silky sand feels wonderful between my toes. The sun hangs low now, painting the sky in hues of orange and pink. And there, silhouetted against the setting sun, is a familiar figure.

As Ryan turns toward me, his lips curve into a slow, sexy smile. "Ditched the girls, eh?"

I return the smile, closing the distance between us. "You know what they say about great minds. You and I think alike so often it's almost supernatural."

Ryan roves his gaze my whole body. "And what exactly was your great mind thinking about?"

I bite my lip, feeling bold in the fading light. "Oh, you know...coconut painting, secrets, the usual vacation fare."

He raises an eyebrow, stepping closer. "Sounds intriguing."

"Not really. Painting a coconut is damn hard. They're slippery buggers."

Ryan's laughter is husky and rich. "I imagine they are. Maybe you should stick with landscape painting."

"I suck at that too. Lila tried to teach me, but I'm hopeless."

"How about a surfing lesson instead?"

My laugh turns into spluttering. "Aren't there sharks out there?"

He shrugs. "Some things are worth the risk."

"Like what?" Am I worth it? I desperately want him to tell me yes.

But Ryan gazes out at the horizon instead, his jaw tightening, a muscle ticking there. The tension I saw there lessens but doesn't evaporate. His voice drops to a rougher tone. "Speaking of surprises, I've got a few of my own."

I can feel the change in his demeanor, but I can't understand it. Maybe he's trying to avoid a deeper conversation. So, I keep my tone light, not wanting to push. "Well, if you'd like to get something off your chest, I'm here to listen."

He knifes a hand through his hair, a gesture I'm beginning to recognize as a sign of his discomfort. "Yeah, I...There's a lot you don't know about me, Meredith."

I take a step closer, drawn by the vulnerability in his voice. "I'm a good listener, if you want to share. I'm also good at keeping secrets—for the right reasons."

Ryan takes a deep breath, his eyes meeting mine. "This isn't exactly first-date material. But then, we blew past that line a while ago."

"Good thing this isn't our first date, then." I'd hoped to ease his tension. Not sure my strategy is working. "You don't have to buy me flowers or chocolates."

He chuckles, but it's tinged with sadness. "Fair point."

While his body tenses up, I wait with the proverbial bated breath, wondering what secrets he might impart to me.

"I...I used to be a Navy SEAL," he begins, his gaze going distant. "There was an accident. A mission that went wrong. Horribly wrong."

My throat tightens. Ryan has never shared this much about his past before. I stay silent, afraid that if I speak, I'll break the spell and he'll retreat back into himself. I want to hold him, but I know I shouldn't, not yet. "Sweetie, you don't have to tell me."

"No, I want to, I need to."

He swallows hard, and I struggle to resist the urge to reach out and touch him.

"We were on a rescue mission in Libya," Ryan continues, his voice low and strained. "Four American archaeologists had been taken hostage at a recently discovered ancient site. Intel suggested it would be a small operation, in and out." He pauses, running a hand through his hair, squeezing his eyes shut. "But the intel was wrong."

The waves crash against the shore, their rhythm a stark contrast to the tension in Ryan's body. I simply listen, sensing he needs plenty of space to tell his story.

"We arrived under the cover of darkness. Everything seemed quiet—too quiet. Just as we approached the temple ruins, all hell broke loose." Ryan's gaze goes distant now, and he's clearly reliving the memory. "We were ambushed. Gunfire erupted from all sides. A terrorist group planned to steal whatever treasures they might find, and they knew we were coming. But there were no riches."

Ryan's whole body tenses, the muscles and tendons visible beneath his skin. Yet at the same time, his lips tremble faintly. He clenches his jaw, the muscles ticking beneath his skin. "We fought hard, but we were outmatched. I made it out alive, but..." He trails off, his voice cracking slightly. "Not everyone did. One of my closest friends got hit and...didn't make it."

The pain in his voice is palpable, and I ache to comfort him. "I'm so sorry, Ryan. I can't imagine how horrific that was."

He shuts his eyes, his shoulders bunching up. "It broke me, Meredith. The guilt, the memories, wondering whether I'd done enough to save my friend...I couldn't face it. Couldn't face myself. That mission changed everything. Afterward, nothing felt the same—relationships, daily life...It was like I'd left a part of myself behind in that desert. That's why came here. To escape my old life."

I step closer, my hand hovering near his arm and my voice barely a whisper. "You're not running now. You're sharing something horrific with me. That takes guts."

He hunches his shoulders. "I don't usually...open up like this."

"I'm glad you did."

Ryan's hand covers mine, his touch gentle, and his voice barely a murmur. "Feels like a two-ton weight has fallen off my chest. There's something about you, Meredith. Something that makes me want to let my guard down and shake off all those old issues."

I grin. "Well, we are on a nude beach. Guards down is kind of the theme."

His laughter is genuine as the tension eases from his shoulders. He clasps both my hands. "You've got me there, baby."

Ryan pulls me into his arms, holding me close. We stand here while the sun dips below the horizon, I feel the shift between us. This isn't just attraction anymore. It's something deeper, more complex. And despite the complications, I find myself falling headfirst into whatever this is becoming. After a moment or two, Ryan kisses my forehead and ambles back to his office. Meanwhile, I send a text to Zara asking where I can meet up with my friends.

We're on the beach, sweetie. Turn right and follow the footprints to the mangrove tree.

Zara's directions get me to my destination swiftly.

"There you are, Mer." Zara exclaims, leaping up. "We were starting to wonder if you'd gotten lost in paradise. Or maybe just lost in Ryan's bungalow."

I laugh, hoping the flush on my cheeks can be attributed to the island sun. My mind flashes back to Ryan's vulnerable gaze. "Get your mind out of the gutter, woman."

We spend an hour on the beach, swimming, splashing each other, laughing, and getting a tan. Then Zara announces that we're all going to a foam party this evening.

I stare at her. "Excuse me? A what party?"

"Foam. You'll understand once you see it. But basically, a machine spews nice, clean foam all over the designated party area—in this case, the big patio."

"Sounds...slippery."

"Oh, it is," Lila proclaims. "And that's half the fun. You haven't lived until you've tried to dance in chest-deep bubbles."

Maya grins. "I can't wait to see everyone sliding around."

As we make our way back to our rooms to get ready, I can't help but wonder if Ryan will be at this foam party. The thought of seeing him there, all soaped up and slippery, sends a thrill through me. But I quickly push the image aside, reminding myself that I need to focus on my friends tonight. What will a nude foam party be like? It sounds crazy, but that's fine with me.

The foam party is in full swing when we arrive, with the patio transformed into a surreal landscape of bubbles and laughter. Music pulses through the air, mingling with excited squeals and shouts as people slip and slide through the knee-deep foam.

"Oh my god, this is amazing!" Maya exclaims, her eyes wide with childlike wonder.

Without hesitation, she plunges into the frothy mess. Lila and Zara follow suit, shrieking with delight as they lose their footing and tumble into the foam. Fortunately, the staff laid yoga mats down on the patio for cushioning. I can't help but laugh at my friends' antics, feeling a surge of affection for these wonderful, uninhibited women.

"Come on, Meredith!" Zara calls out, her face barely visible above the bubbles. "The water's fine!"

Water? I don't see any of that, but I can roll with the wackiness. I take a deep breath and plunge into the foam. As I wade into the sea of bubbles, the sensation is unlike anything I've experienced before. The foam tickles my skin, cool and slippery, and I can't help but giggle as I lose my footing and slide forward.

"Whoa there!" A strong pair of hands steadies me, and I look up to find Ryan grinning down at me with his lips quirked. My heart skips a beat at the sight of him, memories of our earlier conversation flashing through my mind.

"Wasn't sure if I'd see you today," I tell him. "Didn't think the general manager would participate in something as silly as this." I peer into shoulder-high bubbles around us but can't see much. "Are you naked? I can't tell."

"Of course I'm naked," Ryan chuckles. "It's my night off. Even general managers need to let loose occasionally. Besides, how could I resist the chance to see you covered in bubbles?"

Before I can respond, a wave of foam crashes over us, momentarily obscuring my vision. When it clears, I find myself pressed against Ryan's chest, our slippery flesh sliding together. The heat of his body contrasts deliciously with the cool foam, and I feel a familiar spark of desire ignite within me.

"Well, this is cozy," I purr, gazing up at him through foam-coated lashes.

"Very cozy." Ryan's hands slide down to my waist, holding me steady, and I'm now positive that he's naked. His dick just rubbed up against me. "Though I have to say, I prefer our private playtime."

"So do I. But my friends are around here somewhere. We should probably..."

As if on cue, I hear Zara's voice calling out. "Mer! Where are you?"

Ryan and I quickly peel ourselves apart, the foam swirling around us. I catch a glimpse of his regretful smile before he disappears into the bubbles. My heart is pounding as I turn to face my friends and the party.

"There you are!" Lila calls out, emerging from the foam like some kind of bubble monster. She's grinning from ear to ear, her hair plastered to her head. "We lost you for a minute there."

"Yeah, sorry," I laugh, trying to sound casual. "I got a little turned around in all this foam. It's crazy."

Maya slides up next to me, her eyes sparkling. "Isn't it amazing? I feel like a kid again!"

I catch sight of Ryan's head moving away. Soon, he's left the foam behind and begins to wash himself off with the temporary showers the staff had set up for this party. I desperately want to go after him, but I don't want to offend my three best friends.

Zara taps my foamy shoulder. "Go on, sweetie. If I had a hot guy like Ryan waiting to lather me up, I'd ditch the party too." She makes a shooing motion with her hands. "Go, sweetie, right now."

I hesitate for a moment, torn between my desire to follow Ryan and my loyalty to my friends. But Zara's knowing smile and encouraging nod give me the push I need.

"Are you sure?" I ask, glancing at Lila and Maya.

"Go!" They declare in unison.

With a grateful smile, I wade through the foam toward the temporary showers. As I approach Ryan, who's rinsing the last of the bubbles from his toned body, the sight of water cascading down his muscles makes my mouth go water. He has a scrumptious body that any woman would want to feast on.

"Thought you might need some help getting clean."

Ryan turns toward me, dragging his tongue across his lips while his eyes roam over my foam-covered body. "I was hoping you'd follow me."

He reaches out to pull me under the spray with him. The warm water cascades over us, washing away the foam and leaving nothing but slick, bare skin. Ryan's hands glide down my arms, and lower still, until he can cup both of my ass cheeks. I shiver despite the heat, acutely aware of every point where our bodies touch. Then he grasps my hand, leading me away at a swift pace.

We conclude the evening in my bungalow, naked and writhing, moaning and teasing each other. But the most remarkable part of this evening isn't the foam or the orgasms. It's the way we fall asleep together.

Damn, I'm falling for the wounded man lying beside me—and that doesn't bother me at all.

Chapter Twelve

Ryan

I wake to the gentle pressure of Meredith's body against mine, our limbs entangled like vines seeking sunlight. The soft cotton sheets whisper against our skin as I blink away the haze of sleep. Memories of last night flood back—exploring the curves and valleys of her body, breathless laughter whenever I tickled her with a feather, the intoxicating closeness of our newfound bond. But darker images lurk at the edges. Sand and blood and the echo of gunfire. I push the memories away, focusing on the warm weight of Meredith's head on my chest.

Did I snore? God, I hope not.

Her amber eyes flutter open, catching the fragile morning light that streams through the gossamer curtains. A slow smile spreads across her face. "Good morning, handsome."

I brush a wayward strand of hair from her cheek. "Morning, beautiful. Sleep well?"

"Mm, like a baby. You?"

I hesitate, unsure how to answer. Did she notice my restlessness, the cold sweat of nightmares? I decide to sidestep the issue. "Never better. Though I may have snored a bit."

She laughs, the sound as bright as the tropical birdsong outside. "Only a little. It was kind of cute, actually."

Relief washes through me. Crisis averted, for now. I pull her closer, savoring the softness of her skin against mine. "So, what should we do with our day? It's my weekend off, you know. Forty-eight glorious hours of nothing but you, me, and this island paradise."

"Oh, I can think of a few ideas..."

Before she can elaborate, a cheerful knock interrupts us. "Breakfast delivery!"

That's Marley's voice.

I reluctantly disentangle myself, wrapping a sheet around my waist as I answer the door. Marley's grin widens as she takes in my disheveled state.

"Well, don't you look relaxed, boss," she teases, wheeling in a cart laden with covered dishes. The aroma of fresh fruit and coffee fills the air. "You know, this is a nudist resort, and it's your day off. Why not embrace the lifestyle?"

I try to maintain some semblance of professionalism, but I can feel cheeks heating up. "Thanks, Marley. That'll be all."

She winks as she leaves. "Enjoy your day off, you two."

As soon as the door clicks shut, Meredith bursts into laughter. "Your face...You looked like a teenager caught climbing out your girlfriend's window."

I roll my eyes but can't help grinning. "Come on, let's see what culinary delights await us."

We settle on the balcony, the lush greenery of Heirani Motu spread before us like a verdant carpet. Meredith picks up a ripe mango, its golden flesh glistening.

"Open up," she commands playfully.

I oblige, and she slides a juicy piece between my lips. The sweetness explodes on my tongue.

"My turn," I say, selecting a plump strawberry. I trace it along her lower lip before she takes a delicate bite. A drop of crimson juice lingers at the corner of her mouth. I lean in, kissing it away.

"Mm, yummy," she hums appreciatively. "So, what adventure do you have planned for us today, Mr. Resort Manager?"

I consider our options, my gaze drawn to the sparkling waters beyond the beach. "How about kayaking? We could explore the mangrove forests, maybe spot some of the island's rarer wildlife."

Meredith's eyes light up. "Yes! I've always wanted to try that."

As we continue our leisurely breakfast, I find myself marveling at how easy this feels. The weight I've carried for so long seems lighter in Meredith's presence. For the first time in years, I'm allowing myself to imagine a future beyond the next day, the next week.

It's terrifying. And exhilarating.

We begin our kayaking journey after breakfast. The gentle rhythm of our paddles breaking the water's surface fills the air as we glide through the dense mangrove forest, and Meredith's kayak keeps pace with mine.

"Ryan, look!" she whispers excitedly, pointing to a nearby branch. A vibrant kingfisher perches there, its electric blue feathers a stark contrast to the lush green surroundings.

I smile, reveling in her enthusiasm. "Beautiful, isn't it? This island never ceases to amaze me."

We round a bend, and I spot a small inlet.

"How about we take a little detour?" I suggest, steering my kayak toward the shore.

"What's on your mind?"

"You'll see." As we beach our kayaks, I reach for her hand. "I want to show you something special."

We hike through the dense jungle, the air thick with the scent of exotic flowers and damp earth. I hold Meredith's hand securely and remain vigilant for any possible threats. What, like flying monkeys? I roll my eyes at my own asinine thoughts.

"Close your eyes," I instruct as we approach our destination.

"This is exciting. Are we meeting up with aliens?"

"You never know." I guide her forward, positioning her just right. "Okay, open up those beautiful eyes."

Meredith gasps as she surveys the hidden waterfall before us, its crystal-clear water cascading down moss-covered rocks into a serene pool below.

"Ryan, it's breathtaking," she breathes, squeezing my hand.

I watch her face, memorizing every detail of her awe-struck expression. It hits me then, a realization both electrifying and terrifying. I'm in love with her.

Pushing the thought aside, I grin and tug her toward the pool. "Care for a swim?"

As we splash in the cool water, I can't help but marvel at how natural this feels, how right. For the first time in years, I'm not thinking about the past or worrying about the future. I'm simply here, in this moment, with her.

Later, as we dry off on sun-warmed rocks, Meredith points to some markings on the nearby cliff face. "Are those...cave drawings?"

My brows lift. "Good eye. They're believed to be centuries old."

She traces the faded lines with her fingers. "It's amazing to think about the history here, isn't it? Makes you wonder what other secrets this island holds."

I smirk. "Who knows? Maybe next we'll stumble onto buried treasure."

"Well, I think I've already found something pretty valuable here on this island."

My heart skips a beat as our eyes lock. The urge to tell her how I feel is overwhelming, but I hold back. *Not yet,* I tell myself. *Not here.*

Instead, I stand and offer her my hand. "Ready to head back? I've got another surprise waiting for you at my place."

Moments after we've sat down on the sofa in my bungalow, I get a video call from my bosses. Meredith discretely moves to a chair on the other side of the room. I run a hand through my still-damp hair.

James and Holly's smiling faces fill the frame. "Ryan! How's paradise treating you?"

I grin, leaning back in my chair. "Can't complain. How's Florida?"

"Hot and sticky," Holly confirms. "But we're managing. Mom's thrilled to have us here."

While they tell me more about their visit, I find my gaze drifts to Meredith, curled up in that chair, looking sexy and sweet as she skims through a magazine. I'd much rather sweep her up in my arms and carry her into the bedroom. But duty calls.

"Are you still there, Ryan?" James's deep voice jerks me back to attention—and to the video call. "You seem...distracted. Everything all right at the resort?"

I clear my throat. "Yeah, sorry. Actually, there's something I should probably tell you both."

Holly leans forward, her eyes glimmering with interest. "Ooh, I love a good secret. Is this a soap-opera type of deal?"

"Not exactly. I, uh...I've met someone." The words tumble out before I can second-guess myself. "It's a guest. Meredith Hayes. We've been spending a lot of time together."

James's eyebrows shoot up. "Spending time, huh? Is that what the youngsters are calling it these days?"

I tug at my shirt collar, wincing. "It's not just...I mean, yes, but it's more than that. She's incredible."

Holly claps her hands, beaming. "Oh, Ryan! That's wonderful! Tell us everything."

As I share some carefully edited details about Meredith and our adventures, I become more relaxed, especially when I glance at the woman in question. She smiles in the sweetest way and gives me a thumbs-up sign. James and Holly give me knowing smiles. Seeing their genuine happiness for me, I realize how much I've missed having people to confide in. But now I have Meredith—and James and Holly.

"The staff's been teasing me about being 'infatuated with a guest,' " I admit. "They were right about that."

"Well, can you blame them? Blimey, you're practically glowing."

I resist the impulse to point out that men don't glow. At least, none that I've known do.

We wrap up the call with promises that I'll keep in touch more often. I'm actually looking forward to more video calls. As I close the laptop, my phone buzzes. Tucker's name flashes on the screen.

"Hey, Tuck," I answer, waving for Meredith to come over to the sofa. She does that instantly, leaping onto the cushion beside me.

"Ryan, buddy!" Tucker hollers. "How's island life treating you? Damn good, I assume, based on how cheerful you sound."

We catch up, and I find myself talking about Meredith, unable to keep the happiness out of my voice. I even introduce Tucker to Meredith via another video call. As our conversation winds down, my friend grows more serious.

"That's great, Ryan, really. But..." Tucker pauses. "How are you sleeping?"

His question catches me off guard. I hesitate, debating whether to brush it off.

"Ryan?" Tucker prompts gently.

I sigh. "I had a dream the other night. I was back in Libya."

"Shit," Tucker breathes. "Did Meredith notice?"

"Yes, she did," the woman herself announces. "But I didn't say anything. Wasn't sure you'd want me to know."

"Of course I do. I've told you about Libya, but not about the nightmares." I rub my chin, feeling the evening stubble pricking at my skin. "I should tell you, though."

Meredith snuggles closer. "Only if you're ready for that."

"Ryan," Tucker's voice is firm but kind. "You gotta explain it to her. If this is real, she deserves to know. Right, Meredith?"

Meredith raises her hands. "Please don't get me in the middle of this. I don't want Ryan to feel that he has to tell me everything. We haven't known each other long, after all."

"She's right, Tuck. But I will explain everything, I swear—when the time is right."

Once Tucker signs off, I start worrying about what might happen if I tell her about the nightmares. What if it's too much? What if she decides I'm not worth the trouble?

"Ryan?" Her hand touches my arm, warm and grounding.

"Mer, I...I need to ask you something."

She tilts her head, studying me. "Shoot."

"This thing between us..." I gesture vaguely, searching for the right words. "Is it just...I mean, when your two weeks are up..."

Understanding dawns in her eyes, and she crawls onto my lap. Her arms encircle me. "Oh, Ryan. Do you really think I could walk away from this? From you?"

"You have a life back home. A job, friends, family..."

Meredith laughs, the sound as bright as the island sunshine. "A boring job I was planning to quit anyway, and friends who'd be thrilled to visit me on a tropical island." Her expression turns serious. "What about you? Are you ready for something real?"

I swallow hard, realizing this is my moment of truth. "I want to be ready for that. But there are still things about me, about my past, that you don't know."

She silences me with a finger to my lips. "We've all got baggage, Ryan. I'm not looking for perfect. I'm looking for real. Tell me more when you're ready."

The next morning, I wake before dawn, a plan forming in my mind. I slip out of bed, careful not to disturb Meredith, and make a few quick calls.

When she stirs an hour later, I'm waiting with two cups of coffee and a grin. "How do you feel about snorkeling?"

Her eyes light up. "I've always wanted to try it."

"Perfect." I hand her a mug. "Because I've got a whole day planned for us."

We spend the morning exploring the vibrant underwater world surrounding Heirani Motu. Meredith's delight at every colorful fish and the swaying coral is infectious. Her hand finds mine beneath the water, and I realize I've never felt so at peace.

After lunch, we paddle a canoe to a secluded inlet I discovered during my early days on the island. As the sun begins to dip toward the horizon, I build a small fire on the beach.

Meredith leans back on her elbows, watching the flames dance "This is incredible. I feel like I'm in a movie."

I settle in beside her. "Wait till you taste dinner. I packed some local specialties."

While we eat, our conversation flows easily, touching on hopes and dreams, fears and insecurities. With every word, I feel the walls I've built around my heart slowly crumbling.

Once our meal is finished, I know it's time to explain. "Mer, I'm ready to tell you about my nightmares."

She takes my hand, her touch gentle and encouraging. "I'm listening."

And so, under a canopy of stars, I finally let the whole story spill out—the nightmares that often plague my sleep, the lingering guilt over not being able to save my best friend. Even when I explain that my dreams often result in me thrashing and shouting, Meredith listens without judgment. Her presence is a balm to my battered soul.

When I finish, she cups my face in her hands. "Thank you for trusting me with this."

Then she pulls me into a kiss that speaks volumes, more than I could ever find the words to explain.

Later, as we make love on the warm sand, I feel my soul unburdening, lifting the weight that had held me down for so long. The ghosts of my past haven't disappeared, but for the first time in years, I can see a future beyond them—a future with Meredith by my side.

The gentle lapping of waves against our canoe mingles with the rhythm of my heartbeat as Meredith and I fall asleep on the sand. In the morning, we paddle back to the resort.

"Race you to the beach?" she challenges.

I grin, feeling lighter than I have in years. "You're on, sunshine."

We sprint across the sand, laughing like kids. When we reach the main trail, I catch her hand in mine, savoring the warmth of her skin against my palm.

"Last night was..." I start, searching for the right words.

Meredith squeezes my fingers. "I know. Me too."

We walk in comfortable silence, admiring the lush greenery of Heirani Motu. Suddenly, I can see myself living on this island for good, staying on as general manager, not just for a while but forever. I only want to do that if Meredith stays with me. I have a sneaking suspicion she'll love the idea.

As we approach the resort, reality starts to creep back in. I sigh, knowing I need to slip back into manager mode.

"Duty calls?" Meredith asks, a hint of understanding in her voice.

I nod, reluctantly releasing her hand. "I'll find you later?"

"Count on it," she winks, heading toward her bungalow.

I watch her go, my mind already plotting ways to steal more time with her. But as I turn toward the front desk, Mariel's panicked face stops me in my tracks.

"Ryan!" she calls, her usually soft voice pitched high with worry. "We have a situation!"

"What's wrong?" I ask, instantly on alert.

Mariel wrings her hands. "There's a tropical cyclone forming nearby. And Emilio's hurt his ankle badly. He tripped on a root while doing trail maintenance. Marley's out with the nature tour group, and we're short-staffed, and I don't know what to do, and–"

"Breathe, Mariel," I interrupt gently, placing a steadying hand on her shoulder. "We'll handle this. Has the weather service issued any warnings yet?"

As Mariel fills me in on the details, I feel a familiar presence at my side.

Meredith stands there, concern etched on her face. "Sounds like you could use an extra pair of hands. How can I help?"

I hesitate, torn between my desire to keep her safe and the obvious need for assistance. "Mer, you don't have to–"

She cuts me off with a determined look and a raised hand. "I want to do this. Consider me your assistant for the day."

God, I love this woman.

Chapter Thirteen

Meredith

The sun dips toward the horizon, painting the sky in a breathtaking array of oranges and pinks that reflect off the serene, crystal-clear waters of Heirani Motu. I feel the soft, warm sand between my toes as Ryan and I stroll hand in hand along the secluded beach, our footprints leaving trails behind us, like memories being created with every step. The tranquil sound of waves lapping against the shore echoes around us while Ryan and I continue to amble down the shore.

But it does little to calm the queasiness in my stomach. There's a storm potentially barreling toward the island. But for now, for tonight, I'll try to banish those thoughts from my mind.

I sneak a glance at Ryan, admiring the way the fading sunlight accentuates his chiseled features. My heart flutters as I contemplate telling him how I feel—that I want to be with him forever, that I love him. Whether he feels that way...I don't know.

"Meredith, there's, ah...something I need to tell you."

We stop walking, and I turn to face him. But I can't stop myself from ringing my hands, waiting for a bomb to drop. "What is it, sweetie?"

I listen intently, fighting the urge to interject or offer solutions. This is Ryan's moment to express his concerns, and I'm sure he needs to get it all out in one go. So, I focus on the warmth of his hand in mine.

"This position...it's more than just work for me, Meredith. It's been my sanctuary, my haven from the past." He grasps both my hands, facing me, his expression earnest. "I might never have come out of my shell if it weren't for you. I might never have dealt with the pain of that botched mission either. But you saved me, and I'll always be grateful for that."

Why does it sound like he's saying goodbye? "What's wrong? Are you getting fired? Oh god, are you sick?"

He smiles and shakes his head, chuckling softly. "No, Mer, it's nothing like that. I'm trying to say...I love you."

"Huh?"

Ryan clasps my face in both hands. "I'm in love with you, Meredith. You're like a burst of sunshine that lights up the whole world. Your spirit and your sense of adventure—it's infectious."

I suddenly feel like a shy teenager at the prom. "Well, someone's got to keep you on your toes, Mr. Kimble."

"You make me want to be less rigid. To take risks. To seize every day and make the most of it."

"What risks were you talking about?"

He scratches his cheek, seeming almost sheepish. "I have to start with my friend Tucker. For years, he's been my anchor, the one person I could truly confide in, the only one who knew about my nightmares."

"That's understandable. You both experienced that horrific mission."

"I'm trying to explain that I want to share everything with you." He hesitates, then stands up straighter. "I was hoping you might want to become that person for me. If you can handle my baggage."

"Oh, Ryan." I throw my arms around him. "Your baggage is mine too because...I love you."

For a moment, we simply stand here embracing each other. Then we both smile, I realize we both want this—to be together, on this island, always. Is that even possible? Ryan is the interim general manager. James and Holly probably expect to take over again once their vacation is over.

Ryan and I start our trek back up the main trail. My heart feels full, thanks to our newfound intimacy, yet there's also a bittersweet ache as reality creeps in. Less than two weeks. That's all we have left, according to the calendar. I find myself holding out the faint hope that James and Holly won't come back, and that Ryan and I might run the resort together.

We proceed in companionable silence for the rest of our walk, and I find myself making a mental catalog of every sprig of lush foliage, every stunning flower, and every gorgeous creature on Heirani Motu. The vibrant birdsong that usually fills the air has quieted, as if nature itself is holding its breath, waiting to see what becomes of us.

As we approach the main resort building, our steps slow. I know we need to part ways, but every fiber of my being rebels against the idea. Ryan's hand tightens on mine for a brief moment before he lets go.

"I need some time to think," he tells me, his voice husky with emotion. "We both do. After all, I'm only the interim general manager. We shouldn't make plans, not yet."

"You're right," I say, my voice tight. "We'll figure this out, Ryan. Together or...whatever comes next."

He gives me one last look, a mix of tenderness and torment, before turning away. I watch him go, his lean figure disappearing around the corner of the building. The sudden absence of his warmth leaves me feeling adrift.

Sighing, I make my way to the dining hall, my appetite gone but knowing I should at least make an appearance. My friends wave me over, their smiles faltering as they take in my demeanor.

"Mer, what's wrong?" Lila asks with concern etching her features.

I shrug, attempting to seem nonchalant. "Just...a lot on my mind."

My friends exchange glances as if a silent conversation has passed between them. Then Zara stands up. "That's it. We're having an emergency miniten match. Right now."

Before I can protest, they're pulling me toward the beach. While we set up the net, I can't help but scan the beach, hoping to catch a glimpse of Ryan. But he's nowhere to be seen, and the pit in my stomach grows.

"Serve's up!" Lila calls out, snapping me back to the present.

I throw myself into the game, grateful for the distraction. But even as I laugh and dive for the ball, I can't shake the feeling that something monumental is shifting. The paradise around me—the swaying palms, the pristine sand, the crystal-clear water—seems to mock my inner turmoil with its serenity.

By the time the match is over, the sun is setting in earnest. But I can't get excited about the beautiful sunset. As the last rays disappear beneath the horizon, I wonder if Ryan and I will find our way back to each other, or if this magical interlude is destined to remain just that—a beautiful, fleeting moment in time. After a restless night's sleep, filled with dreams of Ryan, I can't take it anymore. The suspense is killing me, and I need to talk to him.

My friends and I are sitting at a table on the auxiliary patio, sipping cocktails that have cute little umbrellas.

I jump out of my chair. "Sorry, girls. I've got to...check on something."

Before they can respond, I'm dashing across the patio, my feet carrying me swiftly toward the main resort building. My heart pounds as I push through the doors, making a beeline for Ryan's office. When I finally reach his door, I'm panting. I knock, but there's no answer. Pushing the open, I find the room empty.

"Looking for Ryan?" Emilio's voice startles me.

I whirl around. "Yes, have you seen him?"

"He's up on the mountain," Emilio announces. "ATV broke down. Guests can't go zip-lining."

"Thanks!" I call over my shoulder, already halfway down the hall.

Although the hike up the steep mountain trail is grueling, my determination propels me onward. When I finally spot Ryan, he's bent over the ATV, tools scattered around him. He looks up, his eyes widening as they meet mine. Sweat glistens on his brow, and a smudge of grease marks his chiseled jaw. He's shed his shirt, and his chest rises and falls with every breath.

"Meredith? I didn't expect to see you out here."

I shrug. "Been looking for you everywhere. The beach, the dining hall, even your bungalow. I was starting to think you'd vanished into thin air." I pause, trying to gauge his reaction. "It was Emilio who finally pointed me in the right direction."

"Just finished," he pronounces, patting the ATV. "Should be good to go now."

I watch as he explains the repairs to the waiting guests, his voice steady and authoritative. Once they've zoomed off toward the zip-line, he turns back to me and wipes his hands on a rag, the muscles in his arms flexing with the motion.

"You hiked all the way up here?" he asks, a note of surprise, maybe even concern, in his voice.

"It wasn't that difficult," I say with a shrug, though my voice is quavering slightly. "Have you, um, reached a decision yet? About us?"

He doesn't respond immediately, and the silence stretches between us like a chasm.

Finally, I can't bear it any longer. "Remember that time we tried to catch fireflies behind the waterfall?" I blurt out, trying to inject some levity into the moment. "I've never seen anyone look so ridiculous covered in mud."

A ghost of a smile flickers across Ryan's face. "I get what you're doing, Mer."

I hold my breath, waiting for him to tell me more. The silence stretches on and on while the sounds of the jungle—chirping insects, distant bird calls, the rustle of leaves in the breeze—fill in the gap. When he takes a step closer, for a moment, I think he's going to pull me into his arms. Instead, he reaches for his shirt and slips it on, his movements slow and deliberate.

My attempt at deflection has crumbled. I'd promised myself no more hiding, no more running from my feelings. Time to live up to that vow.

I stand up straighter. "I need to know what you want, Ryan. Are we a couple or not? We both said the L word."

He just watches me, impassive.

Now it's time to make one last confession, to be sure he understands my limitations. I take a deep breath, steeling myself for what I need to say next. "I was tossing and turning all night, worrying about how you might react to my bombshell. It's something I should've told your much earlier, but I was...afraid. I need you to understand something. I can't have children. And you're young, Ryan. You probably want a family of your own someday. And I—I don't want to hold you back from that."

The words hang in the air between us, heavy with the weight of possibility and heartache.

My pulse pounds as I watch Ryan's face, searching for any sign of his thoughts. He moves one step closer, his body brushing against mine, and I can feel the warmth radiating from his body.

"Meredith, I—" he starts, then stops. His hand reaches for mine, and I feel a surge of hope.

But before he can finish, a shrill ring cuts through the air. Ryan's phone. He hesitates, then pulls it out with an apologetic glance.

"Emilio?" he answers. "What? Slow down."

I watch as Ryan's expression shifts from confusion to concern. "The tropical cyclone? How soon?"

My stomach drops. A cyclone is actually coming? Here? I knew it was a nebulous possibility, but now it seems to be a reality. The idyllic paradise of Heirani Motu suddenly feels fragile.

Ryan ends the call and looks at me, sighing as he wipes a hand over his mouth. "Meredith, I'm sorry."

"I know," I interrupt, forcing a smile. "Duty calls, right?"

He nods, and for a moment, we just stare at each other. The air between us is electric, charged with unspoken words and unfulfilled desires. I want to throw myself into his arms, to tell him to forget about the storm and just be with me. But I can't. That's not who Ryan is, and it's not who I am either.

"Go," I murmur. "Everyone's counting on you. We can finish our conversation later."

Ryan hesitates, then turns to leave. I watch him walk away, his shoulders tense but his head held high. As he disappears around the corner, I can't shake the feeling that I've just lost something precious. I shake my head, trying to clear the melancholy thoughts.

"Get it together, woman. He's got a job to do, and he can't hold your hand while he's doing that."

I pull in a deep breath and blow it out, then I turn and head in the opposite direction, determined to find my friends and warn them about the incoming storm. But even as I pick up my pace, I can't quite silence the little voice in my head that wonders if this interruption has changed things between Ryan and me.

While I make my way down the mountain trail, a breeze picks up, and I experience a pang of anxiety. The cyclone clearly hasn't come close to Heirani Motu yet. But I've never been through a storm like this before, and I wish I had Ryan at my side, holding me close and murmuring that everything will be okay. The once-serene jungle now feels ominous. My mind races, torn between worry about the impending cyclone and the unfinished conversation with Ryan.

I spot Zara and the others still on the miniten court, laughing as they pack up the net and the thugs. Their carefree mood feels jarring against my internal turmoil.

"Girls!" I call out, jogging toward them. "We need to get ready. There's a cyclone coming."

Their smiles crumble as they notice my serious expression.

"Are you sure?" Lila asks, her eyes wide with concern.

"Ryan just got the call," I inform her. "We should head back to our rooms to wait for instructions. Why don't we all hang out in Zara's suite until then? The more the merrier, right?"

My best friends agree with my plan, and we watch silly Australian comedies on TV while we wait for the hammer to drop.

And I pray the cyclone misses the island.

Chapter Fourteen

Ryan

The papers on my desk blur into a sea of meaningless words as Meredith's face shimmers in my mind. Her amber eyes, her sexy smile, the way she throws her head back when she laughs. God, I want to find her right now, pull her into my arms, and kiss her until we're both out of breath. But I can't. There's no time for romantic daydreams when a cyclone might be barreling toward us.

I rub my eyes, then return to studying the weather radar, refreshing it for the hundredth time today. The swirling mass of angry red and orange images on the screen seems to be veering away from Heirani Motu, but I know how quickly these storms can change course. The island's last close call happened during the resort's opening, back when James Bythesea was general manager and Holly wasn't his wife yet. The island got lucky back then. I pray we'll be as fortunate this time.

With a heavy sigh, I push away from my desk. Time to rally the troops. As I stride down the hallway toward the staff room, I smooth my features into a mask of calm authority. No one can see how worried I am, how my thoughts keep drifting to Meredith's safety.

"Okay, everyone," I holler as I enter the staff room, clapping my hands to get everyone's attention. "We've got a situation brewing. There's a cyclone heading this way."

Emilio's eyes widen. "Like the one from the grand opening, boss?"

"Similar, but potentially more severe. We need to be prepared for anything."

As I outline our storm protocols, I can't help but scan the room, half-hoping to see Meredith's familiar face among the staff. She's not here, of course. She's a guest, so she's probably out enjoying the island's beauty, blissfully unaware of the danger. But I have other priorities right now. I'm sure Meredith is fine, probably hanging out with her friends.

I straighten my posture and look directly at each of my employees in turn. "Marley, I need you to start battening down anything that could become a projectile. Emilio, coordinate with housekeeping to ensure all guests are accounted for and informed of emergency procedures."

Everyone nods. Any anxiety they might be feeling has been tamped down, determination replacing the initial fear in their eyes. I couldn't be prouder of my team than I am right now.

"Remember," I continue, "we're prepared, we're capable, and we'll get through this together. Any questions?"

As the staff disperse to their handle their assigned tasks, I still have work to do too. But Meredith's face flashes through my mind. *Where are you, Mer? Please be safe.* The thought of her out there, exposed to the elements, makes my stomach churn. But I push the feeling aside. I have a resort full of people counting on me. I can't let my personal feelings interfere with my duty. With one last deep breath, I stride out of the staff room, ready to face whatever this storm may bring. But even as I focus on the tasks ahead, a part of me remains acutely aware of Meredith's absence, hoping against hope that she'll appear, safe and sound, before the first raindrops fall.

The laptop screen flickers to life, revealing the concerned faces of James, Holly, Eve, and Val. Their furrowed brows and tense postures betray their worry, even through the pixelated video feed.

"Ryan, we've been monitoring the cyclone's path," James begins, his tone solemn. "How are things on the ground?"

I lean back in my chair, projecting an air of calm I don't entirely feel. "We're as prepared as we can be. The staff's been briefed, and we're implementing our emergency protocols."

"What about the guests?" Eve asks. "Are they panicking?"

"So far, so good," I assure them. "We've closed all the storm shutters, secured loose items, and covered the pool and the outdoor hot tubs. The guests have been informed, but we're keeping things low-key to avoid alarming them."

Holly nods approvingly. "Smart move. And the bungalows?"

"Wind and impact-resistant windows, just like in the guest suites," I reply, ticking off points on my fingers. "We've removed all patio furniture and umbrellas. Anyone in beachfront accommodations will be moved to the main building along with everyone else."

Val, ever the pragmatist, leans closer to the camera. "And you, Ryan? How are you holding up?"

The question catches me off guard, but I recover quickly. "I'm fine. Focused on the job at hand."

A low rumble of thunder punctuates my words. The others exchange glances, but I maintain my composure.

"We trust you, Ryan," James finally confirms. "Keep us posted and watch out for your own safety too."

"I will. Thanks for checking in with me."

The call ends, leaving me alone with the growing sounds of the approaching storm. I turn to the stack of paperwork on my desk, more for something to do with my hands than out of any real need.

A soft knock at the door breaks my concentration, but I keep my attention on the documents I'd been pretending to study. I call out, "Come in."

The door swings open, and I hear the unmistakable sound of bare feet padding across the carpet. My pulse quickens, but I keep my eyes fixed on the papers before me.

"Ryan?"

Meredith's voice, soft and sweet, causes the hairs on my arms to lift and tingle. I glance up, and for a moment, I can't breathe. She's dressed in sweatpants and a T-shirt with sneakers too. Her sun-kissed skin almost seems to glow in the dim light of my office. She sashays toward me, hips swaying, before perching herself on the edge of my desk.

A flash of lightning illuminates the room, casting Meredith's silhouette in sharp relief. In that brief, brilliant moment, I see the vulnerability in her eyes. We both know the danger that's approaching. But the storm isn't the only problem. I still haven't found the time to tell her the truth. As thunder crashes overhead,

I realize I'm standing at a crossroads, caught between duty and desire. And as Meredith sits there waiting for me to speak, I wonder if I have the strength to resist the storm that's been building between us since the moment we met.

"Ryan, I can't pretend anymore," she begins. "This time with you...it's changed me. You've changed me. And I need to know if my feelings are reciprocated. Whether I should go home or..."

My heart pounds against my ribs, a rapid drumbeat matching the intensifying wind outside. I should speak, I must speak, and the time has come to act like a man. So, I jump out of my chair. "Maybe I have been anxious about telling you how I feel, but that's over."

The scent of her skin, like coconut and sea salt, envelops me. But it's the look in her eyes that does me in.

I grip her arms, dragging her into me, our lips nearly touching. "I love you, Meredith. No one has ever meant more to me than you do. I don't that you can't have children. I don't care that you're nine years older than I am. *I love you.*"

A deafening crack of thunder drowns out my words, making us both jump.

So, I tell her again, more loudly. "I love you."

"Yeah, I heard you the first time." Her lips curve into a playful smile. "But maybe we should go to the dining hall. That's where everyone is hanging out."

I smirk. "How can I fuck you in the dining hall? The elderly folks might have a heart attack."

"Sorry, sweetie, no sex during a cyclone. My screams of ecstasy might be mistaken for someone in distress."

Despite myself, I feel a smile tugging at my lips. But the moment of levity is short-lived as another gust of wind rattles the windows, reminding me of the very real danger approaching.

I loosen my grip on her arms. "We need to get you to safety. Your bungalow—do you have any weather-appropriate clothes there?"

"I packed some just in case. Jeans, boots, the works."

"Good. We need to hurry. This storm is getting worse by the minute."

As we move toward the door, I worry about the cyclone outside but also how the guests will handle being stuck in the main building for the duration. Before we head for Meredith's bungalow, I take us on a detour to check on all the guests and my staff. Many of the guests who have rooms in the main building had decided to stay in their quarters. The rest took shelter in the dining hall, the game room, and other public areas.

Inside the building, controlled chaos reigns. Emilio's voice rises above the din, his usual cheerful tone replaced by calm authority. "Everyone, please remain calm and follow the staff to the designated safe areas."

The staff volunteered to handle room service. The dining hall is packed with guests who were told to leave their bungalows or rooms in other parts of the resort. Every structure on the island has been storm proofed. But I'd rather have everyone crammed into the main building instead of spread out in various locations.

I catch Marley as she's dashing around helping guests. "You guys have everything under control. I'm taking Meredith to her bungalow. Call me on the walkies if you need me. Cell phones might not work."

"Yes, boss."

A deafening crack rips through the air as we reach Meredith's bungalow. The ground trembles beneath our feet, and I instinctively pull her close, shielding her body with mine as a massive palm tree crashes down mere thirty feet away.

Meredith gasps, her fingers digging into my arms.

"We need to move, now!" I shout over the howling wind. Without thinking, I scoop her up and sprint toward her bungalow. My heartbeat is pounding in my ears by the time I set Meredith down just inside her door and slam it shut. "Are you okay?"

"Yeah, I'm fine. Ryan, that was insane. Like something out of a disaster movie."

"I know."

Now that we're cocooned in her bungalow, the roar of the wind is less noticeable. The mountain and the trees muffle it just enough that we can relax a bit. We have no television, since the signals come from satellites and the storm is blocking them. I have a walkie talkie for communicating with my staff, but otherwise, we have no way to communicate until the brunt of the cyclone moves away from us. Meredith and I pass the time by playing gin rummy—she wins more than half the time—and also by talking. I want to ask about her past, but it feels wrong for me to start that conversation.

Instead, I tell her more about me. Maybe that will encourage her to open up too. We're lying in bed, fully clothes, while the storm rages, though less powerfully than earlier.

"When I took this job," I explain, "I had no idea how my family would feel about it. But they were surprisingly broad-minded about the nudist resort thing. Of course, they still don't know that I've gone naturist too, thanks to a certain bewitching guest."

She feigns innocence. "And that guest would be...Zara, right?"

"Ha-ha." I tickle her belly, which always makes squirm and laugh. "My family would love you."

"Even though I'm a post-menopausal woman who never had any children?"

"Once they meet you, they won't care about your age." I pull her closer. "We could visit family sometime. Then you could get to know my brother and sister, my parents too."

She lays her arm across my chest. "My parents live in South Dakota, but I moved to Seattle with my husband not long after we got married."

"You're divorced, then?"

"Not exactly." Meredith's face pinches up briefly, then she relaxes against me with a sigh. "Brian was very sweet when we were dating and for several years after that. But then he had a stroke and couldn't work, even had trouble walking and speaking. I had to get a second job to pay for his medical expenses. Brian would curse at me and even throw things at me. I knew it was the stroke, but I still felt...defeated. Four and half years ago, he had another stroke and passed away."

"I'm so sorry, Mer."

She shrugs one shoulder. "I know it sounds horrible, but I was...relieved when he died. I quit my second job and stuck with my bank teller position. Then I started going to group grief therapy. That's how I met Zara, Maya, and Lila. They lost their husbands too."

"It's great that you found friends like those ladies. They're amazing, just like you."

We fall asleep in each other's arms, hardly noticing the storm anymore. And when we wake in the morning, it seems like a new day, not just because the cyclone is gone but also because of our conversation last night. The morning sun streams through the windows. Meredith is still nestled in my arms, her warm breath tickling my neck. For a moment, I allow myself to savor this perfect stillness, to imagine waking up like this every morning.

I know this woman. I love this woman. Nothing else matters.

But duty calls. I carefully extricate myself from Meredith's embrace, planting a soft kiss on her forehead before slipping out of bed. She stirs slightly but doesn't wake.

Outside, the storm has left its mark—fallen palm fronds litter the beach, and the usually pristine sand is strewn with debris. There might be more debris in other parts of the island, but I have a feeling the resort will recover quickly. I make my way to the main building, surveying the grounds as I go. A few lounge chairs overturned, some downed trees, and scattered debris.

But now it's time to check to do a thorough, island-wide inspection. I leave a note for Meredith and then head out.

Chapter Fifteen

Meredith

The scent of freshly brewed coffee fills the air as I scan the bustling dining hall, my heart doing a little flip-flop with every new face. No sign of Ryan yet. *Damn.* Where is that man? I might have a heart attack waiting for him to appear. When I spot a familiar trio weaving through the tables, I start toward my friends.

"Have you fallen asleep in your chair?" Zara teases, waving a piece of toast in front of my face. "Are you planning on eating that fruit salad or just rearranging it artfully?"

I blink several times, realizing I've been pushing pineapple chunks around on my plate for the last five minutes. "Sorry, I guess I'm just...trying to grasp the fact that we all survived a cyclone."

The aftermath of last night's storm is evident in the slightly disheveled appearance of our fellow guests, but there's an unmistakable buzz of energy in the air. We survived, and now we're ready to pitch in with the cleanup.

"I still can't believe we slept through most of it," Zara muses, her curls wild from the humidity. "You missed out on charades last night, though I don't blame you for preferring to hide out with the studly Ryan."

For some reason, I feel the need to brag about my honey. "He was a Navy SEAL, you know. Ryan can cope with any disaster."

"Wow, Mer. You bagged a twelve-point buck."

"You hate hunting."

Zara shrugs. "Ken loved it, though. And he made the best venison stew."

Luckily, I'm spared from any deer hunting stories when Emilio's enthusiastic wave catches my eye. He, Marley, and Rene make their way over to us.

"Ladies!" Emilio exclaims. "We can't thank you enough for rallying the troops this morning and for enlisting other guests to help with meal prep. Your enthusiasm and ingenuity were a godsend."

Marley nods, her ponytail bobbing. "Seriously, you're like guest relations superstars. Maybe we should hire you all."

The idea sends a little thrill through me. Could I really stay here? My eyes drift to the dining hall entrance again, hoping to catch a glimpse of sandy blond hair and those beautiful hazel eyes. But I still can't find Ryan in the crowd.

"Oi, Meredith," Rene's voice snaps me back to attention. "You looking for someone in particular, love?"

Rather than admitting I'm searching for Ryan, I change the subject. "So, what's the game plan for cleanup?"

While Emilio outlines the day's tasks, I find myself torn between excitement for the group effort and a gnawing anxiety about my rapidly dwindling time on Heirani Motu. The thought of saying goodbye to this paradise—and to Ryan—makes my chest ache.

"You all right, Mer?" Zara whispers, giving my hand a light squeeze. "You look a million miles away."

"Just thinking about how much I'm going to miss all of this," I admit, my gaze sweeping over the dining hall and the staff who've become like family.

"You know, I was thinking of organizing a beach cleanup later," Marley says. "Maybe we could make it fun, like a treasure hunt?"

"Ooh, I like it!" Maya nods approvingly. "What sort of treasures will we be hunting for? Rene's flip-flops?"

"No, no," Zara interjects. "This is a nudist resort. We should be searching for Ryan's lost shirt. Or maybe his boxers."

Zara winks at me.

And I nearly choke on my coffee in my attempt to stop myself from laughing. I earn concerned looks from the others. "Wrong pipe, that's all."

While the conversation flows around me, my friends share tales of hidden waterfalls and zip-line mishaps, I find my thoughts drifting. Where is Ryan? The dining hall feels emptier without his steady presence, his quiet strength. And I realize, with startling clarity, that I'm not ready for this adventure to end. I'm not ready to leave Heirani Motu—or Ryan. But how can I try to broach that subject if he won't even show his face? I know he must be swamped with the cleanup efforts, but still...

The second we step outside, I gasp. The lush paradise I've come to adore looks like it's been through a blender. Palm fronds litter the ground, and debris from the storm is scattered across the once-pristine beaches. But it's not as apocalyptic as I'd feared.

"Holy coconuts," I mutter, surveying the damage.

Emilio, ever the optimist, grins. "Don't worry. We've weathered worse. This? It's just nature's way of redecorating."

"Well then, let's hope Mother Nature's done with her extreme makeover."

The staff spring into action, directing us with practiced efficiency. I'm impressed by their calm demeanor as they orchestrate the cleanup, all the while ensuring everyone's safety.

"Underground power lines," Marley explains, noticing my puzzled look at the lack of fallen wires. "Clever design, eh? We're online again now, but the backup generator was a lifesaver during the storm."

As I bend to pick up a fallen branch, my mind wanders to Ryan yet again. But my musings end abruptly when there's a stir among the volunteers. Then I see a familiar figure emerging from the direction of the main building.

Ryan.

He's here, looking as gorgeous as ever, his lean body moving with purpose as he surveys the cleanup efforts. Our eyes lock for a moment, and he smiles and winks at me. Every fiber of my being wants to run to him, to throw my arms around him and never let go.

But I can't. Not here, not now.

Zara follows my gaze, her eyebrows shooting up. "No wonder you look like you're walking on air. Your soulmate just walked by."

"I don't believe in soulmates."

"Uh-huh, sure. Come on, girl, I want all the juicy details."

I laugh, and a weight seems to lift off my shoulders. "Later, I promise. Right now, I think I need to talk to him."

While Ryan directs the cleanup efforts, I fall a little more in love with him every minute. Maybe I do want to meet his family. But the one thing I'm certain of is that I want to stay here with Ryan, on this incredible island, forever.

I take a deep breath, gathering my courage, and make my way over to Ryan. He's bent over a large fallen palm frond, muscles rippling as he lifts it with ease.

"Need a hand?" I ask, trying to keep my voice steady.

Ryan looks up, a slow smile spreading across his face. "Meredith. I was hoping I'd run into you."

"Well, here I am." I try to sound casual, but my pulse quickens. "I was starting to think you were avoiding me."

He straightens, wiping his brow with the back of his hand. "Never. I've just been swamped with the cleanup. But I'm glad you're here now."

There's an intensity in his gaze that makes my knees weak. I want to throw caution to the wind, to tell him what I want, but the words stick in my throat.

"Ryan, I don't..." My voice falters. The weight of the words I want to express feels too heavy.

He steps closer. "What's wrong, Mer?"

I take a deep breath and dive in headfirst. "I don't want to leave. I mean, I know I have to go home eventually, but...I'm not ready for this to end. For us to end."

Ryan's eyes widen, a mix of surprise and something else—hope, maybe?—flickering across his face. He glances around, then gently takes my elbow, guiding me away from the bustling cleanup efforts to a quieter spot near the tree line.

He keeps his hand on my arm. "I've been thinking about this too. About you. About us."

"You have?"

"I can't stop thinking about you. These past few weeks have been...incredible. You've awakened something in me I thought was long dead."

I can't help but grin. "Well, I am pretty amazing."

"That you are," Ryan chuckles, his eyes crinkling at the corners in that way that makes my heart flutter. "But it's more than that. You've reminded me what it feels like to be alive, to want something—someone—so badly it almost hurts. In a good way."

I wrap my arms around his neck. "So, what are we going to do about it?"

He pushes a hand through his hair, a gesture I've come to recognize as a sign of his inner turmoil. "I don't know. This isn't exactly a normal situation. You must have a life back home with your parents, and I have responsibilities here."

"But?" I prompt, sensing there's more.

He gazes directly into my eyes. "But I can't bear the thought of you leaving. Of never seeing you again."

"Oh, Ryan, I feel the same way. I can't imagine going back to my old life after everything we've shared here. Our families would want us to be happy, wouldn't they?"

"Yeah, I guess you're right." He pulls me closer, his strong arms enveloping me. The familiar scent of scent of him fills my senses. "What if..."

"What if what?" I prompt, my heart racing.

His mouth puckers for a moment, then all the tension washes away. "What if you stayed? Just for a little while longer. We could figure things out, see if this is real outside of the island bubble."

I can hardly believe what I'm hearing. "Are you serious?"

"Yes. I've never been more serious about anything in my life, Mer. I know it's crazy, but I can't let you go without at least trying to make this work."

"Oh, Ryan, I want that too. Let's give it our all and see what happens." I brush my fingers through his tousled hair. "I already love you, and I know you feel the same. This is going to work out. But you're right, we should give ourselves this time to be sure."

Ryan returns to the cleanup efforts, but he insists that I should have lunch with my friends to tell them the news about us. Their enthusiasm is contagious, and I feel a surge of affection for these amazing women.

"You guys aren't weirded out?" I ask. "Ryan is nine years younger than I am, after all."

"Are you kidding?" Lila grins. "We're thrilled for you! You deserve some island romance with a hot stud, and maybe something more will develop. Who knows? Wedding bells might be calling soon."

I glance back at Ryan, catching him looking our way. He gives me a small, almost imperceptible nod before turning back to his work. And even that small gesture makes me feel like I'm flying above the clouds.

"So, what's the plan?" Zara asks, her voice softening. "Are you going to stay?"

"We're taking the last week of my vacation to sort things out and decide if we want to be more than a holiday fling."

"That's a smart plan," Zara agrees. "Whatever you decide, we've got your back. You know that, right?"

"Of course I do." I feel a lump form in my throat. "God, what would I do without you guys?"

As we stand here, surrounded by the aftermath of the storm, I realize that no matter what happens with Ryan, I've already found something precious here on Heirani Motu. Something that will stay with me long after my friends and I leave this paradise. If I leave.

But I'm not the same woman who arrived here, desperate for a change and a steamy fling.

"Remember when you zip-lined across that gorge?" Maya reminds me. "You were terrified, but you did it anyway. And afterward, you couldn't stop smiling."

"This is your chance to zip-line into love," Zara adds with a grin. "Take the leap, Mer. You've got nothing to lose and everything to gain."

Laughter bubbles out of me, and I clasp each of my friends' hands one by one. "You guys are phenomenal. I never had friends like this until the day I walked into that group grief counseling session. It changed my life—for the better."

Emilio approaches our little group. "Ladies, we could use some help distributing refreshments to the cleanup crews. Any volunteers?"

Lila, Maya, and Zara exchange a look. Then Zara declares, "You've got three recruits here. What about you, Meredith?"

"Count me in. But I really need do something first."

My friends don't ask what that thing is, bless them.

While they follow Emilio, I'm left alone with my thoughts. The island breeze caresses my skin, and I close my eyes, letting the sounds of nature wash over me. I think about the woman I was before coming here—lonely, stressed, stuck in a rut, afraid to take chances. Now, standing on this beach, I feel free and alive as if the universe has opened up for me.

I open my eyes and spot Ryan across the beach, directing a group of guests. His quiet strength and dedication draw me in like a magnet. Taking a deep breath, I straighten my shoulders and begin walking toward him. It's time to take that leap.

As I march across the sand, my heart pounds with every step. Ryan's back is turned as he gestures toward a pile of debris, his tanned skin glistening with sweat. I'm right behind him when he turns, his eyes widening.

"Meredith? What are you—"

I don't let him finish that thought. My arms fly around his neck as I pull him close and press my lips to mine. Briefly, he's frozen. But then he slides his arms around my waist, and he's kissing me back with a passion that makes my toes curl.

Whoops and cheers erupt around us. I break away, suddenly remembering we're surrounded by people. Ryan's cheeks are flushed, and he seems almost embarrassed, the way he ducks his head slightly.

"Well," he drawls, clearing his throat, "that's one way to boost morale during cleanup."

"Sorry, I just...needed to do that."

He takes my hand, his thumb tracing circles on my palm. "Let's talk somewhere more private."

We're barely out of earshot when Rene's booming voice cuts through the air. "Oi, Ryan! We've got a situation, mate!"

Ryan's jaw tightens, but he doesn't let go of my hand. "What is it, Rene?"

The pilot jogs up to us, his blue eyes twinkling with barely contained excitement. "Storm's done a number on our supply lines. We need to make an emergency run to the mainland. Reckon you're up for a quick trip to the Land Down Under? It'll be like old home week for me."

I feel Ryan's grip on my hand tighten slightly. He looks at me, brows raised. "Are you okay with this? Me running away on a supply run? You seemed like you wanted to talk some more."

"Go. We need supplies, and everything else can wait." I surprised myself with how steady my voice sounds. "The resort needs you. We'll talk when you get back."

"I promise we'll finish this conversation."

As Ryan and Rene dash off toward the airstrip, I'm left standing alone. But Ryan will be back soon. That thought cheers me up as I dive back into the cleanup efforts. Sunset arrives faster than I expected, but I guess hard work makes the hours just zip by. After a long day of picking up after Mother Nature, everyone gathers on the beach for an impromptu party. It's in full swing by the time the sun is dipping toward the horizon. Tiki torches flicker in the breeze, casting warm light over the revelers. I sip my fruity cocktail, trying to focus on Zara's animated retelling of her day's adventures, but my eyes keep darting to the darkening sky.

"No more puppy dog eyes," Lila insists, nudging me. "Your sex god will be back soon."

I manage a wan smile. "I know. But it feels like eternity."

Before either of my friends can respond, a familiar rumble fills the air. Heads turn as the small jet appears, silhouetted against the fading light. My pulse accelerates, and I feel a touch lightheaded from sheer excitement.

The party goes quiet as the general manager and the pilot make their way onto the beach. They're grinning, Rene's arm slung over Ryan's shoulder as he regales him with what I'm sure is an inappropriate joke. Then Ryan's eyes lock with mine, and the world seems to fall away. My feet are moving before I realize it, sand kicking up behind me as I run. Ryan matches my pace, closing the distance between us in long strides. When we meet, his strong arms wrap around me, and he lifts me off my feet. I'm laughing, my arms wrapped around his neck while he spins us in a circle.

"God, I missed you," he murmurs, his breath warm against my ear.

"I missed you too," I whisper back, not caring that everyone's watching. In this moment, it's just us—Ryan and Meredith, two people who found something unexpected on this magical island.

He sets me down, keeping his arms around me, and I know we both have decisions to make. But right now, surrounded by the cheers and applause of our makeshift island family, I let myself bask in the joy of this moment, this connection that feels both thrilling and somehow like coming home.

The euphoria of our reunion fades into a bittersweet realization when I wake up the next morning. And for the next six days, we're both too busy to have "the talk."

Suddenly, I realize we have only two days left. The thought hits me like a punch to the gut, and I sit up in bed, running a hand through my tangled hair. We made love last night, and it had been so sweet and sensual that I nearly melted into a puddle.

"You're thinking too loud," Ryan mumbles beside me, his eyes still closed.

I tickle his lips with my fingers. "Sorry, didn't mean to wake you."

He cracks one eye open. "What's going on in that beautiful head of yours?"

I bite my lip, debating how much to reveal. "Just thinking about...time. How little we have left."

Ryan sits up now, his expression serious. "Just tell me what's going on, please."

"Okay." I sit up and wrap my arms around myself. "I want to stay here on the island—with you. Not just for a few days. For good."

"I'm glad you said that, because I want the same thing." He kisses my hand. "You are the love of my life, Mer."

He pulls me close, our bodies entwined. I try to memorize every nuance of every sensation—the warmth of his skin, the taste of his lips, the way his hands fit perfectly on my waist.

Later, as we join my friends and some of the staff for breakfast, the mood is a mix of excitement and melancholy. Everyone's chattering about their plans back home, but there's an undercurrent of sadness at leaving this paradise behind.

"I can't believe we're going home tomorrow," Zara sighs, stirring her coffee absently.

"Yeah, I'll miss you guys," I admit. "It feels like we just got here, doesn't it?"

"Speak for yourself," Lila chimes in, grinning. "I'm ready to sleep in my own bed again. Though I'll miss all you crazies."

"Not looking forward to repeating that thirty-six-hour trip in economy class."

I absently stir my coffee. "Well, at least I won't have to worry about that."

Maya stares at me. "Do you mean..."

"Ryan and I are staying together. Maybe I can get some kind of job here." I toss my Styrofoam coffee cup into the trash can. "But honestly, I'd be happy just to watch him work."

"We've lost her," Zara declares, with sarcastic sorrow. "She's a pod person now."

We laugh, but I catch Ryan's eye across the room. He gives me a small smile, and I wonder what he's thinking.

As the day progresses, I throw myself into every activity, determined to soak up every last drop of island life. My friends and I hike to the hidden waterfall, zip-line through the lush canopy, and lounge on the beach, our bodies bare and free under the warm sun. But as night falls, restlessness takes hold. I slip away from the farewell bonfire, my feet carrying me down to the moonlit shore. The waves crash rhythmically, a soothing counterpoint to my racing thoughts.

As the day progresses, I throw myself into every activity, determined to soak up every last drop of island life. We hike to the hidden waterfall, zip-line through the lush canopy, and lounge on the beach, our bodies bare and free under the warm sun. But as night falls, restlessness takes hold. I slip away from the farewell bonfire, my feet carrying me down to the moonlit shore. The waves crash rhythmically, a soothing counterpoint to my racing thoughts.

I hear footsteps behind me and turn to see Ryan approaching, his silhouette backlit by the distant bonfire. He comes to stand beside me, close enough that our arms brush.

"Penny for your thoughts?" he asks softly.

"I was thinking about us, and what our life will be like from now own. I'm no longer a guest."

"You're so much more than that now." He kisses the top of my head. "My life has done a one-eighty, all thanks to you. I'm grateful, more than you could imagine, to have you in my life. This island wouldn't be half as beautiful without your smile to brighten every day."

As we stand here, bathed in moonlight and possibilities, I know that whatever challenges lie ahead, we'll face them hand in hand. The island may have brought us together, but our story is far from over.

Chapter Sixteen

Ryan

The sun peeks through the slats of our bamboo blinds, painting golden stripes across our bed. I stretch lazily, savoring the warmth of Meredith's body nestled against me. It's been six weeks since we decided to make Heirani Motu our permanent home, and every morning I wake up feeling like it all must be a dream. But it's real.

"Good morning, beautiful," I say, pulling her closer so I can nuzzle her neck.

She yawns and stretches, her sleepy smile gradually widening. "Morning, handsome. Ready to face another day in paradise?"

"Yep. We have the best jobs on earth." I yawn too. "Nothing I'd rather do than hand out sunscreen and condoms to naked people."

We rise slowly, moving through our morning routine with the easy familiarity of a couple who've known each other for years, not months. I brew coffee while she slices fresh papaya and mango from the little garden behind our bungalow. We eat on our lanai, both of us wearing satisfied smiles. The view never gets old—jutting mountains, towering palms, a waterfall in the distance. James and Holly had insisted that Meredith and I move to a different bungalow, one that offers panoramic views of the island. We can hear waves crashing in the distance too.

Once we've finished off our breakfast, we allow ourselves a bit of time to just appreciate where we are. As general manager, however, I'm basically incapable of focusing on only the scenery. Fortunately, the woman I love gets it. She gets *me*.

"I've been thinking," I tell her as I set down my coffee mug. "What if we expanded the nature trails? There's that hidden ledge behind the main waterfall that we haven't fully explored yet. A couple of guests, Craig and Vanessa Hathaway, found it last year."

Meredith leans forward, her eyes narrowing slightly. That means she's thinking. Since Meredith became my right hand at the resort, unofficially, she's been funneling her newfound management skills into eco-tourism initiatives.

"Go on, baby," I encourage. "I can tell you have an idea."

"Remember those deep fissures we stumbled onto last week? I think they could be part of an underground cave system." She taps one finger on her mug. "If we could safely map it out, it could be an amazing addition to the island's attractions. Might even be archaeological artifacts squirreled away there from hundreds of years ago."

I love watching Meredith brainstorm. She almost glows from the excitement of new possibilities. This is the woman I fell in love with—passionate, determined, always seeking new adventures. I reach across the table and squeeze her hand. "That sounds incredible, Mer. And it could be a great way to showcase the island's unique ecosystem. Maybe we could even partner with some researchers to study the wildlife in those caves and in the mangroves on the other side of the island."

"Exactly!" Her expression brightens, and I can practically see the gears turning in her mind. "We could create educational tours, maybe even set up a small research station. It would be a win-win for conservation and tourism."

As we clear the breakfast dishes, I keep glancing sideways at her. It's amazing how far we've come in a relatively short time. Just a few months ago, Meredith was a guest, a stranger, a widow seeking new experiences and craving something wild. I had just taken on a job that I wasn't sure I could handle, on an island full of naked people. But I know now that I belong here with this new family I've forged. My actual family met Meredith in person a few weeks ago—though not here on the island. They aren't quite ready for that. But they're completely fine with my new life.

Now, Meredith and I are building something beautiful together, not just for ourselves, but for this island we've grown to love.

"So, when do we start exploring?" I ask.

Meredith lifts her brows. "Eager, aren't we? How about this weekend? We can pack some supplies and make a day of it."

"Perfect. I'll talk to Cooper and Mila about borrowing some of the resort's climbing gear."

As we finish getting ready for the day, I find myself thinking about what's to come for us. Great things, I know that much. An expedition to a mysterious part of the island is exactly the kind of adventure we both relish these days. And I have the perfect partner by my side.

We make our way down to the main resort area, greeting the early-rising guests with warm smiles. The Au Naturel Naturist Resort South Seas has become more than just a workplace for us—it's our community, our home.

But before we undertake our expedition, I need to do something else.

I suggested to Meredith that she ought to learn all about what goes on in the dining hall behind the scenes. If my idea made her suspicious, she didn't let on that it did. After kissing her goodbye, I jog to the gift shop. Since I don't know how long I'll have to complete my secret mission, I figure I need to get done quickly just in case. My palms are sweaty, though this building does have air conditioning. Memories rush through me—of Meredith's smile, her laughter, the way her eyes crinkle when she's truly happy.

I burst into the gift shop, startling Mariel behind the counter. "I need a ring."

Mariel stares at me blankly. "A ring? Who do you need to call?"

"No, I don't—Never mind." I scan the modest jewelry display. "I need an engagement ring. Right now."

Mariel's eyebrows shoot up. "For Meredith?"

"Yeah." I suddenly feel foolish. "Is it too soon? God, what am I thinking?"

"Relax, boss," Mariel replies, her voice softening. She gestures to a delicate band with a small, sparkling stone. "This one's nice. Simple, but elegant. Like Meredith."

I nod, trying to imagine the ring on Meredith's finger. "Perfect. I'll take it."

As Mariel rings up the purchase, she adds casually, "You know, most women like it when a man gets down on one knee. It's romantic."

I scoff. "That's a bit cliché, isn't it?"

Mariel shrugs. "Sometimes clichés work for a reason."

I pocket the ring box, my mind racing. "Thanks, Mariel. I'll... consider that advice."

Leaving the shop, I head for the dining hall. But only a moment later, I suddenly get a much better idea. I need to rehearse what I'll say. So, I go to our bungalow and stand in front of the bedroom mirror. Proposing doesn't seem that hard. *Marry me*, those words are all I need to speak. But as I glance out the window, I see a familiar figure through the trees, pacing around the hot tub. I freeze, watching her. Meredith stops, her gaze sweeping over the lush landscape. The calls of exotic birds and the distant rush of water fill the air. My chest tightens just from seeing her profile. Her presence always does this to me.

"Time to man up," I mutter to myself. "Go out there and just do it."

Just then, my phone rings. I don't want to answer. Yet my curiosity gets the better of me, and I find myself snatching the phone out of my pants pocket.

Conference room. Now.

The call came from Val Silva. I have to go. My proposal will need to wait a while.

As I burst into the conference room, my jaw drops. Sitting around the table are Val and Eve Silva, along with James and Holly Bythesea—all four of my bosses.

"Ryan!" Val booms, his voice as larger-than-life as ever. "Just the man we wanted to see!"

I struggle to find my voice. "What's going on? I thought you were all back in Oregon."

Eve leans forward, her eyes twinkling. "We couldn't miss this opportunity. Ryan, we want you to become the permanent general manager here at the South Seas resort."

The words hit me like a tidal wave. It's everything I've worked for, everything I thought I wanted. But all I can think about is Meredith.

"I don't mean to be rude, but..." I swipe a hand over my eyes. "You see, I was just about to do something monumental when you guys called. I'm stoked about the promotion, for sure. But, ah, just a few minutes ago, I was on the cusp of asking Meredith to marry me."

"That's wonderful!" Holly and Eve shout at the same time.

James and Val grin and slap my arm.

Then all their faces go blank. James speaks up. "There is a slight problem, Ryan. Didn't Meredith text you?"

"Text me what?"

James glances at the others, then sighs. "Read the text. Now."

I hate cryptic bullshit, but I follow James's orders. I check my texts. There is indeed one from Meredith, but when I see it, my stomach drops. "She's going to Fiji with Rene? On a supply run? And they're leaving in fifteen minutes? Shit."

Eve winces. "Check the time stamp."

When I do that, I throw my head back and groan. "The message was sent six minutes ago. No way can I get to grass strip in time."

"Of course you can," Holly declares. Then she makes a shooing motion. "Run fast, Ryan!"

James chuckles. "What are you waiting for? Rene's jet will be at any moment, and Meredith's on it. Do you really want to wait until she comes back before you propose?"

"Go, Ryan," Eve commands. "Just like Holly said, run fast!"

I'm already racing toward the door when Val's voice stops me. "And Ryan, don't forget to get down on one knee!"

As I sprint out of the room, I can't stop myself from grinning. Maybe being a lovesick moron isn't so bad after all. My heart races as I reach the trail that leads to the grass strip, having already galloped across the resort grounds. The stunning scenery flies by, blurring the trees and grass and even the sky.

The distant hum of an engine spurs me into action. I take off toward the landing strip, lungs burning, legs pumping. Rene's sleek jet comes into view just in time for me to see the door sliding shut.

"Meredith!" I shout, waving my arms like a madman. "Wait!"

Through the window, I catch a glimpse of her face, those warm amber eyes widening in surprise. My voice cracks with desperation. "Please!"

For a heart-stopping moment, nothing happens. Then the door swings open again, and she's there, gorgeous and confused.

"Ryan?" Meredith calls out, uncertainty in her voice.

I can't find the words, and so I simply hold out my arms. She hesitates for only a second before leaping onto the ground, crashing into me with such force we nearly topple over. Our eyes lock, and I see everything I'm feeling reflected back at me—hope, longing, love.

Rene's amused voice breaks the spell. "Oi, lovebirds! Make up your minds, yeah? I've got a schedule to keep."

I barely register the cheers and whistles from a crowd I hadn't noticed gathering behind us. I drag Meredith tightly against me, kissing her with every ounce of passion I possess. When we finally break apart, breathless, I can't wait one second longer.

I drop to one knee, holding out the ring box with the lid up, a sparkling diamond nestled inside. "Meredith Hayes, will you marry me?"

Her answering smile is brighter than the tropical sun. "Yes, you fool, of course I will!"

I sweep her up in my arms and spin round and round until we're both dizzy. Then I kiss her with so much passion that I think even Rene blushed. The crowd cheers. When I glance back, I see several staff members and half a dozen guests observing.

Meredith grins at Rene. "Mind going without a copilot this time?"

Rene grins. "Go on, lovebirds! I'll make do on my own."

Hand in hand, we jog back toward the resort, the jet's engines roaring behind us as Rene lifts off, headed for Fiji.

"What made you do that?" Meredith asks as we jog back to our bungalow. "Proposing in front of everyone? You've never seemed like the dramatic type of guy."

I feel lighter than I have in years, like a huge weight has been lifted. "You might say I got some very pointed advice from the bosses. Turns out they're hopeless romantics."

"Ryan Kimble," she teases, "are you telling me you've gone soft?"

"Only for you, Mer. Only for you."

When we reach the edge of the big patio, I halt abruptly, in need of a short break to catch my breath. Meredith turns to me, clearly as out of breath as I am.

"I have news to share," I tell her, my voice growing stronger. "I was offered the permanent position as general manager."

She crushes her mouth to mine. "Congratulations! You deserve it, sweetie."

A horde of people emerges from the trail, and Meredith and I reluctantly separate. Thunderous applause erupts around us. I'd almost forgotten about our audience, lost as I was in our private bubble of happiness. The faces of guests and staff alike beam at us, their joy palpable.

Mariel, who helped me choose the ring, gives me a wink. "I told you the one-knee thing wasn't too silly."

"You were absolutely right."

Meredith whispers into my ear, "You went full rom-com for me, didn't you?"

"Why not? I would do anything for you, Mer. You bring out sides of me I didn't know existed."

As the crowd continues to cheer and well-wishers begin to approach, I'm struck by how perfectly imperfect this moment is. Here we are, two people who came to this island to escape, only to find a future neither of us expected. The irony isn't lost on me, and I can't help but smile at the beautiful chaos of it all.

I gently tug Meredith's hand, guiding her toward our private bungalow. "Come on, let's take a moment just for us."

As we walk hand in hand along the torch-lit path, the soft sand gives way to smooth wooden planks. The familiar scent of plumeria and sea salt envelops us, a sensory reminder of where our journey began.

"So, Mr. General Manager," Meredith says, "what's our first order of business?"

I sweep her up in my arms, holding her close. "Well, Mrs. soon-to-be Kimble, I was thinking we could start by fucking in our private hot tub."

"Mm, that sounds divine." She taps my nose with her finger. "And after that, we could sneak down to that trail we haven't told anyone about yet. I'll grab the massage oil, and you can get the beach blanket."

"Sounds like the perfect plan."

I pause at the threshold of our bungalow, the warm glow from inside spilling out onto the veranda. "I have no idea what challenges we might face in the future. But I do know one thing for certain."

"What's that?"

I rest my forehead on hers. "Whatever comes our way, we'll face it together. Naked or clothed."

Meredith's laughter, bright and uninhibited, fills the air. "I wouldn't have it any other way."

As we step into the bungalow, ready to begin our new life together, I'm filled with a sense of hope and excitement. The path ahead may be uncertain, but with Meredith by my side, I'm ready for whatever adventures await us on this magical island and beyond.

Chapter Seventeen

Meredith

The big day has finally arrived. Ryan and I are tying the knot today. And it seems appropriate for our wedding to take place on the beach. This resort has become our home, after all. I wriggle my toes to feel the warm sand caressing my feet as I smooth down my wedding dress, its simple elegance a perfect match for this breathtaking beach. The fabric catches the breeze, dancing around my legs like ocean spray.

I gaze out at the surf, letting the gentle rhythm of the waves wash over me. The vast expanse of blue stretches to the horizon, promising adventure and new beginnings. Just like the one I'm about to embark on.

Movement catches my eye, and I turn to see Ryan approaching. I am one lucky woman. He's devastatingly handsome in his linen suit, with his short-cropped blond hair tousled by the wind. My hair is getting plenty tousled too, but I don't mind the strands flying over my face. All I can see is Ryan—the man who changed my life.

He halts just close enough that he can clasp his hands in mine. "You look absolutely stunning. No bride could ever outdo your elegance and grace."

Am I blushing? My cheeks feel slightly warm, so yes, I think I am blushing. It's hard to believe I finally found real love after fifty-two years in this world. "You are the most dashing, sexiest groom any woman could hope for."

He kisses my hand. "Can't wait until the formalities are over and we can go on our honeymoon. A world tour of all the Au Naturel resorts? Gotta be the strangest vacation ever."

"But you love it, and so do I." Maybe it's his fancy suit, but I suddenly feel...like I need to double check. "Sweetie, are you absolutely sure you want to marry me? You're young enough to have children, but I can't give you that."

He gives me a patient smile, then delicately sweeps a lock of hair away from my face. "I'm sure, Meredith. I love my job, and this is definitely not a kid-friendly resort. My siblings have children, which means Mom and Dad won't miss out on grandkids." He kisses my cheek. "My family loves you almost as much as I do."

"Your family is wonderful."

"Now, can we get this wedding going?"

I grin. "Let's get this wedding train rolling."

As Ryan pulls me closer, I marvel at how far we've come. From two broken souls seeking solace on this magical island to soulmates ready to face whatever life throws our way—together.

A burst of joyous laughter draws my attention away from Ryan's face. My heart swells as I take in the sight of my three best friends—Lila, Maya, and Zara—standing just a few feet away. Their vibrant dresses, in shades of tropical coral, sun-kissed yellow, and ocean blue, pop against the lush backdrop of Heirani Motu.

"Oh my, do you ladies look amazing!" I exclaim, feeling even happier because they made it to my island wedding. It was touch and go for a while after a storm in Seattle delayed their flight by several hours. I hug each of them in turn. "I love you guys so much. Never would I have had the gumption to visit a nudist resort alone. Which means you three are responsible for me and Ryan getting together."

Lila smirks and gives me a wink. "Glad we could be of service, Mer."

I twirl once, loving the look and feel of my simple, elegant gown. "Now, which of you will be the next bride to tie the knot on Heirani Motu?"

Maya shakes her head. "Not me, Mer. You know I vowed to never get tangled up in wedding vows again."

Zara conspicuously avoids taking part in the marriage discussion. Instead, she glances around. "I still can't believe you're getting married on a nudist island. Ryan must be a mind-blowing stud in bed to make you want to tie the knot again."

I wag a finger at her. "We all know what you're doing, Zara. It's called deflection. What are you afraid of, sweetie?"

She makes a pained face. "You know the answer. The love of my life kicked the bucket before we even celebrated our thirtieth anniversary."

I give her a squeeze. "That wasn't Stan's fault, and you genuinely loved him. Even if you never remarry, promise me you won't completely give up on love."

"Yes, ma'am." Zara salutes. Then she hugs me fiercely. "Thanks, Meredith. I needed that kick in the rear."

Ryan squeezes my hand, a quiet reminder of his presence. I turn to see him smiling at our friends' antics. "Can we get married now?"

I pat his cheek. "Yes, honey, we can."

I catch sight of James and Holly Bythesea standing a short distance away. James, looking dapper in a light linen suit, offers a polite nod. Holly beams at us, wearing a radiant glow that I suspect means she's pregnant. She does keep laying a hand over her belly.

"Looks like the resort's power couple approves," I murmur to Ryan.

He follows my gaze and chuckles. "James still looks a bit uncomfortable. I bet he's wondering if we're going to strip down after the ceremony."

I playfully swat his arm. "Behave. This is a traditional wedding ceremony—sort of."

But Ryan's brother and sister did not bring their kids to the wedding. It's a naughty nudist resort, after all. His parents are here, though. The family will have another ceremony when Ryan and I visit his parents' home next week.

I feel a delicious shiver run down my spine, thinking of the adventures that await us. Who would have thought that a spontaneous trip to a nudist resort would lead to this moment? Surrounded by friends, old and new, about to marry the man who's brought so much joy and passion into my life.

Ryan offers me his arm. "Ready to do this?"

"More than ready," I reply. "Let's get hitched, island style."

I take a deep breath, feeling the warm sand beneath my feet and the gentle ocean breeze on my skin. This island has become more than just a vacation spot—it's where I found myself, and where I found love.

The officiant steps forward, a serene smile gracing her face. She's draped in flowing white linen, adorned with a lei of fragrant plumeria. As she raises her hands, a hush falls over the gathering.

"Friends, family, and honored guests," she begins, her voice carrying over the gentle lapping of waves, "we are gathered here on the shores of Heirani Motu to celebrate a love that blossomed in the most unexpected of places."

I feel Ryan's hand tighten around mine, and I smile at him. Unexpected is an understatement. Our love was a lightning bolt from the blue.

"Meredith and Ryan's journey," the officiant continues, "is a testament to the value of stepping outside one's comfort zone, of embracing vulnerability, and finding connection in the most surprising circumstances."

I sneak a glance at Ryan, catching the hint of a blush on his cheeks. His eyes meet mine, filled with warmth and just a touch of that signature stoicism that first intrigued me.

"Who would have thought," I whisper, "that all it took was getting naked to break down your walls?"

He leans in, his breath tickling my ear. "You broke them down long before that, Mer. The nakedness was just a bonus."

A melodious trill cuts through the air, drawing our attention to a vibrant bird perched on a nearby palm. Its iridescent feathers shimmer in the sunlight, a living jewel against the lush greenery.

"Even the wildlife approves," I murmur, feeling a sense of magic settle over us.

The officiant's words blend with the rhythmic sound of waves caressing the shore, creating a symphony no other. I close my eyes for a moment, letting it all wash over me.

When I open my eyes, I'm struck by the wonder of this day, of this union. The faces of the people who love us glow with happiness. And at the center of it all is Ryan. His eyes never waver from mine.

"Finding you, finding us, it's changed everything," he admits softly, his voice thick with emotion.

"I'm so glad it happened for us."

As the ceremony progresses, I can't help but marvel at how perfectly Heirani Motu mirrors our journey—wild, beautiful, and full of unexpected treasures. Just like the hidden world we discovered behind the waterfall, our love has revealed depths I never knew existed.

The officiant's words fade into the background as I lose myself in Ryan's gaze, anticipation building for the moment when we'll seal our union with a kiss. Who knew that a spontaneous trip to a nudist resort would lead to the greatest adventure of my life?

I take a deep breath, my heart racing as I prepare to share my vows.

"Ryan," I begin, my voice steady despite the emotions swirling inside me. "When I came to this island, I was searching for adventure, an escape from the pain in my old life. What I found was so much more." I smile as I continue, imbuing that expression with all the joy I hold in my heart. "You've shown me that true excitement isn't just about new experiences, but about sharing life's journey with someone who sees the real you."

I hear a soft chirp from a nearby tree, as if nature itself is encouraging me. "I promise to keep that adventurous spirit alive in our marriage. To explore not just new places, but the depths of our love. To support your dreams as fiercely as you've supported mine. And to always remind you that even on the cloudiest days, there's beauty to be found—just like we found each other."

Ryan's eyes shimmer with unshed tears, and I have to resist the urge to kiss him right here and now. Instead, I finish with a playful wink, "I vow to be your partner in crime, your biggest cheerleader, and your personal sunscreen applier for all our future beach days."

A ripple of laughter spreads through our guests, and I feel a surge of joy. This is us—finding light even in the most solemn moments.

Ryan begins his vows, and I'm struck by the transformation I see in him. Gone is the guarded man I first met, replaced by someone open and contented, sure of his place in the world.

"Meredith," he starts, his voice calm and sincere. "I came to this island to escape, to hide from a past that haunted me. But you...you taught me how to live again."

I lay hand on his arm, offering silent support as he goes on. "I vow to cherish the light you've brought into my life. To face our challenges together, with the same courage you've shown me. To be your safe harbor in stormy seas, and your willing accomplice in every adventure."

His gaze locks onto mine. "I spent so long building walls, but you've shown me the beauty of tearing them down. I promise to always be honest, to share my fears and my joys, and to love you with everything I am."

As Ryan finishes, I feel a tear slide down my cheek. Who knew that the man who once seemed so unapproachable would now be baring his soul to me and our loved ones?

"And I solemnly swear," he adds with a hint of a smile, "to always have your back—quite literally—when it comes to those hard-to-reach sunscreen spots."

I laugh, even as more tears threaten to fall. This beautiful mix of vulnerability and humor, of past pain and future joy, is everything I never knew I needed. While we stand here, surrounded by the lush beauty of Heirani Motu, I realize that our love story is just beginning. And what an adventure it's going to be.

The officiant's voice breaks through my reverie. "The rings, please."

My heart flutters as Lila steps forward, presenting a small wooden box carved with intricate Polynesian designs. I take a deep breath, willing my hands to steady as I reach for Ryan's ring.

"Mer," Ryan whispers, his voice catching slightly. His fingers brush mine as we exchange rings.

I slide the ring onto his finger, marveling at how right it looks there. "With this ring, I thee wed."

Ryan's hands tremble ever so slightly as he takes my ring. As he slips the ring onto my finger, I'm struck by the weight of the moment. This small band of metal represents so much—our past, our present, our future.

"With this ring," Ryan recites, his tone steady and sure, "I thee wed."

The officiant's voice rings out, clear and joyful. "By the power vested in me, I now pronounce you husband and wife!"

A chorus of cheers erupts from our gathered friends and family. I catch sight of James and Holly Bythesea, their faces beaming. Holly whistles. James grins. The sound of applause mingles with the gentle lapping of waves and the calls of exotic birds, creating a symphony of celebration.

"We did it," I whisper to Ryan.

"And we're just getting started, Mrs. Kimble."

I shiver at the erotic promise in his words.

"You may now kiss the bride," the officiant announces, her words nearly drowned out by the crescendo of another round of cheers.

I barely have time to catch my breath before Ryan's lips are on mine, soft yet insistent. His hands cup my face, his thumbs caressing my cheeks as he deepens the kiss. I melt into him, my arms winding around his neck, pulling him closer. The world fades away, leaving only us and the rhythmic crash of waves on the shore.

When we finally break away, breathless and grinning, a third round of applause erupts. I can't help but laugh, giddy with joy and just a touch of champagne from the glasses Maya just handed us.

"Save some for the honeymoon, you two!" Zara calls out.

As the sun begins its descent, we make our way to the reception area—aka the man patio. Tiki torches flicker to life, casting a warm glow over the gathering. Everyone congratulates us at least twice more. Many of them offer their best wishes. Some even ask where we're going on our honeymoon.

"It's a world tour," I say enigmatically.

"I'd like to make a toast," Lila announces, raising her glass. "To Ryan and Meredith, whose love story is as vibrant and unexpected as the way they got married. May your life together be an endless adventure, full of discovery and wonder."

Her words paint a vivid picture in my mind. Yes, our life will be filled with wonder.

"And speaking of adventure..." Zara grabs my free hand. "It's time to get this party started properly."

She tugs me toward the dance floor, her enthusiasm infectious as we shuffle around the floor together.

I glance back at Ryan, who gives me a playful wink. "Go on. Show 'em how it's done, Mrs. Kimble."

Meanwhile, I dance with both Ryan's father and his brother. They're wonderful, and I can't wait to learn more about them. They're both great dancers too.

At last, I get my turn with Ryan. I'm floating on cloud nine as my husband and I weave through the crowd, our hands intertwined like we're afraid to let go. The warm breeze carries the scent of plumeria, tickling my nose and reminding me of the flower tucked behind my ear. And now my husband is adeptly guiding me around the makeshift dance floor, holding me close and nuzzling my ear.

This island, this day, it's all a slice of heaven here on earth.

"Congratulations, you two!" James Bythesea booms, clapping Ryan on the shoulder. "I always knew you were meant for each other."

"Thank you, James," Ryan says, just as James claps his hand down on my husband's shoulder. "We're grateful for the support you, Holly, Eve, and Val have shown us. And we're looking forward to seeing the other Au Naturel resorts on our honeymoon."

"You will love the original Oregon property. It's family friendly." He glances at his wife with pure love in his eyes. "Holly and I met here on Heirani Motu, but now we'll be living near her parents in Florida, running a family-friendly resort there."

Holly grins. "We're having a baby. That's why we're moving to Florida. My parents live there, and Mom can't wait to babysit for us. We were estranged for a while, but there's nothing like a baby on the way to convince everyone to reconcile."

While James and Holly wander away, Maya approaches us. She pulls me into a fierce hug. "I'm so happy for you, Mer."

"You've said that at least twice already, but thank you," I reply, feeling a lump form in my throat. "For everything."

As we continue our circuit, I can't help but marvel at how far we've come. Just a few months ago, Ryan was the stoic, unapproachable resort manager, and I was a lost soul searching for...something.

"What are you thinking about?" Ryan murmurs, his thumb tracing circles on my hand.

I smile up at him. "Just how lucky I am. How lucky we both are."

A soft smile plays on his lips. "I never thought I'd find this. Love. Happiness. You've given me both, Meredith."

"We're both damn lucky, aren't we? We have so many friends who have become like family, and we're free to do whatever we want."

The music fades, and I tug gently on his hand. "Come on. Let's sneak away for a moment."

While we make our way to the water's edge, I glance up at the sky that's dotted with puffy white clouds. But soon, the sun sinks lower and lower, heralding the arrival of stars.

"The sky is so beautiful," I breathe, leaning into Ryan's solid warmth. "Is that the Southern Cross? It's beautiful."

"Yes, it's the Southern Cross." He wraps an arm around my waist, pulling me close. "It's beautiful, but not as spectacular as you."

I laugh, swatting his chest playfully. "When did you get so smooth, Mr. Kimble?"

His expression turns serious, those hazel eyes intense as they meet mine. "When I realized I never wanted to let you go."

I reach up to cup his face. "I'm so thankful for this life I have with you."

"And you've brought light back into my life, Meredith. I can never repay that gift."

We stand here, the gentle waves lapping at our feet, and I experience a sense of peace that's so deep I can't even describe it. The dream I'd given up on long ago has come true at last, and Ryan gave me that.

"Ready to start our next chapter?" I ask, grinning up at my husband.

Ryan's answering smile takes my breath away. "With you? Always."

Just as I gaze up at the stars again, a meteor streaks across the heavens. I can't help but gasp at the breathtaking sight. I point at the sky. "Ryan, look."

He tips his head back just when another meteor streaks by. "It's like the island's giving us a wedding gift."

"Who knew you were such a romantic?"

He chuckles, the sound vibrating through me. "Only for you, Meredith. You bring out sides of me I thought were long gone."

More meteors race across the sky, leaving trails that burn out swiftly. Unlike those heavenly bodies, the love Ryan and I share for each other will never die.

As we stand here, wrapped in each other's arms, I feel a profound sense of rightness. The gentle lapping of waves, the distant laughter of our friends who are still enjoying the wedding festivities, the warmth of Ryan's embrace—it all blends into a perfect moment.

"This is it, isn't it?" I muse aloud. "The beginning of our forever."

Ryan presses a kiss to my temple. "It is. And I can't wait to see where it takes us."

I turn to face Ryan fully. "Ready for our next adventure, Mr. Kimble?"

His answering smile is everything. "Lead the way, Mrs. Kimble."

Chapter Eighteen

Ryan

As we stroll down the beach together on this beautiful day, my mind wanders to our upcoming excursions beyond Heirani Motu. The Au Naturel chain is expanding, and we've booked trips to the newest properties. But first, we'll visit the original Au Naturel Naturist Resort in Oregon. It's family friendly, just like the one being built in Florida will be. I picture me and Meredith lying on the sun-drenched shores of the Sunshine State. They have alligators in Florida. But James and Holly swear there won't be any at the new resort.

Meredith has never looked more beautiful than she does today. Yeah, I say that every day, but so what? It's true.

"Do you think you're ready for that naked sand volleyball tournament yet?" she jokes, waggling her eyebrows suggestively.

I groan, pretending to hate the idea, and try to hide the smile tugging at my lips. "Don't push your luck, Mer."

She sees right through me, of course. Her answering laughter makes my smile deepen. "What are you thinking about, sweetie?"

"Just how unbelievably lucky I am." I pull her closer, relishing the feel of her soft skin against mine. "A year ago, I never would have imagined this life."

"You mean you didn't envision yourself walking naked on a beach with your wife?"

"Not exactly."

She hooks her arm around mine. "Do you remember the day first met?"

I let out a hearty chuckle. "How could I ever forget? You nearly gave me a heart attack on the waterfall bridge."

She pulls back, ducking her chin with mock indignation. "Excuse me, but I believe you were the one who stumbled into my peaceful sunbathing spot."

"Only because I was trying to get a break from the clothes-free guests. It takes a while to fully acclimate to all those bouncing tits."

A warm feeling spreads through my chest as I remember how our initial awkwardness slowly dissolved into curiosity, attraction, and eventually love. "We've both come a long way since then."

"You've changed the most, Ryan. I've watched you learn to truly live again and embrace the unexpected."

We stop walking and face the ocean. I turn to face her, silhouetted against the setting sun. "I have something for you."

"Ooh, I love presents."

From inside a hidden pocket in my beach bag, produce an object. It's a small bracelet made of colorful threads and tiny seashells, intricately woven together. "It's not much, but..."

"That can't be what I think it is."

I gently clasp the bracelet around her wrist. "It's a replica of the one you were wearing the day we met. The one that later got caught on my shirt when I oh-so-gracefully stumbled onto your sunbathing spot in the woods."

She laughs, tears welling in her eyes. "You remembered."

"How could I forget?" My fingers linger on her wrist. "It was the moment everything changed."

Meredith runs her fingers over the delicate shells, each one a reminder of how far we've come. "Ryan, this is beautiful. Thank you."

"So, does this mean you're finally going to forgive me for messing up those perfect tan lines that day?"

She playfully swats my arm. "Hmm, I don't know. That was a pretty big offense. You might need to do more than just apologize."

"I think I can handle that."

Her eyes shimmer with excitement. "Oh, Ryan, won't it be wonderful to visit the original Au Naturel resort? I can't wait for that."

"You do realize we'll be stuck on a plane for a long, long time during the flight to Oregon. It won't be a fun fest."

"Oh, I think we can find ways to make it fun," Meredith proffers. "Maybe we can join the mile-high club."

I laugh and shake my head. "Always the adventurous one. But I'm pretty sure that's frowned on these days."

"Spoilsport," she teases, nudging me with her hip. "Fine, we'll have to settle for some in-flight movies and overpriced airplane food."

We continue our stroll along the shoreline, having no destination in mind, just enjoying this island that has become our home.

She rests her head on my shoulder. "A year ago, I never would have thought we'd be here. Planning our future, feeling...whole again."

"Me neither. But this place had a way of healing us and helping us rediscover ourselves, didn't it?"

"Absolutely. Sometimes I think this place is literally magical."

The beach is deserted now, save for a few birds calling in the distance. Most of the guests are watching the miniten matches on the lawn. I feel a familiar tug of desire as I watch Meredith's hips sway with each step.

"How about we take a little swim," I suggest, "while we have the beach to ourselves?"

Meredith's eyes light up. "I thought you'd never ask."

We race toward the water, laughing like children who just saw their first glimpse of the ocean. The cool waves lap at our ankles, then our knees, and finally envelop us completely as we dive beneath the surface. When we emerge, Meredith's hair is slicked back, droplets of water glistening on her skin in the moonlight.

I pull her close, reveling in the feel of her wet skin against mine. The water laps gently around us as we float together, our bodies intertwined. I brush a wet strand of hair from Meredith's face.

"You're so beautiful," I murmur, tracing my fingers along her jawline.

She nudges my hip. "You're not so bad yourself, Mr. Kimble. Especially when you're all wet and glistening with all those muscles on display."

"Maybe I should stay wet all the time, if it makes you this horny."

She wraps her legs around my waist. "You look downright irresistible right now."

The playfulness in her voice sends a shiver down my spine. I lean in, my lips hovering just inches from hers. "Well, Mrs. Kimble, I can't resist that kind of temptation."

I close the minuscule gap between us to crush my lips to hers. The taste of salt mingles with her familiar sweetness. Her fingers tangle in my wet hair, dragging me closer as the gentle waves lap around us. Finally, we give up each other's mouths, breathless, our foreheads touching.

"Race you to that outcropping," she challenges, nodding toward a small cluster of rocks jutting out from the shoreline.

Before I can respond, she's already swimming away, her lithe form cutting through the waves. I laugh and give chase, my competitive spirit ignited. We splash and play, forgetting for a moment that we're adults who aren't supposed to behave this way. Screw what we're "supposed" to do. I want to chase my wife just for the hell of it.

Soon, the sun dips below the horizon, and my wife suddenly jumps up, stretching languidly. "Hey, why don't we take a moonlit swim now? Before we head back to our bungalow?"

I raise an eyebrow, trying to suppress a smile. "Now? It's getting dark."

She jumps up, pulling me along. "Exactly. It'll be perfect."

"I'm getting kind of tired, Mer. Crawling into bed with you sounds like a much better idea."

"Tired?" she scoffs. "I'm nine years older than you, but I'm not worn out yet."

I give her ass a playful swat. "Careful, Mer. I might decide to spank you."

She bats her eyelashes in an exaggerated manner, knowing full well how ridiculous she looks. "Shall I carry you over my shoulders?"

I smirk and shake my head. "That won't be necessary."

"Are you sure? I wouldn't want you to trip and fall on a seashell because you're wiped out."

She's already racing toward the water. The cool sand beneath our feet gives way to the lapping waves, and she lets out a peel of delighted laughter. I follow more cautiously, my steps measured as I try not to let my bare feet sink into the sand. The second I wade into the water, I can't help letting out a surprised gasp. "Holy crap, it's warm. Not sure why, but I expected the water to be chilly."

"Told you it would be perfect," Meredith teases while splashing me. "It's like stepping into a silky bath."

"You're right," I admit, sinking deeper into the inviting embrace of the ocean. "I forgot how incredible the water is here. It's like we've slipped through a portal to paradise."

The moonlight dances on the gentle waves, casting a silvery glow across the surface. As we venture further from shore, the water caresses our skin, its warmth a reminder that we're on the other side of the world, literally. Tiny bioluminescent organisms sparkle around us with each movement, creating a magical underwater light show.

"This is amazing," Meredith breathes, her voice barely above a whisper. "Don't you feel it, Ryan? Like we're part of something bigger?"

"Only because I'm with you." I swim closer, enjoying the view of her tits floating atop the water. "It's kind of like...all the boundaries just disappear out here."

She smiles as if she understands exactly what I mean. In this moment, we're not defined by our past, our jobs, or even our clothes. We're just two souls, connected to each other and to the vast, beautiful world around us.

I've turned into a sap. Weirdly, that doesn't bother me at all.

My wife floats on her back, her hair fanning out around her like a halo.

"What are you thinking about, Meredith?"

She turns her head to look at me, a soft smile playing on her lips. "I'm thinking about what I'd like to do to you in our bed tonight."

I swim closer, gently lifting her upright so I can wrap my arms around her. The warm water laps at our shoulders as we float together. "I know what you mean. I've got ideas for your body too—once we're lying on that soft bed."

"Who says we have to wait until we're in bed?"

I pick her up and march out of the water, holding her close, and I don't let go until we're standing at the door of our bungalow. "Could you open that for me, baby?"

"Sure thing."

Meredith reaches out and turns the handle, pushing the door open. I carry her over the threshold, our wet bodies dripping onto the polished wood floor. The familiar scent of tropical flowers and sea air wafts through the open windows.

"Welcome home, Mrs. Kimble," I murmur against her neck, relishing the way she shivers in response.

"Why thank you, Mr. Kimble," she purrs, her arms tightening around my shoulders. "Now, are you going to put me down or do I need to take matters into my own hands?"

I chuckle, slowly lowering her feet to the ground. "As tempting as it is to never let you go, I think we both know you're more than capable of taking charge."

She trails her fingers down my chest. "You bet I am. And right now, I'm going to take charge of getting us both dried off."

Meredith saunters over to the bathroom, her hips swaying in a way that makes my dick begin to rouse. I follow after her, admiring the view. She grabs a large, fluffy towel and turns to face me with a seductive smile. "Arms up."

I comply, letting her run the soft fabric over my body. Her touch is gentle yet purposeful, lingering in all the right places. When she finishes, I commandeer the towel.

"Your turn, Mrs. Kimble."

I take my time drying her off, gliding the towel over every curve and dip on her sexy body. I brush my fingers against her skin, eliciting small sighs of pleasure. When I'm done, I let the towel drop to the floor and pull her close.

"You're so damn beautiful," I murmur, roving my gaze over every inch of her body.

Meredith tilts her head, giving me better access to her neck. "Mm, you're not so bad yourself, handsome."

Her hands roam over my back, nails lightly scratching in that way she knows drives me wild. I growl softly against her skin, nipping gently at her pulse point. She pushes me backward toward our king-size mattress.

"Bed. Now."

I fall onto the plush comforter with a soft thump. She straddles my hips while I slide my hands up and down her silky-smooth thighs. The sight of her hovering over me makes my breaths grow heavier. "God, I love you, Mer."

She leans over me, her lips brushing against mine. "Show me."

I flip us over in one smooth motion, pinning her beneath me.

Meredith gasps in surprise, then grins. "Someone's eager."

"Can you blame me?" I drag my tongue along her neck, across her collarbone. "You are a goddess."

My lips continue their journey south, worshipping every inch of her skin. Meredith arches into my touch, soft sighs and moans escaping her. When I reach the apex of her thighs, I glance up to meet her gaze. She tangles her fingers in my hair, urging me to come closer. I oblige, running my tongue along her slick folds. She gasps, her hips bucking against my mouth even while I go on devouring her.

"Ryan," she moans, writhing her hips.

I lose myself in pleasuring her, alternating between long, languid strokes and quick flicks of my tongue. Her thighs tremble on either side of my head as I bring her closer to the edge. When I slip two fingers inside her, curling them at just the right angle, she cries out.

"Oh god, yes!" she shouts.

Her back arches off the bed as she comes undone, waves of pleasure washing over her. I continue my ministrations, drawing out her orgasm until she gently pushes my head away, oversensitive.

I crawl back up her body, every luscious inch of her along the way. When I reach her lips, Meredith pulls me in for a passionate kiss, tasting herself on my tongue. Her hands roam over my back, nails lightly scratching.

"My turn," she purrs, flipping us over.

She straddles my hips and rocks against me teasingly, the wet heat of her core sliding along my length. I groan, gripping her waist with my hands.

"Mer, please," I beg, desperate to be inside her.

She smirks, clearly enjoying having me at her mercy. "What do you want, Ryan?"

"You," I breathe. "Always you."

With agonizing slowness, she sinks down onto me. We both moan at the sensation of finally being joined. Meredith begins to move, setting a languid pace that has me gritting my teeth with the effort to hold back. I don't want to go off until she does. Her hips roll in a mesmerizing rhythm, and I'm transfixed by the sight of her above me, bathed in moonlight streaming through the bungalow's windows.

"God, you're perfect," I murmur, running my hands up her sides to cup her breasts.

She leans into my touch, increasing her tempo. "So are you."

I thrust up to meet her, matching her rhythm, our gasps and shouts filling the room, growing louder every moment. The sound of skin slapping on skin mingles with our moans and grunts. Meredith braces her hands on my chest, using the leverage to ride me harder.

"Ryan," she gasps. "I'm almost there."

I push a hand between us, finding the sensitive bundle of nerves that I know will push her over the edge. Her movements become erratic as I circle her clit with my thumb, rubbing it roughly. Meredith's head falls back, her mouth open in a silent cry of ecstasy. I can feel her inner walls fluttering around me, bringing me closer to the edge.

"Let go, baby," I encourage, increasing the pressure of my fingers. "I've got you."

With a keening moan, Meredith comes undone above me. The sight of her in the throes of passion, combined with the rhythmic clenching of her body around mine, sends me over the edge. I thrust up twice more, harder than ever, then bury myself deep inside her as I follow her into that blissful release.

We stay connected for a moment, both of us panting and trembling with aftershocks. A sheen of sweat glistens on our bodies. Meredith collapses onto my chest, and I wrap my arms around her, holding her close. I press a tender kiss to her forehead as we lay tangled together, our breathing slowly returning to normal. The gentle ocean breeze drifts through the open windows, cooling our flushed skin.

Meredith traces lazy patterns on my chest, a contented sigh escaping her lips. "That was unbelievable. You never cease to amaze me with your sexual prowess."

"Same for me," I reply, tightening my arms around her. "You give me more kinds of pleasure than I knew existed."

We fall into a comfortable silence, basking in the afterglow. As I run my fingers through her silky hair, a thought occurs to me. "Hey Mer, remember that hidden ledge we heard about?"

She props herself up on an elbow. "Of course. We still haven't gotten around to exploring that."

"Why don't we make that our mission for tomorrow?" I suggest, tracing lazy circles on her back. "We could pack a picnic, make a whole day of it."

The excitement in her expression is adorable. "Oh, that sounds perfect! I've been dying to see what's on the other side of that waterfall."

"I know. You've been talking about it non-stop since I told you about it."

"Can you blame me? A hidden world just waiting to be discovered...it's like something out of a storybook."

I pull her closer, nuzzling her hair. "As long as I'm with you, every day feels like an adventure."

"When did you get so sappy, Mr. Kimble?"

"When I met you, Mrs. Kimble." I kiss her forehead. "On the day I first saw you, when you were ripping your clothes off and grinning like a kid in a candy store, that's when I melted into a sappy puddle for you."

She wriggles on the mattress, getting into position to sit up facing me. "So, what do you think we'll find behind that waterfall? Maybe some ancient ruins? Or a tribe of people who've never seen the outside world?"

"Who knows?" I pull her on top of me. "But won't it be fun to find out?"

Meredith grins. "It'll be a blast."

Chapter Nineteen

Meredith

I toss a vibrant turquoise sarong at Ryan, the shimmering fabric floating through the air before landing draped across his broad shoulders. He smirks as the fabric catches the light. I pick up a scarf, prepared to fling that his way too, but then someone knocks on the door.

"You might need this," I tease.

He wags his eyebrows. "For modesty's sake?"

"If that's what floats your boat, sweetie."

Ryan's eyebrows lift, his lips quirking. He snatches up the sarong, letting it slide sensuously down his muscular arms.

I laugh, turning back to our suitcases. "More for sun protection. You know how easily you burn. Can't have that beautiful dick turning beet red."

The warm island breeze drifts through our open windows, carrying the sweet scent of white ginger lily. I pause in my packing, distracted by the view of turquoise waters stretching to the horizon. Our room at Au Naturel is a slice of paradise, and sometimes I still can't believe this is our home now.

"Speaking of sun protection," I muse, eyeing the collection of hats spread across our bed. "Which one do you think I should bring? The floppy straw one or the chic fedora?"

Before Ryan can respond, someone knocks on the door.

"I'll get that," he offers. "You have important hat decisions to make."

He slings the sarong around his hips as he strides toward the door, deftly swinging it open. "Hello, ladies. How are you this morning?"

"Good morning, Mr. Kimble," comes Maya's cheerful voice. "We're just dropping off some last-minute items for your trip."

Why are my three best friends here? It's simple. They're jealous of me because I get to live on a stunning tropical island with an equally stunning husband. Okay, the real reason is that my friends are on their way to Australia for a group vacation. They stopped over for a night on Heirani Motu to see me and Ryan before we begin our transoceanic journey to see all the Au Naturel resorts.

I peek around Ryan's body to see Zara standing in the doorway while Maya and Lila loiter behind her. All three of my friends wear similarly smug expressions, as if they know a wonderful secret but don't care to share it.

Ryan steps aside. "Please come in, ladies. And it's just Ryan, remember? Mr. Kimble is my father."

The trio casually walks into the bungalow, and I can't help but notice that my friends' eyes widen slightly when they realize what Ryan is wearing. Even with the sarong, there's no hiding my husband's sculpted physique—or the bulge beneath that flimsy fabric.

"What a lovely surprise," I say. Since my friends are fully clothed, I consider grabbing a light sundress. But I nix that idea. These ladies already know what Ryan and I look like naked.

My husband ties the sarong around his hips—to make sure it doesn't fall off, no doubt. I shake my head at his meticulous nature. Even after all this time, his attention to detail never fails to amuse and impress me. "Uh, sweetie, what occasion requires a sarong at a nudist resort?"

"You never know," Ryan replies with a wink. "Maybe I'll start a new fashion trend."

The mental image of Ryan strutting around a nudist beach wearing a sarong sends me into a fit of half-suppressed snorts. "Oh, I'd pay good money to see that."

Zara is clearly struggling not to laugh. "Better make it a see-through sarong. Otherwise, he'll be violating the resort's rules."

"He's the general manager," Lila points out. "He wears clothes whenever he's at work."

"Fair point."

Maya settles onto the edge of our bed, careful not to disturb the array of hats. "Speaking of paying good money, you'll never guess what we saw this morning."

I raise an eyebrow, my curiosity piqued. "Okay, you have got to tell me about it."

Zara and Lila exchange knowing glances, barely containing their excitement. Maya leans in, her voice dropping to a conspiratorial whisper. "You know that silver fox who checked in yesterday? The one with the designer luggage and the fancy watch?"

"Yes, I remember," I tell Maya, recalling the distinguished gentleman who'd arrived on the last flight. He'd certainly cut an impressive figure, even sans clothing.

"Well," Maya drawls, her grin widening, "we spotted him down by the lagoon this morning, and he wasn't alone."

"Oh, it's even better than that," Zara asserts. "He was with none other than Mrs. Hemsworth."

My jaw drops. "No way. Elaine Hemsworth? The one who's always complaining about the buffet and curling her lip at the idea of eating at a 'common trough,' as she calls it?"

Lila nods emphatically. "The very same. And let me tell you, she wasn't complaining this morning. In fact, she looked positively radiant."

Ryan chuckles, crossing his arms as he leans against the doorframe. "Let me guess. Mrs. Hemsworth found some company at the Coconut Bar last night."

"Got it in one."

I have trouble picturing prim and proper Elaine letting loose with our mysterious new guest. "Well, good for her. Maybe she'll find her next husband on the island and learn how to chill out."

"Speaking of relaxation…"—Maya extracts a small package from her bag—"we brought you a little something for your trip."

I lean in closer as Maya hands me a beautifully wrapped package tied with a silky ribbon. "What's this?"

"Just a little bon voyage gift," Zara explains with a wink. "Something to help you two lovebirds make the most of your travels."

I glance at Ryan, who's watching with equal interest, before I carefully untie the ribbon. As the wrapping falls away, I let out a delighted laugh. Inside is an assortment of massage oils, scented candles, and what appears to be a book of sensual games for couples.

"You guys!" I exclaim. "This is...wow."

Ryan peers over my shoulder, his warm breath tickling my cheek. "Well, it looks like we won't be lacking for entertainment on our trip."

I feel a flutter in my stomach at his steamy tone, imagining all the ways we could put these gifts to use. I turn to my friends. "Thank you all. This is so thoughtful."

"We just want to make sure you two have a memorable time," Lila says. "After all, it's not every day you get to tour nudist resorts around the world."

"Speaking of which," Zara chimes in, "we should probably let you finish packing. Your flight leaves in a few hours, right?"

I bite my lip, suddenly aware of how much we still need to do before heading to the airport. "Yes, we should really get back to it. But thank you again for stopping by and for this lovely gift. We'll definitely put it to good use."

While my friends file out of the bungalow, giving us hugs and well-wishes, I turn back to Ryan, who's watching me intently. He lets the sarong slip to the floor as he approaches me. "So, shall we test out some of those massage oils before we go?"

"Tempting as that is, we really do need to finish packing."

He pulls me close, his hands warm and deliciously rough on my bare skin. "Are you sure? We could always pack later and take an earlier flight tomorrow."

"Better not. We have obligations, after all."

Ryan sighs and goes back to packing.

For a moment, I simply bask in the glow of knowing a hot younger man loves, until his brow furrows slightly. He reaches for his tablet, pulling up a detailed checklist.

"Speaking of our upcoming adventure," he begins, his voice taking on that familiar, focused tone, "we should review the resort operations before we leave."

I smile and shake my head. Even on the brink of our grand excursion, Ryan's mind is on Heirani Motu. It's endearing, really.

"All right, Mr. Responsible," I tease, peering over his shoulder. "What's first on the list?"

Ryan scrolls through the items, his eyes scanning each point meticulously. "Staff schedules, inventory, maintenance...oh, and we need to brief Mariel on handling guest inquiries."

"Okay, that's a good idea." But I really just want to get on Rene's jet and start our big trip. But I am his right-hand woman, so I will indulge him. "We should also remind the activities team about the new sunrise yoga sessions. And maybe we could ask Rhonda to lead an extra snorkeling tour while we're gone? Guests love those."

Ryan looks up at me, a hint of surprise and admiration in his gaze. "Good thinking, Mer. I'll add that to the list."

As he taps away on the tablet, I can't resist. "You know, if you keep adding to that list, we might never leave."

"Says the woman who just suggested two new items."

I laugh, playfully nudging his shoulder. "Touché. But seriously, Ryan, part of what makes you an amazing general manager is your obsessive need to check things five times."

"Someone has to balance out your wild spontaneity."

I gasp in mock indignation. "Wild spontaneity? I'll have you know my escapades are carefully improvised."

Ryan chuckles, a rich, warm sound that never fails to make my heart skip. "Carefully improvised? Only you could make that work, Mer."

"Admit it, you love my carefully improvised adventures. They keep you on your toes."

"They certainly do." He cups my ass with one hand, humor glinting in his eyes. "And I wouldn't have it any other way."

I glance at our packed suitcases. "I think we're as ready as we'll ever be."

Ryan is about to speak when his phone dings. He has a new text. My husband's brows furrow as he reads the message. "We've been dawdling for too long. Rene just pinged me. He said we should get our 'arses' out of bed and hurry to the jet. Otherwise, he'll take off without us."

We gather our luggage, which showcases our dual personalities—a mishmash of bright floral prints and Ryan's more subdued neutrals. As I hoist my bag, Ryan's hand brushes mine.

"Let me get that," he offers.

"Such a gentleman," I tease, handing it over. "But don't forget, where we're going, chivalry might be the only thing you're wearing."

He pats my bottom. "I think I can handle that."

We make our way through the resort, the familiar paths now tinged with a sense of impending exploits. At the main entrance, our staff has gathered to see us off.

Leilani, our effervescent new activities director, rushes forward to envelop me in a hug. "Have an amazing time, bosses! Bring back lots of scandalous stories!"

I laugh, giving her a quick hug. "We'll do our best to maintain our professional dignity."

"How boh-ring," she stage-whispers, winking at my husband.

Ryan clears his throat, a hint of pink touching his cheeks. "The resort's in good hands with Emilio as interim general manager, not to mention you and the rest of the staff. We appreciate your hard work."

As we say our goodbyes, I'm struck by the genuine affection in everyone's faces. This place, these people...they've become family.

Finally, we're jogging toward the grass strip, ready to jump onto the smaller jet.

"Can you believe we're really doing this?" I ask.

Ryan's arm wraps around me, pulling me closer. "Embarking on a tour of naturist resorts? Where we'll either go clothing-optional or clothes-free? I hear there are horses at the Oregon resort. So yeah, it does seem a bit surreal."

I slap his chest. "You know what I mean. This adventure, just us, exploring new places, new ideas..."

"I know, Mer. And I'm looking forward to every minute of it."

Ryan gallantly offers his hands to help me board the jet. Soon, we're flying toward Fiji. As we touch down at the Suva airport, the possibilities of what lies ahead fill my mind. I never could have imagined I would become the guest services manager at a nudist resort, much less one where almost anything goes. Even Ryan enjoys going au naturel these days.

The Suva airport terminal buzzes with activity as we weave through the crowd, our carry-ons trailing behind us. Ryan's hand rests lightly on the small of my back, guiding me through the chaos.

I smile affectionately at the man who's determined to hustle me into an airliner as quickly as possible. "You know, for someone who runs a nudist resort, you seem awfully keen on keeping me covered up."

"Just protecting my investment. Can't have you causing an international incident before we even take off."

My laughter draws curious glances from nearby travelers. "Me? I'm fully clothed, sweetie."

"Right," he drawls, his hazel eyes twinkling. "And I'm the King of Switzerland. That sundress barely covers the parts of you that belong to me."

"Switzerland doesn't have a king, Ryan."

As we approach security, I can't resist one more jab. "Well, Your Majesty, I hope you're ready to strip for these fine TSA agents."

"They don't need to strip anyone, Mer. They've got computers that can erase your clothing and turn everyone into a nudist."

While we make our way through security, our banter lightens the tedium of the process. Once we're through, we find ourselves with time to spare before boarding.

Settling into seats at our gate, I turn to Ryan. "You know, this trip...it's more than just a vacation for us."

He nods, his expression thoughtful. "I know. It's about growth—personal and professional."

"Exactly." I touch his thigh. "Can't stop imagining all the possibilities for Heirani Motu. The things we might learn, the ideas we could bring back..."

Ryan's fingers twine with mine. "I've been thinking the same thing. This could be a turning point for the resort."

As we discuss our hopes for the future, I'm struck by how in sync we are, how our visions align. It's not just about business, though. We've had a passionate connection since the day we first met, and our marriage only strengthened that bond.

"Ryan," I whisper, "I'm really glad we're doing this together."

He kisses my hand, his smile telling me everything I need to know.

The overhead speakers crackle to life, announcing our flight. A thrill of excitement courses through me as I stand, gathering my carry-on.

"Ready for takeoff?" I ask Ryan, watching as he smoothly rises to his feet, radiating quiet strength.

"As I'll ever be," he replies, a hint of a smile playing at the corners of his mouth.

As we make our way to the boarding area and join the queue, Ryan keeps his hand curled around mind. I rest my cheek on his arm. "I never thought I'd be jetting off to naturist resorts as part of my job description."

"Do you ever miss your job as a bank teller?"

"Oh, hell no." I rest my cheek on his upper arm. "I could never go back to my old life."

As we hand over our boarding passes and make our way down the jet bridge, I can't help but feel like we're on the cusp of something momentous. It's not just about the trip or the resort—it's about us, about the potential of what we achieve on Heirani Motu. We will certainly learn a lot from our current adventure.

We find our seats, stowing our bags before settling in. As the plane begins to fill with other passengers, I reach for Ryan's hand, giving it a gentle squeeze. He turns to me, his hazel eyes searching mine.

"Nervous?" he asks softly.

"Excited. A little scared, maybe. But in a good way."

"Me too." Ryan drums his fingers on his thigh. "There's a lot riding on this trip."

"It's not just about the business, though, is it?" I ask, my heart racing a little as I broach the subject we've both been dancing around.

Ryan's thumb traces circles on the back of my hand, sending shivers down my spine. "No, it's not just about the business. This will be our second honeymoon too."

"I was hoping you'd say that."

The plane begins to taxi, and I relax into my seat, though I'm still holding Ryan's hand. The jet engines roar to life, vibrating through the cabin, and I feel a familiar flutter in my stomach. As we accelerate down the runway, I steal another glance at my husband.

"You know, sweetie, I never thought I'd be jetting off to tour nudist resorts with my business partner—my husband."

Ryan's lips quirk into that half-smile I've come to adore. "Life's full of surprises, Meredith. Especially where you're concerned."

The plane lifts off, giving me a brief sensation of near weightlessness. My throat tightens as I watch Heirani Motu shrink beneath us. The lush green of the island, ringed by pristine beaches and turquoise waters, slowly fades into the vast expanse of the South Pacific.

"It looks so small from up here," I murmur, a sudden pang of nostalgia hitting me.

Ryan has his gaze fixed on the window. "But it's given us so much."

I think about the trails we've hiked, the hidden waterfalls we've discovered, and the countless sunsets we've shared. Each memory is a thread, weaving us closer together. "Do you think we'll find what we're looking for out there?"

"I think we might find more than we bargained for."

As we climb higher, leaving our island paradise behind, the vast sky stretches out before us. Whatever comes next, I know one thing for certain—with Ryan by my side, I'm ready for anything.

Chapter Twenty

Meredith

As we had stepped off the plane in Redmond, Oregon, the first thing I noticed was a crisp breeze. It had sent my hair swirling around my face like a mini cyclone. The journey from Redmond to the Au Naturel Naturist Resort had taken longer than I expected, but I'm excited to finally see the original resort that set off a chain reaction of nudist hijinks.

A beautiful, tanned god opens the passenger door of the pickup truck that had brought us here. "Welcome to Au Naturel. It's lovely to meet you, Meredith. I am Val Silva. And that is my wife Eve over there, preparing to explain the rules to a new batch of guests."

Val's Brazilian accent is hot, but I prefer Ryan's voice.

Ryan steps out of the truck first and gives me a helping hand. We both glance around, curious about our new environment.

I fake a shiver and wrap my arms tightly around myself. "Brr! Quite a change from the warm, sunny paradise we just left, huh?"

"Seriously? It's not that cold," Ryan informs me sarcastically, taking my hand as we follow Val. "Look at those senior citizens playing miniten in the buff. If they can handle it, so can we. This place definitely has charm, don't you think? I hear there's a hot spring too."

Well, that does sound wonderful. Hot spring sex? Count me in.

Ryan's gaze veers to a family nearby—the parents nude, the kids a mix of clothed and not. "Interesting crowd. I've gotten used naked adults twenty-four seven."

I follow his line of sight, taking in the diverse group of travelers. An elderly couple strolls by hand in hand, smiling and waving to Val—and by extension, me and Ryan too. A little girl, maybe five or six, gleefully skips ahead of her parents with not a stitch on. Her ebullient giggles echo off the buildings.

"Welcome to Oregon," I proclaim, linking my arm through Ryan's. "Land of the free, home of the bare."

He chuckles softly at my joke as we make our way to toward a lovely little cottage that's set apart from the other buildings. I can't help but compare this bustling resort in the heart of America to our secluded island home. No lush jungle or pristine white beaches here. Instead, I see Ponderosa pines, western hemlock, Indian hawthorn. Still, there's an undeniable beauty and energy here.

When we reach the little house, I notice it's labeled "Caretakers Cottage."

Val pounds on the door. "Wake up, *amorzinho*! Our guests have arrived." He throws a smirk over his shoulder at us. "Don't worry, Eve is in there. She's pregnant again and needs a good amount of rest." He pounds again. "*Amorzinho*! I'm about to kick the door in."

Ryan and I exchange awkward looks, then turn our attention to the large lawn. I spot a young man with a buff bod who's wearing...well, not much. Just a small apron emblazoned with the resort logo. I sneak a glance at Ryan, noticing the slight furrow of his brow.

"Everything okay, sweetie?" I ask.

"Hell yeah. Don't worry about me, Mer."

The door to the cottage swings open at last, and a strawberry blonde greets us with a big smile. "Welcome to Au Naturel Oregon, our original resort. Ryan I've met, virtually. And you must be his other half. Ready to explore the place where naturism found its home?"

"I'm so ready. My name is—"

"Oh, we know all about you and Ryan." She steps aside to make room in the doorway. "I'm Eve Silva, by the way."

A dark-haired woman rushes up to me and Ryan, grinning broadly—and wearing clothes. "I'm Mara Jackson. My hubby, Ollie, is busy with other stuff, so I thought I'd greet you guys."

"It's wonderful to meet you, Mara. We've heard so much about this place."

"Well, prepare to have your expectations blown away," Mara advises us with a teasing smile. "Let's start with a quick tour, shall we?"

Eve and Val join our little group. As we all follow Mara through the resort, I can't help but notice the stark differences between our little slice of paradise on Heirani Motu and this part of Oregon. Here, the air is crisp and pine-scented, a far cry from the tropical breeze we've grown accustomed to. Families and couples of all ages mingle freely, some clothed, some bare, all seemingly at ease.

Ryan keeps hold of my hand as we pass by a group of clothed staff members. This resort is just like Heirani Motu in that respect.

"And here's our pride and joy," Mara announces, gesturing toward a winding path that disappears into a thick grove of pines. "This is the 'Naked in Nature' hiking trail. It's a favorite among our guests. Anyone up for a little something different?"

I had been casually admiring the scenery, but I perked up at Mara's question. "Oh, that sounds amazing. What do you think, Ryan?"

Rather than responding to my query, he asks our guide, "How long has the resort been here? Was it always clothing-optional?"

Mara grins. "You're a curious one, aren't you? The resort's been around for about a decade, and yes, it's always been clothing-optional."

I'm fascinated to hear more, and I find myself soaking up every detail as we tour the facilities. There's a swimming pool, complete with mini water slides and a splash pad. Ryan raises an eyebrow at the sight of naked kids frolicking in the water but doesn't comment.

"It's so different from Heirani Motu," I whisper to him as we come out of the woods to see a mini-golf course. "It's, uh, more structured?"

He nods while scanning our surroundings. "Definitely geared toward families. Different vibe entirely."

After the tour, we're led to a conference room where Eve, Val, Holly, and James are waiting, along with some unfamiliar faces—presumably the other resort employees. We meet Ollie, Heidi, and Damian, who are also bigwigs at the resort.

While introductions are made, I notice Ryan's posture straightening. He's slipping into business mode. I admire his ability to compartmentalize, even as I fight the urge to squirm in my seat. Clothes feel strangely confining after our time on the island.

The meeting flies by in a blur of spreadsheets and projections. As we're wrapping up, Mara whistles to get our attention.

"Don't forget, the 'Naked in Nature' hike leaves in an hour!"

I grab my husband's arm. "Ryan, we have to do that."

He scrunches up his mouth. "I don't know, Mer. It sounds like a long hike."

I employ my best seductive voice to change his mind. "Come on, it'll be fun. When's the last time you went hiking au naturel?"

A reluctant smile tugs at his lips. "Never, actually. We should do that when we're back home again."

"Why not try it right now? Don't tell me my husband, a former Navy SEAL, is squeamish about hiking in the nude with strangers."

One corner of his mouth stretches upward into a smirk. "Okay, you got me. Can't have anyone thinking I've gone soft."

"Then it's settled." I declare triumphantly. "We're going."

As we head back to our room to change—or rather, un-change—I find myself wondering what other new experiences await us here and at other resorts in the Au Naturel chain. More importantly, how might these experiences change us? For the better, I'm sure.

We hold hands as we set out on the trail with the cool Oregon air kissing our skin. The sounds and scents around us are both invigorating and freeing. I catch myself grinning at the woods even while my feet crunch on the pine-needle-strewn path. Ryan walks beside me, his initial hesitation melting away with every step.

"Isn't this incredible?" I whisper, nudging him playfully.

"Well, it's...different. But not in a bad way."

Peripherally, I notice a young woman trailing behind the group, arms wrapped tightly around herself. Her eyes dart nervously, never quite meeting anyone else's gaze. My heart goes out to her. I'd been a little anxious the first time I stripped naked in public, though I was never as nervous as she is.

I slow my pace, falling in step beside her. "First time at a nudist resort?"

She winces. "Is it that obvious?"

"Only because I remember feeling exactly the same way. I'm Meredith, by the way. My husband, Ryan, and I run the Au Naturel Naturist Resort South Seas."

"I'm Stephanie," she replies, her posture relaxing slightly.

"You know, my first nude beach experience was on a little island called Heirani Motu. I was fifty-two at the time. Boy, was I terrified at first, but I quickly realized something important." I lean in to whisper, "Baring it all made feel freer than I ever had before."

Sarah's eyes widen. "Really? How did you get over the nerves?"

I grin, gesturing at the lush forest around us. "By realizing that this"—I indicate my body—"is just as natural as the trees, the earth, and the wildlife. We're part of nature, not separate from it."

Okay, I fibbed a little. I was never that nervous on day one at the South Seas resort. Stephanie needed encouragement, so I consider my little white lies to be all for a good cause.

As we chat, I can't help but marvel at the stark difference between this landscape and Heirani Motu. Where the island was all sun-drenched beaches and vibrant tropical flowers, here the air is crisp and pine scented. Towering evergreens create a cathedral-like canopy overhead and dappled sunlight filters through the trees.

"It's so...green," I murmur, more to myself than anyone else. "And quiet. Peaceful too."

"A different kind of beauty," Ryan, overhearing my conversation with Stephanie. "It makes you appreciate the diversity of the natural world."

Though we're far from our island paradise, we're discovering new wonders together. And isn't that what life's all about?

Even after the guests hike back to the resort proper, Ryan and I linger on the shores of the lake that resides within the confines of the resort's land. The sun dips lower and lower on the horizon, and soon, we'll need to head back to the main area. But Ryan and I stretch out on the sandy shore briefly to wiggle our toes and feel the cool grains against my skin.

"This place has such a different vibe," I muse, turning to face Ryan.

He raises an eyebrow. "How so?"

"No monkey-faced bats, no dolphins, not even one cockatoo." I gesture toward the spot where a family had built a sandcastle earlier. "It's more...communal, I guess? Back home, it's all about luxury and decadence. Here, it feels like summer camp for all ages."

"Summer camp where clothing is optional."

I wriggle around to face him, cross-legged. "But doesn't it make you think about what we could do with the South Seas property?"

He eyes me sideways. "Your mind is always dreaming up ideas, isn't it?"

"Anything wrong with that?"

"Nope. It's what I love about you."

Something like a cowbell clatters from the direction of the main resort area. A male voice shouts through a megaphone, "Dinner! Get the grub while it's hot."

We race up the trail, arriving just in time.

The main building's dining hall is quite similar to the setup back home. Although, it's bustling with energy, more like an indoor picnic. Laughter and the clink of utensils fill the air as we make our way to an open table.

"Well, this is certainly lively," Ryan comments, his eyes darting around the room.

I grin, already feeling the pull to mingle. "It's fantastic, isn't it? Look at all these people, just being themselves."

A young couple approaches our table, wearing a friendly smile. "Mind if we join you?"

"Please do." I gesture to the empty chairs. "I'm Meredith, by the way, and this is Ryan."

"Tim Smithers," the man introduces himself, "and this is my wife, Mindy."

As we settle in, I can't help but notice how at ease everyone seems, despite their state of undress. It's a beautiful reminder of why we do what we do.

"So, what brings you two to Au Naturel?" I ask, genuinely curious about their story.

Mindy's face lights up. "Oh, it's our annual getaway. We've been coming here for years. It's like a second home now."

A lot of people we've met today told us the same thing. It's extraordinary how faithful to the resort these guests have become. And it reveals a lot about Eve's original vision for Au Naturel, as well as what she and Val have done to explain the brand.

As the evening progresses, we're joined by another couple, Damian and Heidi Petrescu, who we met earlier today. The conversation flows easily, touching on everything from favorite hiking trails to the challenges of running a naturist resort.

I can't help but think how perfectly this moment encapsulates what I love about the naturist lifestyle—the openness, the connections, the feeling of belonging. As I catch Ryan's eye across the table, I see a spark there that tells me he's thinking the same thing. James and Holly turned Heirani Motu into a glittering treasure in the middle of the South Pacific, honing the grand until it became the hottest destination for naughty nudists. But now, it's time for me and

Ryan to take their vision and set it ablaze—in the best way. When I look around at the smiling faces, the animated conversations here in this dining hall, I know we're on the right track.

Damian has begun gesturing animatedly as he regales us with tales of his Ludar gypsy heritage. His dark glitter with humor, and I can't help but be drawn into his storytelling.

"You know," Damian begins, wiggling his eyebrows, "I've got a special talent for palm reading. It's all part of the show I do in my gypsy wagon."

"Really?" I ask, intrigued. "That sounds fascinating."

Ryan raises an eyebrow, his skepticism evident. "Palm reading, huh?"

Damian grins. "Oh, it's legit. I've got what we call 'Ludar lidar.' It's kind of like radar, but it's for reading people."

I burst out laughing. "Ludar lidar? I love that."

As the laughter subsides, I turn to the woman sitting beside me, a first-timer at the resort. "So, what made you decide to try naturism?"

Wendy blushes slightly. "Honestly? I wanted to challenge my-self. Push past my comfort zone, you know?"

"I get that. It can be intimidating at first, but it's so liberating once you embrace it."

"Exactly," Wendy agrees. "I never thought I'd feel this comfort-able being naked around strangers. It's freeing."

Later, as Ryan and I walk back to our room hand in hand, I can't help but sigh. "I miss Heirani Motu."

"Me too. It feels like home, doesn't it?"

I sigh, surprised by the intensity of my longing. "There's just something about the island...the freedom, the dirty escapades."

"The condoms in terra cotta bowls?"

"Among other things."

Ryan pulls me close as we reach our door. "I get what you mean, though. But you know what? I've been thinking that maybe we should take a real honeymoon. Explore some places neither of us has seen before."

My heart leaps at the suggestion. "Really? That would be in-credible!"

Once we're inside our bungalow, we both fall asleep swiftly. It's been a wonderful, if exhausting day.

I watch Ryan's chest rise and fall as he drifts off, a contented smile playing on his lips. My fingers itch to trace the line of his jaw, but I resist, not wanting to disturb his peaceful slumber. Instead, I drink in the sight of him, marveling at how quickly he's become such an integral part of my world.

"Who would've thought?" I whisper to myself. "Me, Meredith Hayes, falling head over heels for the stoic resort manager."

As the room grows quiet, save for Ryan's gentle breathing, a sense of solitude washes over me. It's not loneliness, exactly, but a moment of introspection. I think back to the woman I was before Heirani Motu—always searching, never quite satisfied. And now?

"I'm happier than I've ever been," I muse, snuggling closer to Ryan's warmth.

After a while, I surrender to sleep.

Then a thunderous pounding on our door jolts me awake.

"Get up, lazy heads!" a familiar voice booms. "No rest for the wicked, or in this case, the naked!"

Ryan bolts upright, his eyes wide. "Tucker? Is that you?"

"Better believe it. Time to rise and shine."

I can't help but laugh at his expression. "Looks like your best friend's come to join the party."

We throw on some clothes and open the door to see Tucker's beaming face. Ryan told me about his Navy SEAL buddy, but I didn't have the chance to meet him.

Until now.

"Tuck the man is here!" Ryan exclaims, pulling his friend into a bear hug. "What are you doing in Oregon?"

"Couldn't let you two have all the fun," Tucker winks at me over Ryan's shoulder. "Now, who's hungry? I hear this place does a mean breakfast spread."

As we make our way to the dining hall, I can't stop smiling. Watching Ryan and Tucker banter feels like witnessing a piece of my husband's past come to life. It's a side of him I haven't fully seen before, and it's utterly captivating.

"So, Meredith," Tucker says as we find seats at a table, "has this grump been treating you right?"

I laugh, reaching for Ryan's hand under the table. "Oh, he's nowhere near as grumpy as he once was. I loosened him up a bit."

Ryan rolls his eyes, but I can see the happiness radiating from him. As Tucker launches into a story about their college days, I find myself imagining a future filled with moments like this—laughter, love, and endless possibilities.

"You okay?" Ryan whispers, noticing my distraction.

"Never better." And I mean that with every fiber of my being.

He slips his fingers between mine. "This seems like the right time to tell you both what I've realized recently."

Tucker moves closer to us, waiting to hear more—just like I am.

Ryan shoves his hands into his jeans pockets. "I haven't had a nightmare since the day I proposed to you. And I've stopped worrying about whether I'll ever suffer another bad night." He kisses my cheek. "But if I ever do, I know you'll be there to talk me through it. My burden has been lifted, after all these years. That's due in large part to you, Mer."

That might just be the best compliment I've ever received. Our life together will be full of joy, humor, and hot sex from this moment on.

Epilogue

Ryan

The moon hangs low over Heirani Motu, casting a silvery glow across the gentle waves lapping at the shore. My fingers intertwine with Meredith's as we stroll along the beach, our bare feet sinking into the sand with every step. A breeze rustles the palm fronds in a hypnotic rhythm that fills the comfortable silence between us. I glance at my wife. Her profile seems angelic in this light, as she's become a heavenly spirit. Even after all this time, her beauty takes my breath away.

She catches me staring. "What are you thinking about, sweetie?"

"Just how lucky I am to be here with you."

Meredith leans her head on my shoulder as we walk. "I'm the lucky one."

My mind drifts back to when we first met, how guarded and closed-off I was. If someone had told me then that I'd be here now, happily in love and at peace, I would have scoffed. But Meredith's unwavering warmth and patience slowly chipped away at the walls I'd built around my heart.

"Remember how grumpy I was when you first arrived at the resort?" I ask, shaking my head at the memory.

Meredith laughs. "Oh yes, Mr. Stern and Serious. I thought you might be allergic to smiling."

"Hey now," I protest with a grin. "I smile plenty these days, thanks to you."

She reaches up to trace my lips with her finger. "And what a gorgeous smile it is."

I capture her hand and press a kiss to her palm, marveling at how natural such affectionate gestures have become. For so long, I shied away from any hint of vulnerability or intimacy. The guilt and pain from my past seemed an insurmountable barrier. But Meredith's love has been a balm to my battered soul, helping me rediscover joy and learn to trust again.

We come to a large rock on the beach, and I boost her up onto it. I'll take any excuse to lay my hands on Meredith. We sit side by side on the boulder, letting our gazes roam over the endless ocean before us.

I slide an arm around her waist to hold her close. "Do you regret that we gave up our big tour of the new Au Naturel properties? I did promise you we'd do that."

"How could I be disappointed? I'm with you. And we'll make that trip later on." She snuggles closer, and the feel of her breast rubbing against me is making me horny. "Besides, there was an emergency at home."

I try to stifle a laugh, but it mutates into a snort. "Emergency? You're stretching the truth a bit, Mer. The resort ran out of condoms and sunscreen. It's not like a great white shark was eating the guests. And Rene flew to Suva to get more supplies."

"Okay, maybe I used the condom 'emergency' as an excuse." She moves her hand down to my groin, cupping my dick. "I missed our island, Ryan. I'm sure Holly and James will send us lots of pictures of those new resorts."

I peel her fingers away from my dick. "The only thing I want to talk about is all the ways I want to fuck you right here on this boulder."

"Speaking of us," she says, leaning to coil her tongue around my earlobe, "have you thought more about James's proposal to expand the resort?"

I furrow my brow slightly, considering her words. "I have. It's a big decision, Mer. More responsibilities, more guests...and there's also the space issue. An island only has so much land."

"True. But we could come up with more activities and outings off the island." She taps her chin, and I swear I can almost hear her thoughts. "Think about all the new adventures we could offer. There's that buggy tour you've mentioned, maybe even a natural waterslide option."

I chuckle and shake my head at her boundless enthusiasm. "You always see the adventure in everything. But you know, I heard about something really unusual that could be amazing—bioluminescent kayak tours. That's done with kayaks that have clear bottoms, which lets you see the glowing water."

"That would be unbelievable. I bet nobody else in the Au Naturel chain has thought of it." She gives me a quick, firm kiss. "You're a genius."

The moment our lips meet, I feel a fire explode within me. It's not just the warm island breeze, but the warmth of her touch that consumes me. I move my hand to the small of her back, then slide it down to cover one ass cheek. She cradles my face in her hands, and I feel the familiar softness of her touch against my stubble.

As I gaze into her eyes, I mull over all the possibilities. "Adventure, huh? I think we can come up with some hot ideas."

"Of course we can." Meredith trails her fingers down my chest with a feather-light touch. "Any specific plans in mind, Mr. Kimble? We should try out some of your ideas before implementing them. Wanna have sex in the bioluminescent water?"

I shake my head, grinning. "You read my mind, Mrs. Kimble. But why wait for the kayaks when we have a perfectly good ocean right here?"

"We aren't really going to do it on the boulder, are we?" she asks. "Rocks are quite...scratchy."

"You're right." I slide off the boulder, pulling Meredith along with me. She laughs as I scoop her up in my arms, her warm, naked body nestled against mine. The moonlight dances across her skin as I carry her toward the water's edge, determined to fuck her immediately.

I walk us deeper into the water until it reaches my chest, then let Meredith's feet touch the sandy bottom. After a moment, she wraps her legs around my waist, pressing herself against me. I can feel the hard points of her nipples against my chest. Her legs tighten around my waist, and I groan softly as I feel her heat against me.

Then I skim my hands up her and down her back. "I think this might be better than any bioluminescent kayak tour."

"I don't know, Ryan. Those glowing waters sound pretty magical."

"More magical than this?" I slide one hand between us to cup her breast. When I brush my thumb over her nipple, I feel it harden even more under my touch.

She gasps, arching into my hand. "Okay, you might have a point."

In response, I capture her lips in a searing kiss. I roam my hands over her body, reacquainting myself with every curve and dip. The water laps gently around us, adding a sensual rhythm to our movements while I trail kisses down Meredith's neck.

"Oh god, Ryan, I need you inside me."

No further encouragement is required. With one smooth motion, I lift her slightly and guide stiff cock into her welcoming heat. We both gasp at the sensation as Meredith clutches my hips with her legs, drawing me deeper inside her body. I begin to move, slow and steady at first, relishing the way her inner muscles conform to my cock. The moonlight catches the droplets of water on her skin, making her glow like a goddess.

"You're so stunning," I murmur against her ear.

Meredith's eyes flutter closed as she tilts her head back, exposing the graceful curve of her neck. I can't resist tasting her skin again, trailing my lips along her throat as I continue to move inside her. The water swirls around us, creating a sensual cocoon that heightens every sensation.

"Faster," she gasps, her fingers digging into my shoulders. "Faster, please."

I oblige her, a slave to my wife's desires, and increase my pace as I grip her hips tightly. The sound of our heavy breathing mingles with the gentle lapping of the waves. Meredith meets my thrusts, her body undulating against mine in perfect harmony. It's as if we were made for each other, two halves of a whole finally united.

Our lips collide in a ravenous kiss, our grunts and moans mingling. The warmth of the water, the coolness of the night air, and the heat between us create an intoxicating blend of sensations. I can feel Meredith beginning to tense, her inner muscles fluttering around me as she nears her peak.

"Let go, baby," I encourage, increasing the pace and power of my thrusts. "I've got you."

With a soft cry, she comes undone, her body shuddering against me. The sight and feel of her pleasure pushes me over the edge, and I follow her into blissful release, burying my face in the crook of her neck as waves of ecstasy wash over me. We cling to each other as our breathing slowly returns to normal.

Then it's time to go back to our bungalow and get some rest. Another crop of guests will arrive in the afternoon tomorrow. Meredith and I do everything we can to help the staff prepare for the inevitable tumult to come. I love my job and enjoy giving the welcome speeches. But I know I won't see much of my wife after the introductions are over. Still, I manage to spirit Meredith away from the preparations just long enough that we can enjoy a picnic lunch at our favorite waterfall. It's the one where I found Meredith on her first day at the resort.

But now we need to get back to work. A general manager's life is never dull.

We've just left the waterfall trail behind and are ambling toward the main path, in no hurry to return to our jobs. It's as if we're the only two people in the world. Until a commotion in the distance catches our attention. The peaceful afternoon air is suddenly filled with excited chatter, girlish squeals, and the unmistakable sound of camera shutters clicking rapidly.

"What on earth?" I squint to see what's causing the fuss.

But we're too far away. So, I grab Meredith's hand, virtually dragging her toward the main patio at a good clip. A throng has taken over the space, making it hard to pinpoint anyone.

Until the crowd parts.

Meredith stands on her tiptoes, craning her neck. "Is that...no, it can't be."

But it is. As we draw closer to the resort's main entrance, we see none other than international rock sensation Miles Roydon sauntering down the path, surrounded by an entourage of assistants and bodyguards. His dark hair, slicked back, gleams under the resort's soft lighting. Even from this distance, I can see the impish glint in his ice-blue eyes.

Oh, yeah. He's trouble for sure.

Meredith grips my arm. "Oh my god. It really is Miles Roydon. What's he doing here?"

"I'm not sure. James didn't mention any celebrity guests."

As we approach, I notice Emilio hurrying toward the rock star, looking flustered. Marley trails behind him, her eyes wide and glittering with excitement.

"Mr. Roydon," Emilio declares. "Welcome to Au Naturel. We weren't expecting you until tomorrow."

Miles flashes a roguish grin. "Change of plans, pal. Thought I'd surprise you guys."

His gaze sweeps over the gathered crowd, lingering on the nude bodies with unabashed interest. When his eyes land on

Meredith, he gives her an appreciative once-over that makes my jaw clench. I instinctively step closer to her, wrapping my arm around her waist protectively.

"And who is this knockout?" Miles asks, sauntering toward us with the easy confidence of a man used to getting what he wants. "Maybe you guys rustled up some groupies for me."

Before I can respond, my wife extends her hand. "Meredith Kimble. I'm the guest services manager here at Au Naturel. And this is my husband, Ryan, the general manager."

Miles Roydon claims Meredith's hand, holding it for a beat too long. "You're one hot chick, baby. Come to my suite later and we'll have some fun."

She's my wife, you jackass. Those are the words I want to snarl at him, but it's my job to cater to every guest—even the assholes. However, that catering does not include screwing my wife. If he makes another pass at Meredith, I might deck him, to hell with my job.

I feel my jaw tense as I struggle to maintain my professional demeanor. Meredith gently squeezes my hand, a silent reminder to keep my cool.

"Thank you for the compliment, Mr. Roydon." Meredith smoothly extracts her hand from his grasp. "But I'm afraid I'll have to decline. As I mentioned, I'm married. Very happily married."

Miles shrugs, seemingly unfazed. "Can't blame a guy for trying. So, what's the deal with this place? Heard it was clothing-optional, but I didn't expect everyone to actually be naked."

I step forward. "Au Naturel is a clothes-free naturist resort, Mr. Roydon. Our website and all our brochures, not to mention our social media ad campaigns, describe the resort as such."

"No shit?" Miles's eyebrows shoot up. "Well, when in Rome, I guess." With a casual shrug, Miles starts unbuttoning his designer shirt. "My people didn't research this place thoroughly enough, I guess."

Everyone in Roydon's entourage seems embarrassed. Because they screwed up? Or because of the naked people?

I clear my throat. "Mr. Roydon, perhaps we should continue this conversation in private. We have a VIP check-in area where we can discuss the resort policies and amenities."

Miles pauses, his shirt hanging half-open. "Sure, whatever you say, boss man." He turns to his entourage. "You guys hang tight. I'll be back in a few."

As we lead Miles away from the crowd, I catch Meredith's eye. She gives me a reassuring smile, but I can see the tension in her shoulders. This isn't going to be an easy guest to manage. In the privacy of my office, I explain the resort's rules and philosophy to Miles. He listens with surprising attentiveness, nodding occasionally.

"So, no cameras, no gawking, and no unwanted advances," Miles summarizes, leaning back in his chair. "Got it. And everyone's really cool with just..hanging out in the buff twenty-four seven?"

"That's right," I assure him. "Our guests come here to embrace an alternative lifestyle and connect with nature. It's about freedom and acceptance—and exploring your sexuality, if you choose."

Miles runs a hand through his hair, seeming thoughtful. "Huh. Well, that's...actually kind of cool. Different from what I'm used to, but cool."

"We're glad you think so," Meredith concurs. "We have a variety of activities if you're interested. Yoga, nature hikes, water sports, and soon a bioluminescent kayak tour."

"Did you say water sports?" Miles grins. "Now that sounds totally based."

I resist the urge to roll my eyes. "We have kayaking, paddleboarding, and snorkeling available."

"This place does sound pretty awesome." Miles slants forward, smirking. "So, what's the craziest thing that's ever happened here? I bet you've seen some wild stuff."

I resist the urge to deck him with great restraint. "We respect our guests' privacy, Mr. Roydon. What happens at Au Naturel stays at Au Naturel."

"Fair enough." He winks at me. "But come on, you can call me Miles. Mr. Roydon makes me sound like my old man."

Meredith steps in smoothly. "Miles, why don't we give you a tour of the resort? We can show you our amenities and introduce you to some of our activities."

"Sounds good to me, gorgeous," Miles winks at her.

I feel my jaw clench again, but Meredith squeezes my hand under the desk. Her touch grounds me which is the only reason I haven't decked him yet. So, I take a deep breath, reminding myself to stay professional. "Let's begin with the main areas of the resort."

As we exit my office, Miles saunters ahead, already slipping out of his clothing. His toned physique draws appreciative glances from nearby guests.

"So, where to first?" Miles asks, cocking his hip in what seems like a deliberate attempt to show off his dick.

"Let's begin with the pools and beach area," Meredith suggests. "It's a great place to relax and mingle with other guests."

While we walk, Miles peppers us with questions about the resort's history and our personal experiences. Despite my initial reservations, I find myself enjoying his genuine curiosity about...everything.

"You know, this place is pretty crazy," Miles confesses as we stroll along the beach. "I came here looking for a private getaway, but I didn't expect to feel so...free."

"That's what draws many of our guests," I tell him. "The freedom to just be yourself, without judgment."

Miles knifes a hand through his hair, suddenly thoughtful. "Yeah, I get that. In my world, there's always someone watching, judging. It's exhausting sometimes."

For a moment, I see a glimpse of vulnerability in the rock star's eyes. It reminds me that beneath the bravado, he's just a person seeking connection like anyone else.

Meredith smiles. "You're welcome to stay as long as you like. We have plenty of activities to keep you entertained."

Our new guest freezes abruptly, his entire demeanor shifting as something past my shoulder grabs his attention. One corner of his mouth kinks upward. "Could we skip the rest of the orientation bullshit? I see something I need to check out."

When I glance back, I see what he's talking about—a beautiful blonde with a killer body. "Sure, Miles, orientation can wait. Go have some fun. That's what Au Naturel is all about."

As Miles makes his way toward the bombshell in question, I sling my arm around Meredith's shoulders. "I think that man is going to be trouble with a capital T."

"Definitely. But just imagine the exposure the resort will get from having a celebrity vacationing here."

Oh, yeah, our lives will never be boring ever again. And we wouldn't want it any other way.

Bonus Chapter

Holly

As we step off the plane in Redmond, the crisp Oregon air fills our lungs, and the scents of the wilderness envelop us. James squeezes my hand, a sparkle in his blue eyes that makes me want to jump him right now. We've been too busy to have fun—until today.

"Ready for our grand tour, darling?" he asks, his sexy British accent making even the most mundane words sound hot. "Ryan and Meredith did vow that we must see the original Au Naturel resort as well as the newer ones."

I salute. "Ready to go, skipper."

He chuckles. "I do love your enthusiasm, Holly."

I get horny just listening to his voice, even if all he does is read a grocery list. My hubby is one hot tamale.

Our first stop is the original Au Naturel resort. It offers family-friendly, clothing-optional fun nestled in the lush forests of the Pacific Northwest. The scent of pine and damp earth envelops us as we drive up the winding road. Towering Douglas firs create a natural privacy screen, their branches swaying gently in the breeze. James and I had taken over the onerous task of checking out the whole chain when Ryan and Meredith preferred to stay home—meaning at the South Seas resort.

Yeah, it's rough work visiting lush resorts.

As we pull into the parking lot, I can't help but smile at the sight of families playing miniten, their laughter echoing off the trees. James, ever the professional, immediately starts inspecting the facilities, but I can't resist tugging him toward the trail that leads to the hot spring.

"Come on, sweetie-pie. We're here to experience the resort, not just inspect it."

James rolls his eyes. "We're meant to meet with Eve, Val, and the others in the conference room."

"Not right this minute. We have some wiggle room."

James hesitates, his brows furrowing. "Holly, we have a schedule to keep—"

"Schedules are made to be broken," I inform him with a wink, already shimmying out of my sundress. "When was the last time we actually enjoyed one of these resorts? Other than the South Seas property."

His gaze roams over my newly exposed skin, a familiar heat kindling in their blue depths. "Well, I suppose a quick dip wouldn't hurt..."

Within minutes, we're both submerged in the steaming water, the tension melting from our muscles. James lets out a contented sigh, his head tilting back against the rocky edge.

"This was a brilliant idea, love," he tells me, while his fingers trace lazy circles on my thigh under the water. "I'd forgotten how magical this place can be."

I snuggle closer to him, relishing the warmth of his skin against mine. "See? Sometimes it pays to be spontaneous."

James drags me closer, his lips brushing my ear. "You've always been the adventurous one, darling. What would I do without you?"

"Probably work yourself into an early grave," I tease, but there's a hint of truth behind my words.

His arms tighten around me. "I know I've been...difficult lately. With the baby coming, I just want everything to be perfect."

"James, our life is already perfect. This little one," I guide his hand to my barely swollen belly, "is just going to make it even better."

A giggle and a chuckle from nearby lets us know we're not alone. Then a young couple saunters up to the hot spring. The man eyes us with a touch of humor in his expression. "Hey, sorry, didn't know anybody was here. We'll visit the lake instead. Have fun, guys."

As soon as the couple has left the vicinity, it's time for me to seduce my hubby.

"You know," I whisper, my lips brushing his ear, "we're all alone out here. No one would know if we..."

He stops blinking. "Holly, we can't. What if someone comes?"

I grin wickedly. "That's kind of the point, sweetie-pie."

Before he can protest further, I straddle his lap, relishing the way his breathing becomes labored. His hands instantly grip my hips as his resolve crumbles. I can feel him hardening beneath me, and I roll my hips provocatively.

"Holly," he groans, his dick stiffening more every second. "You're impossible to resist."

"And you love it."

I nibble his lips briefly, then plunge my tongue between them, swirling and licking until James is grunting and roughly fondling my tits. While our tongues twine, his hands roam my body with even more fervor. Breaths bluster out of my nostrils while James grunts and growls, the sounds reverberating off the trees. The hot spring bubbles around us, providing a delicious contrast to the cool air on our exposed skin. I reach between us, guiding him to my entrance.

James peels his lips away from mine. "Are you sure?"

I rise just enough to let him think I might stop, then sink back down inch by mind-blowing inch. My gasp mingles with the steam as the exquisite fullness of his cock stretches me. His head falls back, a guttural moan spilling from his lips, and his fingers dig into my hips with a need that mirrors my own. I catch my lip between my teeth, relishing the way he fills me so completely and the water sloshes around us in a gentle, erotic rhythm.

The heat of the spring contrasts with the cool air, making every touch, every movement, electric. I lean forward, my breasts grazing his chest, as I kiss the line of his jaw. His hands slide up my back, pulling me closer, and I can feel every muscle in his body tense with restraint. Every subtle shift of our bodies unleashes another wave of pleasure that ripples through me, and I have to fight to keep from crying out.

"God, Holly," he groans while he goes on fucking me. "You feel better than anything in the world."

I nip at his earlobe. "So do you, baby. I've missed this...missed us."

"You are a wanton goddess, luring me into your temple of decadence, making me your willing slave." His hands glide up my back as he pulls me closer. "I'm sorry I've been so distracted lately. You deserve better."

I silence him with another kiss, pouring all my love and devotion into the lip-lock. I increase my pace, chasing the climax that's mounting inside me. James' hips buck up to meet mine, driving deeper with every powerful thrust. The water around us churns, mirroring our passion. I can feel my orgasm approaching as its tingling heat spreads through me and straight into my core. His cock feels so damn good inside me, hot and hard and pulsing with the need to come. James senses it too, his fingers finding my clit and circling it with practiced precision.

"That's it, darling," he murmurs against my neck, his voice rough. "Let go for me."

His words push me over the edge, and I erupt with a cry that echoes through the air, my body clenching his cock in pulsating waves. Half strangled cries burst from my lips. James follows soon after, pounding into me like a maniac until he finally releases a deep, groaning shout as he spills everything he has inside my body.

We cling to each other, panting and laughing tenderly as we come down from our high. I rest my forehead against his, savoring the intimacy of the moment.

"I love you so much, James."

He places a gentle kiss on my lips. "I love you too, Holly. More than anything. Can't wait to meet our first child."

"Me too. But we'll have to wait several more months for that."

We stay entwined for a few minutes more, basking in the afterglow and the warmth of the spring.

Eventually, James glances at his watch and sighs. "We really should get going, love. Eve and Val will be wondering where we've got to."

"I guess you're right. But this little detour was worth it, wasn't it?"

He sweeps wet hair away from my face. "Absolutely, pet. Though I fear I'll be distracted all day now, thinking about an encore performance."

We climb out of the spring, the cool air raising goosebumps on our damp skin. As we dry off and get dressed, I can't help but admire the way James' clothes cling to his still-damp body.

He catches me staring and winks. "Later, darling. I promise."

We make our way back to the main building, our skin still flushed from our encounter in the hot spring. As we approach the conference room, I smooth down my sundress and run a hand through my damp hair. James adjusts his collar, trying to look presentable.

"Do you think they'll notice?" I whisper, suddenly feeling like a teenager sneaking in after curfew.

James chuckles. "Darling, we work for a chain of naturist resorts. I doubt Eve or Val will be scandalized by a bit of post-coital glow."

As we enter the room, we find the big bosses already seated at the large oak table, heads bent over a stack of papers. They glace up as we approach, wearing identical knowing smiles.

"Well, well," Eve drawls. "Looks like someone decided to attend the meeting after all."

Eve's knowing smirk should probably make me blush, but I rarely get embarrassed. The things I did with James when we first met...ooh-la-la. If that didn't mortify me, nothing will.

"We were just getting reacquainted with the facilities," I say breezily, taking a seat across from the bosses while James settles into a chair beside me. "Gotta make sure everything's up to snuff, huh? I assume that's why we're here."

Val snorts. "I'm sure you conducted a very thorough inspection."

Though Val has a sexy Brazilian accent, it can't compete with James's British accent.

My hubby clears his throat, all business now as he smooths down his slightly rumpled shirt. "Right then, shall we get started? I know you want to review the quarterly numbers first and then discuss any maintenance issues. Correct?"

While James launches into his agenda, I find my mind wandering. The warm glow from our hot spring rendezvous still lingers, and I can't help but steal glances at my husband. His brow is furrowed in concentration as he pores over spreadsheets with Eve and Val, but there's a newfound lightness to his demeanor. I catch his eye, and he winks.

"So, as you can see from these figures," James is explaining, "our occupancy rates have increased by fifteen percent since last quarter. The new yoga retreat package has been particularly successful. With Meredith and Ryan at the helm these days, the South Seas property has a bright future ahead."

I snuggle up to my honey. "And we can't wait to take on the Florida resort. James and I are so excited about this project. Another family-friendly property is exactly what the chain needs."

My hubby kisses my cheek. "Precisely, pet."

Now it's time for us to move on to the Caribbean resort that's heading into the final phases of construction. Once we've said goodbye to the staff, Eve and Val take us aside for a private chat.

"We know the South Seas resort is very naughty," Eve acknowledges. "But the Caribbean version looks to be, well...even naughtier. We gave the general manager carte blanch to mold it into something spectacular."

Before we can ask any questions, Val and Eve walk away. They wear strangely knowing smiles as they leave us.

After our overnight stay, it's time to move on. And we bump into some old friends who will be working with us at the new the Florida project.

"Vanessa! Craig!" I shout with genuine joy. "Come on over here. It's been too long since we saw you guys. Look, James, the Hathaways are here."

James grins at the sight of our old friends. "Well, bugger me. What a lovely surprise."

Vanessa and Craig Hathaway make their way over to us, both sporting deep tans and easy smiles. Craig's salt-and-pepper hair is tousled from the ocean breeze, while Vanessa's chestnut locks are pulled back in a bun. They seem blissfully relaxed and happy, a far cry from the stressed-out couple we met last year at the South Seas resort. They'd been divorced back then, but they remarried not long after their time on Heirani Motu.

"Holly! James!" Vanessa exclaims, pulling us both into a warm hug. "We were hoping to run into you two lovebirds."

Craig shakes James's hand before giving me a friendly peck on the cheek. "How've you been? We heard about the little one on the way. Congratulations."

Vanessa gives me a big hug. "I'm so happy that you and James will be running the new resort. You guys played a big part in helping me and Craig realize we should never have divorced. Our children were thrilled that we remarried, and so were our grandkids."

After an update on the new resort and an overnight stay, it's time to visit the final property on our itinerary—the Caribbean resort.

As our plane descends toward the sparkling turquoise waters of the Caribbean, I can't help but feel a flutter of excitement in my stomach. This new resort is our most ambitious project yet, and I'm eager to see how it's shaping up.

James wraps his arm around my shoulders. "Well, pet, are you ready to see the most audacious Au Naturel property ever conceived?"

"You bet, sweetie-pie. I have a feeling this one's going to be extraordinary."

The moment we step off the plane, the balmy air envelops us like a warm embrace. Palm trees sway in the gentle breeze, and the scent of tropical flowers fills the air—different flowers from what we're used to on Heirani Motu.

Our driver, a cheerful local called Miguel, greets us with a wide smile. "Welcome to the Caribbean, Mr. and Mrs. Bythesea."

"We're so happy to be here," I declare.

Miguel loads our bags into a sleek convertible. "All the employees are eager for your arrival. Not everything is up and running yet, mostly the forward-facing areas. But you'll be amazed by what the boss has done."

As our car winds along the coastal road, the lush landscape unfolds before us. Pristine beaches give way to verdant hills, and colorful bougainvillea spills over stone walls. I can't help but feel a sense of pride. We chose this location well. Eve and Val won't be disappointed.

The resort comes into view as we round a bend, and I gasp. It's even more stunning than I imagined. Elegant white buildings with red-tiled roofs nestle into the hillside, cascading down toward a crescent-shaped private beach. Lush gardens bursting with tropical flowers surround the property, creating an air of secluded luxury. But as we slide into a parking spot, I realize just how incredible this new addition to the Au Naturel world will be. No one, not even a clairvoyant could guess what's coming.

But my oh my, everyone is going to love this resort. That's a certainty.

Anna Durand is a bestselling, multi-award-winning author of contemporary and paranormal romance. Her books have earned bestseller status on every major retailer and wonderful reviews from readers around the world. But that's the boring spiel. Here are the really cool things you want to know about Anna!

Born on Lackland Air Force Base in Texas, Anna grew up moving here, there, and everywhere thanks to her dad's job as an instructor pilot. She's lived in Texas (twice), Mississippi, California (twice), Michigan (twice), and Alaska—and now Ohio.

As for her writing, Anna has always invented stories in her head, but she didn't write them down until her teen years. Those first awful books went into the trash can a few years later, though she learned a lot from those stories. Eventually, she would pen her first romance novel, the paranormal romance *Willpower*, and she's never looked back since.

To get exclusive content, join Anna's Facebook group, Anna's Romance Addicts, or sign up for her newsletter.

VISIT ANNADURAND.COM TO SIGN UP.